Lucifera:

The Anomaly

I0552882

Copyright Page

Lucifera: The Anomaly
A Novel by Ken Konet, M.Ed., MBA & Ibrahim Roble.

Paperback ISBN: 978-1-966703-13-6

KDP eBook ISBN: 978-1-966703-10-5
First edition: 2025
Cover art by Ken Konet, M.Ed., MBA
Published by Humbolton Press; Dallas, Texas

Table of Contents

Acknowledgments

This story was born from dangerous questions—whispers most people are too afraid to follow. But you did. To every reader who's grown weary of simple answers and black-and-white justice: I see you. Keep questioning. Keep burning.

Special thanks to my mother, Paulette Konet, who helped breathe fire into Lucifera before the rest of the world ever saw her. She was there at the very beginning—helping to shape ideas, asking hard questions, and pushing me beyond safe storytelling. Her passing in 2018 made it difficult to return to this world, but *Lucifera* became a labor of love—an act of memory, defiance, and unfinished magic finally brought to life.

Paulette also helped give voice to Mercy, the heart of *Mercy Is Blind*, the companion novel that forms Book Two in this four-part series. After her passing, Ibrahim was brought into the fold to perfect both Lucifera and Mercy; his storytelling expertise has been invaluable in making Lucifera come true in ways I could only hope.

If Lucifera is fire, Mercy is truth—and watching them collide in Book Three has been one of the most rewarding acts of storytelling Ibrahim and I have ever undertaken. Book three will be completed sometime in late 2025 or early 2026.

And we're not done yet.

In Book Four, a new voice joins the rebellion. One more powerful soul to challenge power, confront systems, and stand in the flame. We can't wait for you to meet them in 2026.

Thank you for walking through the fire with us.

—Ken Konet, M.Ed., MBA & Ibrahim Roble

Foreword

There are stories that entertain, and there are stories that excavate. *Lucifera* was not born from a desire to amuse but from the relentless, sometimes painful need to confront the machinery of judgment—divine, systemic, and personal. What began as a dark fantasy mythos evolved into a crucible for questions long left to rot in sacred shadows.

This book asks: What if the villain you feared was the only one telling the truth? What if redemption required fire, not forgiveness?

Written during a time of cultural upheaval, *Lucifera* is a tribute to those who have been failed by systems built to protect them—and to those who dare to light the match.

Let it burn.
Let it reveal.

—Ken Konet, M.Ed., MBA

Every story needs a hero. We wrote a story that needed a reckoning.

Lucifera is not a savior sent to soothe our fears; she is a mirror forced upon a world that refuses to look at itself. She is the uncomfortable truth that judgment is not about piety or power, but about consequence. In her fire, we see the reflection of a world where institutions of faith have become fortresses for the corrupt, and the righteous are left to burn.

Collaborating on this novel was a journey into the shadows—not to find monsters, but to understand the systems that create them. We wanted to explore the space between rigid, divine law and raw, human justice, and to ask what grows from the ashes when both fail.

Ken's foreword speaks of the fire that reveals. This story is what we hope to find in that light: a new, more honest foundation, forged in the heat of a truth that can no longer be ignored.

—Ibrahim Roble

Chapter 1 – Ashes and Pleas

The alley stinks of piss and broken promises. Lucifera steps into it like she owns the darkness, her boots clicking against wet pavement that reflects the city's neon wounds.

Lucifera steps forward with a fierce inevitability, a spark searching for dry kindling. Her eyes blaze, searing light onto flickering streetlamps, painting long, skeletal shadows that dance like specters on the graffiti-scarred brick.

The predator, a man whose name the world once respected, stumbles backward, his tailored suit no armor against this. He is a cornered rat, his heart a frantic drum against his ribs. He can feel the air bending around her, growing heavy, oppressive, and scalding. With each deliberate, unhurried step, she dismantles his illusion of escape, of power, of the life he thought was his to command.

"You can't do this," he gasps, the words a pathetic shred of his former authority. His voice breaks, not with fear, but with the sheer indignation of a king being challenged by a ghost.

But Lucifera hears the truth beneath the lie, the false bravado that fear sharpens into a weapon.

She stops, tilts her head. Studies him the way a coroner studies a corpse—cataloging damage, calculating cause of death.

"Do you think," she says, her voice a low, melodic thing, each word enunciated with deliberate, surgical cruelty, "that the walls you built with the bones of others will save you now?"

He doesn't understand. He opens his mouth to retort, to threaten, but no sound comes out. He is a creature of concrete and influence, of backroom deals and silenced screams. He doesn't believe in this. In her.

With a flick of her wrist, she summons light from the dark, the ancient runes etched into the scarlet leather of her jacket flaring to life.

The sudden, incandescent glow catches the sheen of sweat on his face, reflecting a universe of terror in every drop. "Your lies," she repeats, her smile an exhalation of fire, a beautiful, terrible promise, "are about to burn away."

The first fingers of flame curl around him, gentle in their lethal embrace. They are not like any fire he has ever known—they are silent, colorless, a heat that feels more like an absolute cold.

They are supernatural and unyielding, bypassing the fine wool of his suit, the silk of his shirt, aiming straight for the rot beneath. His clothes remain untouched as the fire works its way inward. He howls, a raw, guttural sound of disbelief and agony that echoes up the alleyway, mingling with the sharp, psychic crackle of purifying heat.

The fire grows, voracious and knowing, a sentient thing that traces the paths of his corruption with terrifying accuracy. Where it touches, truth erupts.

His body jerks against the wall as the sins he thought buried, the secrets he thought protected by power and money, blaze across him in searing, undeniable detail. The liar, the thief, the predator—all the hidden parts of him are reduced to simple, unendurable honesty. He sees the faces of the girls he trafficked, their eyes burning into his from the heart of her flame. He feels the terror of the rivals he had eliminated, their last, choked breaths filling his own lungs.

The fire flares once, twice, as if inhaling its own completion, then dies down to embers. Lucifera stands over the remains, a monument of unchallenged will. The alley is quiet now, save for the pop and fizz of dying embers that hiss on the damp ground. She looks down at the fine, gray ash, and for a moment her gaze softens, a fleeting shadow of a sorrow so ancient it has no name passing across her features. She turns to leave, the heat of her judgment lingering in the night, a promise to the city's sleeping monsters.

Puddles bloom red and blue as sirens scream down the alley, their wails tearing through the pre-dawn calm.

The photo had been in his desk drawer for three years, four months, and sixteen days. Ezra knew because he'd stopped counting after the first year, then started again on the anniversary.

Sarah Martinez. Eight years old. Dark hair in pigtails, gap-toothed smile, holding a drawing of her family. The drawing was still in evidence storage. The family was in Holy Cross Cemetery.

"Another dead end, Voss?" Detective Rayne dropped a case file on his desk, scattering the reports he'd been pretending to read. "The Martinez thing again?"

Ezra slipped the photo back into the drawer. "Following up on some leads."

"Three-year-old leads in a case the brass closed." She leaned against his desk, studying his face. "Father Miguel had an alibi. The whole parish vouched for him."

"Twelve kids, Rayne. Twelve kids in three parishes, all with the same story. All recanted after talking to their 'spiritual advisor.'"

"You know what your problem is? You think every priest is a predator and every victim is telling the truth."

Ezra's jaw tightened. "I think the Church protects its own, and kids like Sarah pay the price."

The Martinez case had been his first real corruption investigation. A little girl's desperate accusation against a beloved priest. Physical evidence that mysteriously vanished. Witnesses who suddenly remembered things differently. A district attorney who decided the case was "too circumstantial" to prosecute.

Sarah's parents moved away. Father Miguel got a promotion. And Ezra learned that some kinds of evil wore halos. "Let it go," Rayne said, not unkindly. "Some fights you can't win."

But as she walked away, Ezra pulled out his phone. Three missed calls from an unknown number. He almost deleted them, then noticed the timestamp— all from the same night Sarah had died in that car crash. The crash that happened two days after she'd tried to speak to him again.

He pressed play on the voicemail.

"Detective Voss?" A child's voice, scared, whispering. "It's Sarah. I... I need to tell you something. About Father Miguel. About the others. They said if I talked again, something bad would happen, but I can't... I can't keep quiet anymore. I'm scared, but you believe kids, right? You believe me?"

The message ended. Ezra stared at his phone, his hands shaking.

Sarah Martinez had died before she could tell him the truth. But now, three years later, another child was dead. Another priest was involved. And this time, there were burn marks.

Detective Ezra Voss pushes his way under the yellow tape, his trench coat a familiar shroud against the drizzling rain. He scans the chaos with eyes that miss nothing and, lately, understand even less. The scene is a carnival of dissonance: rain-soaked detectives barking orders into radios, their voices tight with a frustration that has become a constant companion, and forensics hunched over a blackened husk of what was once a man, curled like an apostrophe. Everything around the corpse is untouched by flame. No accelerant. No burn radius. A perfect, impossible circle of annihilation. Precision that whispers an impossible forensic poetry.

"This is the third one this month," Rayne says, her voice blunt and uncompromising as she steps up beside him, snapping her gum with a rhythm that defies the grim tableau. "Rich, powerful, and now very, very dead. What do we know?"

One of the techs, a kid named Miller who still had the misfortune of looking surprised by things, looks up, his face pale and slightly singed. "No accelerants," he says, disbelief coloring every

13

syllable. "No surrounding damage. It's like the fire knew exactly where to burn."

Ezra takes a long drag on his cigarette, the smoke curling around him in gray tendrils, mingling with the steam rising from the asphalt.

A fire that knew.

The thought settles into him, a cold, hard stone in the pit of his stomach.

He's seen the pattern, a thread of righteous violence weaving its way through the city's elite. Judges with a history of buried cases. CEOs whose factories poisoned entire communities. Bishops who traded in the souls of choirboys. Powerful men who had found salvation in bribes and sealed investigations. Until now.

"Heard a witness say it went up like a matchstick," Rayne offers, her voice skeptical, her pen scratching against her notepad. "Some old homeless guy, rambling. Said a name. Lucifera."

Ezra stands back, the word thundering through his brain like a prophetic hymn. An angel's name. A demon's.

The others say it too, but as an urban legend, a fable of revenge told in half-believing whispers around the precinct's burnt-out coffee machine. He had dismissed it, filed it away with the other ghost stories that haunted the city's dark corners. But seeing this, this impossible, surgical violence, and hearing the name spoken by a man with nothing to lose and no reason to lie... Ezra almost wishes he could believe.

The scene gnaws at him, a pit bull on a bone. He can feel its teeth, its persistence, its refusal to let go.

The official investigation was already a ghost, dead on arrival. Forensics would find nothing, the brass would bury it, and the only lead was a name that sounded like a myth. But myths and whispers were currency in the city's underbelly. If the system had no answers, Ezra knew he'd have to find them in the places the law forgot—in the stories told by men who traded in regret.

The tip from the old journalist was a long shot, a dying man's last gasp of relevance, whispered over a cup of greasy diner coffee: "If you're stupid enough to chase this, check the docks. Lotta things burn there, and not all of 'em are accidental."

The security office at the docks was a cramped space that reeked of stale cigarettes and desperation. A relic of a TV cast a ghostly, flickering light across Ezra's tired face as he scanned hours of grainy, cycling footage. The truth was a phantom on the screen. Nothing. And then—a flare of impossible light in a forgotten corner of the shipyard. A figure of terrible beauty, wreathed in flame. Lucifera. Her form moves with a liquid, predatory grace. Her scarlet coat flares behind her like a wing of fire. Her eyes, even in the grainy black and white, seem to blaze with a divine, consuming judgment as she raises a hand toward a figure cowering before her.

The video pulses like a living thing, like Ezra's heart as he slows the footage, catching every exquisite detail. She is the sum of all impossibilities, beautiful and merciless, and she haunts him now more than ever. Revelation grips him.

The holy truth of it shakes him to his core, strips away doubt like burning skin. He watches again. And again. Her presence shatters everything he knows, the neat, orderly world of evidence and procedure, rebuilding him from the ashes of disbelief.

He's seen the fire, the light, the woman. He's seen what none of them dare believe. His feet take him forward, out of the suffocating office and into the night, his movements slow and deliberate, but his heart races.

They might all think he's mad. Maybe he is. But at least now he's seen her. He is no longer just a detective. He is a witness. An acolyte. And he has just found his faith.

Chapter 2 – The Architectural Pattern

A charred ruin of a man, skin cracked like burnt leather, lay folded in the alley's filth.

Detective Ezra Voss squats beside it, eyes tracing the seared spine, the blackened ribs that thrust skyward in perfect symmetry. Everything around the corpse is untouched by flame. No accelerant. No burn radius. The annihilation was so clean, it left a scar of perfect, chilling artistry. This is the third one this month. He listens to the techs talk in hushed, fearful tones, but their words become static in his ears. A shape begins to form in his mind, though he doesn't know it yet—a shape behind the flame.

In this gritty urban artery, the hushed whine of distant sirens sings backup to a buzzing streetlamp. Alleyways branch off like veins, dark and crawling with whispers. Ezra finds the same improbable logic at each new scene. Always some man with more power than conscience, lying incinerated among beer cans and alleyway graffiti. He should have known the pattern. He should have cracked this by now. It feels like God playing dice, but with fire instead of dice. He scratches his stubble, eyes narrowing to razors, cutting through the odds.

Static. The techs keep muttering behind him, scanning the scene with digital indifference. Words leak into his consciousness. "No DNA." "No fucking way." "Pyromaniac freak." They're just as rattled as he is, reaching for anything solid to hold onto. He smirks, though the gesture is devoid of humor, bitter as it is exhausted. Maybe they're right. Maybe there is no understanding this. But understanding is the only thing he has left.

The world outside the ribboned perimeter moves at the pace of disinterest, bystanders crowding for a look at urban carnage. He watches them for a moment, a sea of gray faces lit by cell phone glow. Curious and hungry for the next tragic headline, but he knows they'll forget by tomorrow. He lets them drift away, focusing instead on the impossible in front of him.

"Hey, Voss!" A fellow detective, cigarette pinned to his lip, stands silhouetted by the flashing red-and-blue disco of a squad car. "You coming in, or you gonna stare that thing to death?"

Ezra stands slowly, feeling the creak in his knees. He stuffs his hands in his pockets, feeling the tug of leather gloves he forgot to put on. "Looks like death's already had its say."

The detective flicks ash into the night. "You'd know. Some of us are heading back, calling it a night. No prints, no evidence, no suspect. Just the usual."

"Yeah," Ezra mutters, more to himself than anyone else. "The usual." He takes one last look at the charred punctuation mark of a man, wondering what it means to be part of this unfinished sentence. He turns and leaves the techs to their useless routines, useless hopes.

The whispers around the precinct had solidified into a ghost story: Lucifera. The name echoed in his mind, both a hymn and a heresy.

It's only when the sounds of the alley fade that Ezra notices the sweat beading his forehead. It feels like a fever in slow motion, creeping up on him in his obsession. As it should. His life is now this fever.

His steps take him toward the beating heart of the city. Streets are neon arteries, glistening with the same oily darkness he finds in himself. The lights blur, movement bleeds into stillness. This place—filthy and familiar, home and crime scene—is his true companion. The only one he has left. It mocks him with empty promises of leads, and clues, and truth, but it's better than nothing. Better than going back to the loneliness of a small apartment and the echo of his failures.

Ezra walks, not caring where, not caring how long. Faces pass by, sneering in judgment. Or maybe he's imagining that. Maybe he imagines a lot of things these days. Like angels with fire in their eyes, doing the job he should be doing. His mind wanders and returns, circles back on itself like an animal chasing its own tail. What are you? it asks the dark city. Who are you?

It takes him hours, or maybe a lifetime, to get the answer he wants.

Lucifera.

Ezra adds another face to his wall of the damned, the fresh pinprick a new wound in the plaster. His office is a furnace. Files piled high, cluttered like a pyromaniac's kindling, heat up with each new report. His brain, his prison cell, simmers under the weight of a hundred unspoken names. This is not random. The coroner reports are unholy scripture, writing themselves anew every day. His feet burn from the endless pacing, but he can't stop now. This pattern is his gospel.

He steps back, eyes scanning the faces of the guilty. The first photo stops him cold. Judge Patricia Hendricks, her smile frozen in campaign poster perfection. Ezra remembers her from the Martinez case—how she'd dismissed the evidence with surgical precision, citing "procedural irregularities" that materialized from nowhere. Sarah's testimony ruled inadmissible. The physical evidence deemed "compromised." Case closed before it could begin.

He traces the red thread connecting her photo to the others. Each connection tells a story of systematic corruption, of power protecting power while children paid the price. Senator Morrison, who'd pushed through the budget cuts that gutted child protective services. District Attorney Walsh, who'd somehow lost three separate investigations into Church abuse. Bishop Torretti, who'd transferred Father Miguel to a new parish instead of a prison cell.

The pattern wasn't random—it was architectural. A carefully constructed wall of complicity that had taken him three years to map and Lucifera less than three weeks to start tearing down.

Ezra picked up another photo. Father Miguel himself, his kind eyes and reassuring smile a mask Ezra now saw through completely. The priest was still out there, still "serving" his new community. Still untouchable under the protection of the same network that had silenced Sarah Martinez.

His hands trembled as he pinned another thread to the wall. Not from fear, but from the weight of finally understanding the scope of what they were fighting. This wasn't just corruption—it was a machine designed to devour innocence and shit out justifications.

Judges, CEOs, bishops. Powerful men who found salvation in bribes and sealed investigations. Until now. Until this fiery retribution. It's so obvious to him, glaring in its simplicity. He imagines his fellow detectives' voices like an itch in the back of his skull. "Wealthy guys get murdered all the time." "Forget it, Voss. This ain't biblical." They might as well have said, "Forget your career."

Reports cover his desk, falling in a defeated heap to the floor. The air is thick with their ghosts, taunting him with unfinished confessions. They add heat and pressure, but he thrives in this inferno. Each new file—a cross to bear, a brick in his prison—binds him closer to his revelation. Ezra's eyes dart to a printout: "Evidence of foul play—None. Circumstantial—Plenty." His teeth clench. Plenty. The word rattles like a cynical laugh.

This is no coincidence. This is precision and punishment, judgment without apology. Ezra breathes in the stale scent of ink and sweat, feels the walls close in, a choking intimacy. This is personal. His own soul trial.

Ezra sorts through photos, each one like a lover's betrayal. The familiar faces—burned into his memory, like scars—mock him from their perch. Pins trace a map of flame and fury. He fights back the claustrophobic choke of doubt, the doubts that others have planted and that he's too tired to uproot. He paces. It's a ritual now, worn smooth with repetition. No trace of accelerant. No sign of forced entry. No witnesses. No hope, according to anyone who isn't him.

Beneath it all, he can see it. A woman's name, though he's not yet desperate enough to say it. That fire burns too close, too consuming, even for him. He breathes through it.

He catches the scent of singed paper, and his gaze whips to a report perilously close to the heating vent. Not quite going up in flames yet, but it might as well. He imagines their secrets kindling in the heat, the truth searing through the lies. He's tried everything, every angle. That none of the others have is a wound that refuses to heal.

"Voss." The sound is muted, as though afraid to enter this sacred space. Ezra barely acknowledges it. "Voss!" Louder this time. Unafraid. A rap at his door shakes the room.

Detective Rayne leans against the doorframe, nonchalance painted in sharp, dismissive lines. Her arms cross, her gaze taking in the mess with calculated skepticism. "Don't you ever go home? This shrine to your obsession is getting bigger every time I see it?"

He doesn't answer, doesn't look away from his wall of faces. It feels like defeat to even blink.

Rayne pops a new piece of gum and surveys his inner sanctum. "What's all this?" She approaches, dodging precarious stacks of files. "Your murder wall have a baby?"

"Coroner report came in on the third vic," Ezra says, holding up the curled photo. The blackened husk. The familiar scrawl of corruption revealed. He waves it like a priest with a Bible. "Just like the others."

Rayne arches a brow, unimpressed. "Rich. Dead. Got it."

He closes the distance, the scent of fresh nicotine making him light-headed. He wonders if this is how angels feel in the clouds. "Powerful. Filthy. There's a method. A reason."

"Yeah, well." She gestures to the chaos around her, unimpressed. "Sure doesn't look like it from here."

Ezra pins the last photo with conviction, his determination louder than anything he could say. The implication hangs thick between them. Someone—or something—is delivering judgment, and it's not the justice system.

She rolls her eyes. "Not this again. The cosmic crap?"

"You know I'm right, Rayne. Admit it." His voice carries a desperate edge, the sound of a man already standing trial.

"What I know," Rayne says, unfazed, "is you need sleep. Maybe a vacation. Definitely an intervention."

She crosses her arms, stance a mixture of empathy and steel. "Voss, come on. You've been down this road before. It didn't end with promotions."

"That's not what this is about."

"No? Sure as hell looks like it." She nods to the wall, the shrine to Ezra's devotion, to his faith in more than a paycheck.

Ezra turns away, a stubborn set to his shoulders. "It's a pattern. It's intentional. And it's not human."

"Let me guess," she says, feigned wonder dripping from each word. "Lucifera?"

The name cuts through him, pure and dangerous. It is everything he believes and nothing he can prove.

" Get your head out of the urban legends, Voss. We're in this job to catch criminals. The kind that bleed. Remember?" Her words sting like antiseptic, cold and precise.

"You think that's all there is?" he fires back, voice tight with conviction and fatigue.

Rayne shrugs. "I think it's all that matters." She checks her watch, her cue to leave him to his madness. "Gonna catch hell if I don't drag you along for another homicide meeting. With actual suspects."

Ezra grinds his jaw. She's wrong. She has to be.

"Alright." Her voice is distant now, already moving on. "But don't say I didn't try. You know where to find us when you're done." Rayne shoots him a look—half pity, half warning—and strides out.

Ezra's office is suddenly vast, painfully empty. Just him and his endless piles of burnt offerings.

He steps back, lets the fire of files and faces sear into him once more. It is almost beautiful, this

24

infernal mosaic. But not as beautiful as the thought of finally pinning Lucifera to the wall.

The journalist sits hunched over, as collapsed and hollow as the old diner booth he calls home. His beard, wild and gray, quivers when he speaks, like the words themselves want to escape. He's a relic, a leftover from an era when truth didn't get buried along with the bodies. Ezra listens as he shoves papers across the table. Files from a past life. Each one a confession, a regret, an unsolved murder.

The diner buzzes with the indifference of faulty neon. It's empty except for them, two ghosts conducting a seance with the past. Grease-stained wallpaper peels from the walls, tired of pretending that anyone still cares. The city moved on decades ago. So did the world.

But not Ezra. He picks up the first file, inspects the scorched edges and water-damaged print. The old man watches him, eyes dull and hopeless, as though seeing his own failure reflected in the young detective.

"They shut me down before I got anywhere near the truth," the journalist mutters. His voice is sandpaper and whiskey, worn rough with years of disuse. "Now you show up like a goddamn ghost, waving badges and promises."

Ezra smirks, bitter and humorless. "Promise is a strong word." He flips through the pages, recognizing patterns among the smudges. Abusers. Traffickers. Murderers. The city's finest. "Looks like you were onto something."

25

"Too bad the something didn't pay." The journalist scratches at his beard, as if the action could stir life back into his skeletal form. "Used to be this town had morals. Values. Truth was worth more than a fucking cigarette."

He sparks a match, inhales smoke and nostalgia. Ezra imagines that life—journalism, the relentless pursuit of truth—gnawing away at him like a cancer. He imagines the two are not that different.

"You know anything," Ezra says, lifting his gaze, "about the woman?"

The journalist freezes, and for a moment, the words hang in the stale air between them. "Heard the rumors. Same as everyone else."

"So, you're not everyone else," Ezra says, hoping, pushing.

"A goddamn ghost story," the journalist grumbles, though his hands tremble. "Myths and angels. Justice in flames." His laugh is a hollow thing. "Some folks called it Lucifera. Some called it bullshit."

Ezra leans back, disappointment washing over him like old news. He fights to keep sarcasm from spilling over his lips. "And you're a true believer, right?"

"I believe in what I see." The old man's eyes dart to the scattered files, to his own broken history. "What I saw was rich bastards getting exactly what they deserved."

Ezra taps the edge of a yellowed newspaper clipping. He recognizes the names, and the heat of conviction burns through him. "This all ties back to one of my vics. The bishop." He scans another page, the words blurring into clarity. "Looks like you got pretty close."

"Closer than anyone wanted." There's pride there, but it's buried beneath years of disappointment. Beneath the doubt that chokes this dying town.

The journalist leans in, voice lowered, fragile as an old man's bones. "Had myself a source once. A good one. Thought I'd found the next big story." His eyes flicker, catching a momentary spark. "Fire got to him too."

"Maybe it was the right fire," Ezra suggests, but the words are acid on his tongue.

The journalist shakes his head, a slow and mournful gesture. "Not if you believe in justice. Not the kind with badges."

Ezra spreads the clippings like tarot cards on the table, reading his future in their burnt edges. The story is there. Not just the bishop. More names. More crimes. Each one a link in the unholy chain he's obsessed with. He can see himself unraveling it, a priest at the altar of justice.

"Good luck," the journalist scoffs, as though seeing Ezra's conviction naked and exposed. "The whole goddamn thing's rotten."

"You were onto something," Ezra repeats, softer this time. More to himself than the ghost across from him. "And it's still there." He packs the files into his bag, and it feels like theft, like sacrilege.

The journalist leans back, defeat etched in every line of his sagging face. "Maybe." He drags the word out, a dead body in tow. "Got one last tip. Free of charge."

Ezra raises an eyebrow, torn between suspicion and hope.

"If you're stupid enough to chase this," the old man says, "check the docks. Lotta things burn there."

Ezra nods, letting the fragile optimism settle into his bones. It feels dangerous. "Appreciate it."

"Sure." The journalist grinds his cigarette into the ashtray, resignation as thick as the smoke that surrounds him. "Bring me a piece of the truth when you're done."

Ezra stands, shoulders heavy with conspiracy and vengeance. He walks to the door, the diner a wasteland in his wake. The tip, like the files, will consume him. The tip, like the files, might be worth nothing.

The journalist watches him go, sadness playing across his face like an old, familiar tune. "Kids," he mutters to the empty room. To the ghost in his booth. "Always think they can change the world."

The security office reeks of cigarettes and desperation. A small TV, a relic from the last century, casts ghostly light across Ezra's tired face. He squints at the static, at the grainy footage. The truth is a phantom on the screen. Nothing. Nothing. And then, a flare of fire and a figure of terrible beauty. A goddess of vengeance. His pulse hammers like a dying star.

Ezra leans forward, the brittle plastic of the chair creaking in protest. The rest of the station buzzes with familiar disinterest, but here—here in this cramped and flickering sanctum—is all that matters. He rewinds the tape, eyes hungry and wide. Nothing. Static. Then there, captured in ghostly fragments: Lucifera. Her form moving with liquid grace. Her coat flaring behind her. Her eyes, blazing with a divine, consuming judgment.

The video pulses like a living thing, like Ezra's heart as he slows the footage, catching every exquisite detail. She is the sum of all impossibilities, beautiful and merciless, and she haunts him now more than ever. More than the fire. More than the unanswered questions. This is the answer he didn't dare hope for.

Revelation grips him. The holy truth of it shakes him to his core, strips away doubt like burning skin. He watches again. And again. Her presence shatters everything he knows, rebuilding him from the ashes of disbelief.

"Hey, Voss!" a voice barks from outside the makeshift temple, from the real world, which has grown pale and thin. Ezra barely registers it, the muffled intrusion a lifetime away.

A uniformed cop nudges open the door, stepping into Ezra's world with the gracelessness of the uninvited. "Rayne's been looking for you, man. We're not your babysitters, you know."

Ezra's gaze doesn't waver from the screen, from his divinity in 24 blurred frames per second. "You gotta see this," he says, words hushed and reverent. "It's all here."

The cop squints at the screen, shrugs with casual disdain. "Looks like crap to me. Grainy as hell. What am I supposed to see?"

Ezra's eyes blaze, a reflection of Lucifera's own. "Everything," he whispers. But the word echoes without landing, without sticking. The cop mutters something about wild goose chases and a paycheck, then leaves Ezra to his vision quest.

He doesn't care. Let them doubt. Let them follow leads as cold and useless as old newsprint. He's seen the fire, the light, the woman. He's seen what none of them dare believe.

Ezra cycles through more tapes, hands shaking with a holy fever. Other murders. Other places. The same terrible beauty captured for a fraction of a second, a phantom of justice that shatters the logical world. He plays them in reverent sequence, the footage skipping like a heartbeat. Each new glimpse of Lucifera sets him ablaze.

Her image is etched into him now. He can see it when he closes his eyes, when he opens them again to the same grainy film. But something in the footage bothers him—a detail he can't shake. In the moment before the flames erupted, she hesitated. Just for a fraction of a second, her hand wavered. Her eyes closed, as if steeling herself for something distasteful rather than relishing it.

He rewinds, watches again. There—that flicker of something almost human crossing her features. Not bloodlust. Not divine wrath. Something closer to... regret?

Ezra leans forward, studying her face in the pixelated freeze-frame. He's seen that expression before, in the mirror after closing cases that left him feeling hollow despite the conviction. The look of someone doing what needs to be done, not what they want to do.

"You don't enjoy it," he whispers to the screen. The revelation sits heavy in his chest. "This isn't vengeance for you. It's work."

He imagines her in every pixel, every frame, every unsolved case in his career. And he is filled with wonder, consumed by its terrible promise.

Outside the tiny office, the city waits. Its grays and blacks muted further by Ezra's sharpened, bright belief. He steps into the street, dazed, drunk on certainty. People move around him, ghosts of flesh and doubt. The wind cuts sharp against his cheeks, the only thing cold enough to penetrate the fire inside.

Urban legends bleed into reality. Ezra's world shifts. He stands at the intersection of myth and truth, and he knows there is no going back.

His feet take him forward, slow and deliberate, but his heart races. They might all think he's mad, that he's seeing what isn't there. Maybe he is. But at least now he's seen her.

A staccato burst of grainy light fills the apartment, rewinding itself into an endless loop. It bleeds into Ezra's brain like divine radiation. She's not just an urban legend. She's real. Each new pass of the footage strips another layer of certainty from his exhausted mind. Her face flickers in the flame. Ezra rewinds the tape again. "What are you?" he whispers. And then: "Who?"

The glow of the old TV paints the walls with faded, frenetic strokes. Ezra sits among empty bottles and stale, suffocating air, eyes locked on the flickering image. Lucifera. She stands at the center of the inferno, face lit by judgment and fire. Her stance isn't rage. It's resolve. Her eyes blaze with purpose, with clarity. They fill the room with light and shadows, with doubt and belief.

Ezra rewinds, plays it back, the action more compulsion than choice. His fingers work like the gears of a broken clock, unstoppable, imprecise. The static seeps into his skin, his breath, his bones. Each grainy pass of the tape pulls him closer to the truth, pushes him further from sanity. His own question echoes back to him. Who? What?

The footage is a comfort. The footage is a torment. He watches it on endless loop, lets it become his pulse, his rhythm, his salvation. Lucifera's face flickers in the flame. It haunts him, saves him, tears him apart. Her beauty, terrible and unearthly, fills his head and leaves room for nothing else.

He mouths the words now, too dry and tired to give them voice. What are you? He feels the distance between the question and its answer. He feels the distance between himself and his certainty. She is not a myth. She is not a story. She is a phantom. A truth. She is here, and she is not. Ezra is close, so close, but still a lifetime away.

The world outside his apartment is a different reality. It whispers of doubt and practicality, and it fades the moment he closes the door, turns the volume up, rewinds the tape. His doubt has no foothold here. He's seen her, more clearly than ever, more clearly than anyone. The disbelief of the others only strengthens his faith.

He pauses the footage, watches the still frame, watches her face, watches his own certainty reflect back at him like light from a burning sun. The silence in the apartment is loud, oppressive, before he lets the tape run again, faster this time, as though speed will deliver him the final answer. His mind is a blur of flame and need and bright, beautiful chaos.

Lucifera

The name bursts behind his eyes like fireworks, a storm, an inferno. It blazes across the screen and through his consciousness. He watches her emerge from the shadows, burn likc prophecy, disappear and emerge again. She is his heartbeat. She is the light at the end of the tunnel. She is everything the world said he couldn't believe.

Ezra lets the tape loop, lets the tape become his reality. It is all he needs. All he wants. It fills the cracks in him like molten gold, like beautiful, binding certainty.

She moves across the screen with terrible precision. She moves through his soul the same way. His

33

breath catches, tangled in the burning weave of his belief. "What are you?" he whispers. Louder this time. More desperate. He sees the way her face shifts in the light. He sees the answer in its molten glow.

"Who?"

Chapter 3 – Heaven's Orders

In the Celestial Decree Chamber, a space where perfection casts long shadows, the sacred silence is a breath held far too long. A robed archon, faceless and silent, breaks Heaven's austere quiet with a chilling mandate.

"She's become a problem we can't ignore." The archon's voice was flat, businesslike. "Lucifera needs to be dealt with. Permanently."

Oren stands before a vast mural of sculpted divine order, his silver armor gleaming, wings like blades poised for flight.

The last time Oren had unleashed his true power, three-star systems had gone dark.

It was not a memory he revisited often, but the Void Leviathan had required nothing less than absolute force. The ancient creature had been older than galaxies, a primordial thing that fed on the space between spaces, growing fat on the dreams of dying worlds. When it had begun to devour the Proxima cluster, consuming entire civilizations in its hunger, the High Council had sent their most perfect weapon.

Oren had materialized in the creature's path, a single point of silver light against the cosmic dark. The Leviathan, vast as a solar system, had regarded him with eyes like black holes, each one capable of swallowing planets whole.

The battle had lasted seventeen minutes.

Oren's first strike had been a blade of pure creation-force, drawn from the fundamental laws that held reality together. It carved through the creature's hide like light through shadow, spilling ichor that crystallized into new constellations as it fell. The Leviathan's scream had shattered three moons and left a psychic scar across the galaxy that mortals would interpret as the Wailing Nebula for millennia to come.

But the creature had been ancient, cunning. It had wrapped itself around Oren like a living galaxy, each tentacle the size of a planetary ring, squeezing with the force of collapsing stars. Lesser beings would have been crushed into quantum foam.

Oren had simply expanded.

His divine essence had erupted outward, a sphere of absolute order that rewrote the laws of physics in a billion-mile radius. Matter obeyed. Energy submitted. The Void Leviathan, a creature that had devoured gods, found itself suddenly, impossibly, defined—given boundaries, limitations, mortality.

And then Oren had contracted, pulling all that stolen power back into himself, leaving nothing but a perfectly spherical void where the ancient horror had writhed moments before.

The High Council had been pleased. Three star systems were a small price for cosmic security.

Standing now in the Celestial Decree Chamber, Oren flexed his fingers, feeling the echo of that absolute power thrumming through his armor. The anomaly—Lucifera—burned bright, yes, but she was a candle compared to the star-forge of his true strength. She was a local problem, a rogue spark that had gotten out of hand.

She was not worth his personal attention. Not yet.

He is a masterpiece of martial elegance, a statue carved from Heaven's most unyielding stone. He nods once, accepting the command, his steel-blue eyes unbroken but not untroubled.

The High Council's will was absolute, but this task required surgical precision.

He turns, his gaze sweeping across the chamber until it lands on a lone figure kneeling in the shadows. **The Justicar.**

An angel forged for a single purpose: to be the final word in Heaven's judgment. Unlike Oren's radiant glory, the Justicar is clad in stark white robes, his wings the color of storm clouds, his face obscured by a silver mask that betrays no emotion. He is Heaven's most precise and silent weapon.

"The Council's decided," Oren said, his tone sharp with frustration. "Lucifera's made us look like fools. IIcr little fire show has mortals questioning everything we've built. Find her. End this."

The Justicar does not speak. He rises in a single fluid motion, his head bowed in assent. In his hand, a blade materializes—not of radiant light, but of solidified silence, a weapon that cuts souls more cleanly than it cuts flesh.

He is an instrument of pure, unconflicted will, and as he turns to depart, Oren feels a flicker of something he cannot name: the chilling certainty that the Justicar will not fail... or falter.

The High Council had demanded a subtle solution, a quiet erasure to avoid spooking their mortal flock. This was subtlety.

This was a scalpel, not a sword. For now.

A blaze of celestial luminescence parts the rain-soaked sky, and **the Justicar** emerges, an angel in a city far from Heaven.

The divine realm dissolves behind him, a ghost of purity swallowed by urban decay. He descends like an alabaster dagger, sharp and pristine, cutting through the filth.

His storm-cloud wings fold seamlessly against his back as his feet touch the wet pavement, his presence a ripple of cold order in a world that knows none.

He takes on a human form, the transition seamless, his angelic aura condensing into an almost unbearable stillness.

He is a phantom in a simple gray coat, yet the air around him remains charged, sterile. Cold streetlights cast harsh neon reflections on the glistening pavement. His armor is gone, but the divine precision remains, carving a path through the city's ruin.

The streets are desolate, deserted as though even the damned have left them behind. His footsteps are silent, leaving no echo. In this dark, shimmering landscape, the remnants of Lucifera's presence loom large. Brick walls marked with scorched symbols speak of infernal interventions; ash swirls in the wake of his passage, ghosting the air with memories of fire.

The Justicar scans the chaotic remnants with eyes that miss nothing.

He is a hunter, and this is his new terrain. Each charred outline, each burned impression on brick, is a signpost in the dark, leading him ever closer to his target. Residual ash clings to his boots like the world's failed absolutions, yet he remains unswayed.

"Order will be restored," the Justicar murmurs, his voice a brittle promise, the words fragile against the backdrop of steel and stone. The phrase is not a prayer, but a statement of fact. His mission is all that exists.

Night holds the city in a breathless grip, its corruption wrapped tightly around every crumbling facade.

The Justicar moves through this desolate landscape like a whisper made solid, his silent footfalls absorbing the echoes of the city's decay. The air is heavy with unfulfilled promise, a tension that coils with every deliberate step he takes. He is not a ghost; he is the absence of ghosts, a void of purpose moving through a world of chaos.

He stops before a monument of ruin—a dilapidated church, its once-majestic walls now scarred by time and neglect. Stained glass lies shattered on cracked pavement, colorful confessions strewn about like unkept oaths. This is a center of chaos, a locus of past judgments where Lucifera's fire has left its indelible mark. The Justicar surveys the damage with the dispassionate eye of a predator assessing a kill site. He moves with a solemnity that borders on the mechanical. His gloved fingers graze the burned inscriptions that mar the stone, but he feels no reverence, no regret.

He is reading, not mourning. The unique, volatile signature of Lucifera's flame still clings to the air, a scent only he can perceive. It is a trail of infernal defiance and celestial betrayal, and it is beautifully, damningly clear.

The physical and moral decay is pervasive, but to the Justicar, it is merely data. Each scorched marking, each singed edge, tells a story of her methods, her power, her proximity. His mind processes this, relentless and unwilling to be distracted by the mortal tragedy of it all.

He finds a single, unburnt feather near the altar—not angelic, but something other. He pockets it without a second thought. The wind kicks up, and a swirl of ash circles his feet, a grim ballet that dances in time with his cold thoughts.

The Justicar whispers into the heavy air, "Order will be restored," an affirmation that falls with the finality of a blade. The terse words are both powerful and absolute, a decree and a promise.

He turns, leaving behind the remains of the shattered sanctuary. The hunt is on, and he has found the scent. He walks on, every silent step an echo of a judgment already passed.

Chapter 4 – Scarlet Jacket, Smoking Gun

Lucifera surveys the empire of guilt from a corner of darkness. She stands at the top of the grand balcony, shadow and light dancing across her like reluctant partners. Below, pews stretch in neat, endless lines, pinning the congregation in place like rare insects for study. Father Hale orchestrates from the stage, his voice weaving through the crowd like an artful con. Eyes fixed on him, worshippers ignore the blood on their neighbors' teeth, the sins on their own hands. To Lucifera, this place smells of ash. This place smells like home.

The room pulsates with excess, where stained glass windows and gilded statues bear silent, jeweled witness to the drama below. Candles flicker along the walls, casting halos on marble columns that strain under the weight of their own splendor. Her amber gaze is the only witness from the upper tier. It burns like an afterthought, unblinking in the dim.

The pious stare at Hale as if transfixed.

"Rejoice!" he says, the word tumbling from his mouth like a precious gem. It skitters across the floor to nestle in every heart. "Rejoice, for salvation is at hand."

Lucifera suppresses a bitter laugh, arms crossed against her chest like a judge on the bench.

He stands bathed in righteous light, arms open wide to the flock. The grandeur of his robe shimmers in time with his cadence. It glitters, pure and white. She can see the poison it conceals, seeping from the man himself, corroding all that he touches.

Behind Hale, an enormous crucifix looms, its suffering carved into exquisite detail. Lucifera sees the irony there. His hands dance as he spins promises from air, working the crowd into a hypnotic lull. His words echo off walls that soar, gaudy and ornate.

"For He sees beyond your sin," Hale continues, his voice dropping to a tender whisper. "Forgive yourself, and He will too."

Lucifera's contempt flares like a stoked ember. Her presence flickers in and out of the light, an angelic ghost haunting the living. This temple to human ego, its very structure an arrogance, strains towards heaven but sinks to Hell.

In that distortion, she is her truest self.

She focuses on Hale, whose smile could ransom a thousand guilty souls. He believes his own lies, she realizes. It is the ultimate deceit, one that deceives even the deceiver. His congregation devours his empty truths, washing them down with greed and self-pity. How hungry they all must be.

Her eyes wander over the worshippers, dissecting their veneration. Silk and diamonds hug their bodies; guilt and arrogance cling to their souls.

This crowd knows sin. They wear it with the comfort of old clothes.

In their faces, she sees self-righteousness veiled as piety. Many have soiled others to keep themselves clean. She knows this because it's always the same. The fires of absolution burn coldest where they're least welcome. Here, amid pews and scripture, they are frozen solid.

A man in the front wipes a single tear from his cheek. Behind him, a woman raises both hands in fevered devotion, her fingers laden with jewels and desperation. Lucifera takes it all in, each precious trinket, every counterfeit conversion. Each would barter their soul to have it handed right back.

Her gaze sharpens to a razor's edge. They'll learn.

The familiar rage simmers beneath her skin, seeking release. She is a coiled flame, waiting for the air to ignite her, the powder to spark. It would be so easy, she knows, to burn this monument to its foundations, to watch the sermons turn to cinder and the saints melt like wax. So damn easy.

And that, she understands with bitter clarity, is why she doesn't.

Too familiar, too predictable, too futile.

She has traveled this road, its circular twists as treacherous as any serpent. It's an Ouroboros of mission and penance, each circuit less distinct from the one before. There are times she longs for the release of quitting, times she dreams of the silent oblivion that only surrender would bring. But dreams are for those who can sleep.

Hale's assistant, a young woman in a soft pink dress, emerges from a side door. She rushes to his side with something resembling admiration. Too close, Lucifera thinks. She knows a spider's lure when she sees it. Hale gives her a small, proprietary smile and resumes the show.

"Join me in prayer," he commands.

The congregation complies with a collective sigh, heads bowing in synchronized shame. His murmured words settle over them like a shroud. The young woman looks up at him, lips forming silent words of her own. Their meaning is clear to everyone but herself.

Lucifera grips the rail, skin hot against the cool metal. Enough of this, she decides.

She watches as Hale pats the assistant on the shoulder, then guides her through the side door. The crowd lifts their heads, and she reads the need in their eyes. Their cravings turn inwards, unsatisfied.

The righteous begin to disperse.

Lucifera moves like smoke across the balcony, steps quiet as condemned souls. She descends the grand staircase, a whisper in the falling dark. Soon, there will be new judgment, and new ash.

He recognizes her before she even speaks. Standing in the entrance of the ornate chapel, a molten vision, she watches him with an intensity that pierces his careful composure. "Who let you in?" Hale sneers, though his voice shakes like a bad liar's hands. His assistant cowers behind him, all big eyes and bitten lips. Lucifera advances slowly, words like embers. "You did." Hale flinches but recovers, eyes flicking to the chapel door. "I see," he says, summoning a confident smirk. "Another sinner." "We'll see," Lucifera replies.

The assistant trembles, a frightened lamb caught between a wolf and an inferno. Hale shifts, trying to maintain his poise, but his gaze darts like a cornered animal's.

"Who are you?" he demands again, the edge in his voice betraying him.

"Your last chance," Lucifera says, unblinking.

He laughs, hollow and unconvincing. "What do you want? Money? Repentance?" He gestures dismissively, the bravado slipping from his fingers. "Go back to your gutter, girl."

The chapel feels smaller with every step she takes, shadows retreating from her path. She holds Hale's eyes, an executioner in no hurry. "She didn't agree to your absolution," Lucifera says, nodding toward the assistant.

Hale's mask falters, eyes wide for a split second before the sneer returns. "You think you know something? You think anyone will believe—"

"You," Lucifera interrupts. "I believe you do."

His confidence falters. She can taste the fear rising off him, bitter and satisfying. The assistant's gaze flickers between them, trapped and desperate. Lucifera's presence burns the air. The young woman shudders, feeling the heat of the coming fire.

Lucifera tilts her head, a small, terrifying gesture of acknowledgment. "He doesn't own you," she says softly to the girl. Then, turning her full attention back to Hale, "Does he?"

The assistant recoils, a mixture of hope and disbelief. Hale clenches his jaw. "Go," he says to the girl, voice tight with anger. "Wait in the car."

She hesitates, caught in Lucifera's burning eyes.

"Now!" he barks, shoving her toward the door.

The girl runs, leaving Hale alone with his hunter.

Lucifera stands silent, her condemnation a palpable force between them. Hale backs away, pretending indifference, his movements a series of stumbles disguised as steps. "What's the price?" he asks, cornered. "Name it. We can make a deal."

"You had thirty pieces of silver in mind?" Lucifera's words are soft and lethal.

Hale's face flushes with rage. "You have no idea who you're dealing with."

Her laughter echoes, pure and cutting. "On the contrary." She pauses, letting the stillness sink into his bones. "I know you exactly. Hypocrite. Coward. Worm."

Each word hits him like a lash.

She takes another step forward. "Your guilt radiates," she says. "How long did you think you could hide behind your sermons?"

"You think you can just walk in here, accuse me—"

"You did this," she interrupts again. "I'm simply here to watch you confess."

Hale's composure splinters. He lunges for the chapel door but freezes when Lucifera raises a single hand, runes glimmering along her arm.

"You're not the first who's tried," she warns.

Hale hesitates, torn between anger and terror.

"Admit what you are," she urges. Her voice is almost tender, almost.

He hesitates, hatred battling with desperation. "A man," he says, spitting the words. "A sinner, just like you!"

"Just like me?" Lucifera's smile is molten metal. "I think not."

"Your threats mean nothing," Hale blusters, but it sounds like a plea.

Her eyes narrow, the heat around her growing. Hale sweats, the slick panic beginning to show.

Lucifera closes the distance between them, a lioness eyeing the wounded gazelle. She lets her silence hang like an anvil, waiting for gravity to do its work.

His shoulders sag, and he slumps against the wall, gasping for breath that sounds more like a sob.

"It must be a relief," she says.

"What?" His voice cracks.

"Finally to be caught."

Hale shakes his head, hands clutching at nothing, seeking some last bit of control.

"There's always mercy," he says, the bravado all but gone, voice naked with fear. "I could have you arrested. This is breaking and entering. I'll—"

"Keep lying?" she says, and the words ignite the very air. "You're out of practice."

Her hand reaches for him, judgment in physical form. He shrinks back but has nowhere to go.

She lets her gaze burn into him, unyielding. His knees hit the floor with a dull, pitiful thud.

The assistant watches from the hall, uncertain whether to run or scream. She does neither. Instead, she clutches her dress and stares, spellbound.

Lucifera towers over him, the full power of her presence brought to bear.

"We'll see what kind of sinner you are," she says, sealing his fate.

Hale lurches forward, arms wrapped around his gut like he's trying to keep it from spilling out. He collapses to his knees, forehead pressed to the floor. Lucifera's eyes follow his every move, hungry and patient. "Please," he says, voice cracking like old plaster. "I'm sorry." She steps closer, heat radiating from her like justice itself. Hale springs to his feet, desperation and adrenaline fueling a reckless surge for freedom. Lucifera barely moves, yet somehow blocks him, scorching his path to escape.

"Try again," she says, but something in her voice wavers—a hairline crack in her certainty. Hale falls once more, a crumpled, quivering heap. As he hits the ground, Lucifera sees not the predator, but the broken thing beneath. For a moment—just a moment—she remembers what it felt like to beg. To plead for mercy that never came. The thought disturbs her. She pushes it down, but it clings like smoke. "You can't do this!" Hale screams, the sound ricocheting off the walls. "I'm a man of God!" "You serve no one but yourself." The words come automatically, but they taste different now. Hollow. She's said them before, to others like him. When did her truth become a script? She shakes her head, refocusing. He is guilty. The flames know guilt like a bloodhound knows scent. There is no mistake here. So why does her fire feel colder than it should?

"I confess! I confess!" he blurts, but the words are weak, like damp wood refusing to kindle. "Forgive me!"

"Try again," she repeats, each syllable striking with deliberate calm.

He collapses again, grabbing at her ankles like a child in the throes of a tantrum. "I'm just a man! Everyone sins!"

"Not like you," she replies. Her presence towers over him, unyielding as prophecy.

Hale flinches at her words and at the power crackling through the air between them. Panic paints his face in raw, frantic strokes. Lucifera stands silent, a beacon of certainty against the chaos of his cowardice.

His mind races, grasping for a tactic, a trick, a miracle.

He finds nothing.

"I confess," he whispers, eyes wild and unsure. "I'll change, I swear."

"Then why do you still stink of lies?"

Hale screams, a shrill, primal noise. He leaps to his feet and lunges, driven by terror more than reason. The chapel walls close in as he makes for the door. It should be so close, just steps away. It might as well be a thousand miles.

Lucifera takes one step, then another, measured and implacable. The very air bends around her. He slams into it as if it's made of iron.

She doesn't even touch him, but his skin blisters with proximity.

"Again," she says, the word soft and inexorable.

Hale collapses. He weeps openly now, tears streaking his red face.

"You're a demon," he accuses, desperate for a response. "Hell sent you! Or heaven! I don't care which! Get away from me!"

He scrambles backwards, his suit a crumpled mess. His sweat hits the floor in frantic patters.

Lucifera watches, unmoving, eternal as time.

"No one sent me," she says. "I came because you called."

"I confess! It was me! I confess! You win!" Hale's voice shreds under the strain of false contrition. He tries to find her eyes, tries to believe his own salvation. But the words come too easily, and he can see she knows it.

She shakes her head, the slightest movement, but it strikes like a thunderclap. "Not good enough."

"You're wrong!" Hale protests, his voice climbing to heights of impotent rage. He looks more like a petulant child than a preacher, more worm than man. "I'm a sinner! I admit it! I confess! What more do you want?"

She lets the silence follow her steps. "You," she says, closing the space between them. "I want you."

Hale's face blanches as he stumbles back. He hits the wall, shoulders shaking. "This is madness! You'll never get away with it!"

Her smile is almost gentle. "I already have."

Hale springs again with adrenaline-fueled fury, a last attempt to crash through the inevitability surrounding him. Lucifera's eyes never leave him, tracking his flight and flailing, her expression an infinite calm.

He fights, claws for purchase against a world collapsing inward.

He's never known what it is to fail. Never believed it could happen to someone like him. Now, it crushes him, leaving nothing but dust and the charred husk of pride.

"Please," he says, the single word stripped of pretense.

Lucifera stands over him, her shadow larger than the crucifix's. She extends her hand, fingertips almost touching. He is so still he might already be a corpse.

His breath is shallow and frantic, an injured bird's. "Forgive me," he tries again. "I confess." His eyes close, unable to face the truth.

He says it over and over, words falling like dying sparks. "I confess, I confess, I confess."

"Still lying," she replies.

This time, she laughs, a bright sound like the crack of a match in a room filled with gas.

Lucifera lets him see the futility. Lets him taste it, feel it in his marrow. Her runes burn a molten orange, her breath a blast furnace. He has a moment to realize what it means, what it all means, before she lets herself ignite.

Fire, glorious and precise, envelopes him.

Hale's scream is lost in the roaring blaze, his voice consumed long before the rest. He burns bright and hot, and for the first time, he is pure. Pure flame. Pure pain. Purest of all, judgment.

He collapses, a blackened heap, while the chapel barely smolders.

Lucifera stands amid the scorched pews, smoke rising from her skin. She knows how easy it would be to make this a habit, a routine. There are days when it almost is.

The thought twists her heart, an organ that she tries to forget she has.

She thinks of her mission. She thinks of how much there is left to do. She thinks of the weight of this life, the unending chain of guilt and fire.

But most of all, she thinks about the inevitable futility of it. And that's what gives her the strength to go on.

She is her own greatest rebellion. The thought cuts deeper than any blade Heaven could forge. She was made to be their perfect weapon, but perfection, she's learned, is just another word for predictable. And she refuses to be that anymore.

Lucifera turns from the husk of a man and exits the chapel. Her steps are tired and slow, leaving trails of heat on the cold stone floor.

She lets the rain have her. It meets Lucifera with a rush of cold fury, soaking her in the angry downpour of an ungrateful world. Her scarlet jacket hisses with steam as she emerges, fresh-burned, from the scene of her latest execution. Lucifera ignores the hurt and lets it mix with all the other pains—old ones, sharp ones, ones she wishes she could set ablaze. A twinge of satisfaction tempts her mouth into a defiant, weary smile.

The city sprawls ahead, arrogant and immense. Rain pounds every surface, baptizing the guilt and grime in a relentless cycle of cleansing and filth. She walks with slow, deliberate steps, each a declaration against gravity and despair. The downpour could soak through her bones, but still she'd burn from the inside out.

Steam curls around her like a taunting halo.

She knows how easily this mission could become an obsession, a cycle as predictable as the sins she hunts. Some days, it is. Some days, she thinks about what it would mean to quit, to let the corruption run unchecked until it eats itself whole. But every sinner who falls into her arms reminds her why she goes on. They believe they have an escape, and that is why they never will.

It's Lucifera who's trapped. It's Lucifera who should confess.

She quickens her pace, letting the rain strike like penance.

Her existence is its own kind of hell, caught between the infernal and the divine, but she doesn't care. If neither Heaven nor Hell wants her, that means she answers to no one. And that, at least, is something.

Lucifera stops beneath a skeletal tree, its bare branches clawing at the sky. She catches her breath and shakes off the water, a futile gesture that feels like the rest of her life.

There are thousands more like Hale. Some wear robes and stand behind pulpits. Others hide in plain sight, behind screens or desks or wedding bands. Each is convinced they'll never be caught. She knows better. She catches them all.

A bitter laugh escapes her lips and vanishes in the rain.

She pictures the world like this: a sprawling metropolis of sin, burning bright in the dark of the universe. It draws her like a moth. It repels her like an oath.

Lucifera closes her eyes, trying to shut out the image. Trying to shut out the inevitable, the impossible, the infinite.

She can't.

Her knees tremble, but they don't give. Not yet.

Water drips from her hair, tracing lines down her face that feel almost like tears. She wonders what that would be like—to cry without burning the very air around her. It would be a relief. It would be a betrayal. She doesn't know which, only that it would be impossible.

She forces herself to take another step, and then another.

This city, this mission, this life. It's all she has. It's all she'll ever have.

The ground trembles beneath her, a rumble that echoes deep in her bones. She looks up, but it's only the sky shifting its weight. This time.

Lucifera breathes in, lungs raw from smoke and judgment. Breathes out, refusing to stop.

Her world narrows to the street ahead. She sees each puddle as a lake, each drop of rain an ocean. They saturate everything, but they don't touch her fire.

Never that.

She wants to hate it, this compulsion, this duty that she never chose but can never refuse. Instead, she feels its comfort, its permanence, and hates herself for that instead.

The city's bright lights pierce the gloom, and she thinks of eyes. Judgmental eyes, heavenly eyes. Watching. Waiting for her to fall.

She won't.

They think she's nothing but their burned angel, but she'll show them. She'll make them see.

The rain lessens, and her steps quicken. She imagines the voices of a thousand like Hale, calling to her in fear, in anger, in surrender. They sound like music. They sound like Hell.

Lucifera braces herself for the next firestorm. For the next betrayal. For the next confession.

And in the flicker of a lightning bolt, she sees it: herself, alone against legions, the heavens split wide open, the hordes of hell on her heels.

There is no doubt where the storm will strike.

Her mouth curves into a stubborn, reckless smile. She never expected it to be easy.

"I confess," Lucifera says, challenging Heaven itself. "I'll never quit."

The clouds rumble, and she walks headlong into the rising wind.

Chapter 5 – Heaven's Cold Call

Crime scene lights splinter the night, red and blue falling like divine hammers on the urban street. Ezra stands alone among uniformed bodies, an island of trench coat and unsolved obsession. To one side, forensic apostles murmur over the dark testament of charred bone, speculation and incense rising. His green eyes, weary saints, scan the crowd with a fanatic's intensity. He knows what he's looking for. The holy writ of this massacre. The revelation he hopes is truth. An officer, young, unmarked by life, approaches with a thumb drive offering. "Surveillance," the kid says, jittery with too much caffeine or too much conscience. "You won't believe it."

Ezra takes the drive with a rough nod, like accepting a cigarette from an old enemy. The kid looks too eager, too naive to see the black seam running through this night. Ezra flicks open a leather-bound notebook, snaps it shut again—no ink will match the urgency of this. "Laptop. Where?" He dismisses the rest, words buried under the shuffling of uniformed bodies.

"In the car. I, uh, queued it up," the officer adds, his voice lost in the roar of the scene's machinery. Ezra is already in motion, a lean silhouette slicing through the crowd.

The mobile command unit throbs with half-light and radio static, a shrine to human limitation. He slumps into a chair, the brittle thing groaning beneath him. The laptop's screen flickers to life, and with it, his hopes. Ezra leans in, ghostlike in the glow. He has been down this road too many times—always hoping, always unsure until the end credits roll.

Then it begins. Black-and-white grain gives way to moving figures, a tableau of light and dark, innocence and sin. Ezra watches as Lucifera enters the church, her flame the only color against the monochrome desperation of the pews. The footage shows her standing over a kneeling man, an apostate's prayer frozen in his mouth. Her hand moves like a conductor's, and then the flame.

He leans closer, oblivion swallowing the world outside the screen. Fire erupts, incinerating the man in a brief and silent scream. Walls and wood remain untouched, sacred symbols unscarred. Lucifera walks away as the embers cool, molten eyes staring into the camera. As if she knows. As if she always knows.

He plays the clip again, hunger and disbelief wrestling in his gut. The scarlet leather, those runes that pulse with damning grace. There's no hesitation in her judgment. No excess. This is not murder. It's precision. The words—mythic, terrible—echo in his skull as he replays her breath before the ignition, the flicker of something almost human in her eyes. Is it regret?

An officer nudges him back to the living. "Shouldn't we, you know, get backup or something? She's nuts. Taking out priests now, for God's sake."

Ezra's voice slices through the kid's nervous rambling, blunt and serrated. "That wasn't a priest. That was a rapist with a savior complex. You'd know if you read the files."

The kid steps back, deflected, and Ezra's gaze returns to the screen, devotion burning the doubt from his eyes. She fascinates him, he knows this. Not because she kills, but because her fire is a gospel only he seems to understand.

He shuts the laptop with a finality that startles him. The flame has seared itself onto the back of his eyelids, a confession that only he seems willing to hear. "This is more than you think," he tells the young officer, though the words feel as much for himself as for the kid. "Much more."

He steps out of the car into the cathedral of night, red and blue lights coloring the smoke of the holy. They make him think of candles, makeshift shrines left to burn out on their own. A witness, unmoored, stands wrapped in the blanket of the too-close and too-lucky. Ezra approaches, his coat sweeping behind him like the wings of a fallen angel. The man looks up, shaky but with enough resolve to hold Ezra's stare.

"I need your account," Ezra says, no comfort in his words.

The witness rubs the fringe of the blanket between trembling fingers. "I already told them," he starts, but something in Ezra's posture silences the objection. "She walked in like she owned the place. We all thought it was part of the show, you know?"

Ezra's brow furrows. "Show?"

59

"Yeah, one of those confession night things," the witness continues, words spilling out like loose change. "We sit and pray while he gives a speech. 'Fire and the Father,' he called it. Pretty intense stuff, even without her."

Ezra scrawls in his notebook, thoughts moving faster than his hand can record. "And when she acted? What then?"

"She looked right through him. Like she could see..." The witness hesitates, ghosts of memory playing across his eyes. "He wasn't what he said. She called him a liar. A destroyer of the innocent. Then it just happened. Boom. An angel, man. An angel wrapped in hell."

The phrase lands like a stone in Ezra's gut. "What did you see?" he presses, softer now, as if gentleness might tease the truth from this reluctant soul.

"She knew. Just knew," the witness says, shaking. "Never seen anything like it. The fire only touched him." His voice dwindles, the enormity of the experience rendering him suddenly, utterly small.

Ezra backs away, leaving the man to the solace of his trauma, the blessing of his disbelief. A reflection—of himself?—in the church's dark windows catches him off guard. The notes, the footage, this fevered witness: they're everything the law isn't. Exacting. Unyielding. An Old Testament kind of right. A realization too dangerous to dwell on lances through his mind: She is not the problem. She is the solution.

The remaining officers huddle near the smoking remains, moral compasses spinning in disoriented circles. "We call it in? Manhunt? Something?" one suggests, voice punctuated by uncertainty.

A more seasoned officer shakes his head, gaze flicking to Ezra and then back to the ground. "Voss will get her. Or get us all fired. Or both."

Ezra stays close, far enough to remain an outsider but near enough to feel the edges of their doubt. He cherishes it, like old regrets. "Write it up," he says, offering no more guidance than that. It's a whisper of command, a challenge and a promise rolled into one.

The scene clears, life and light bleeding from the night. Only Ezra remains, alone in the flickering glow of what has passed and what is yet to come. He kneels by the corpse, touches the untouched pew. The quiet is deafening, his certainty louder still.

"Angel wrapped in hell," he murmurs, the words a confession. His own. His eyes burn with something like belief as he rises, a dark apostle in the shadows. The last to leave, the first to understand.

Ezra stands in the shifting glow of Lucifera's recorded flame, an altar of charred case files and dying bulbs. She is his religion now, he knows this. The dark pulse of her compulsion echoes through him like a heartbeat not his own. In each pixel, in each flicker of incandescence, he searches for answers she cannot give. Each breath she takes is a challenge. Each movement, an accusation. He plays it again. Over and over until the boundaries of self begin to blur. Until the borders between his chaos and her order crumble, and he can no longer tell who is looking back at whom.

She commands the screen with an aura both terrifying and exquisite, an anomaly that distorts more than just light. Ezra's green eyes, predatory and pleading, follow her every move. She approaches the man with all the calm of a sinner before the confessional. Ezra sees it in slow motion, the moments before impact, the milliseconds before ignition. Her gaze, unflinching. Her silence, deafening.

His focus is brutal, an interrogation more desperate than any suspect he's ever grilled. He leans into the screen's phosphorescent hum, each frame searing into him like confession. Lucifera's unhurried blink. Her hand at her side. Each gesture pulls him further from certainty, deeper into obsession.

The ghost of a voice echoes in his head, his own voice: "Who are you?" It spirals into the silence, bouncing off cracked plaster walls and twisting back into his chest. A challenge. A plea. He presses pause on a single frame: her face, half-turned, unreadable.

"This isn't random," he mutters to the empty room, as if the world has the power to disagree. The words hang there, the only sound in the void of her judgment.

He falls into the chair behind him, a mess of limbs and adrenaline, gaze never leaving the screen. She is not what they think she is. She is not what he should think she is. It is both humbling and terrifying to understand, to be the one who knows.

His apartment is an echo of his mind: chaos and desperation dressed in yellowed paper and glowing pixels. Half-drunk coffee cups stand like bitter sentries among stacks of reports. Everything about the place feels alive, pulsing with the same urgency that beats in his chest.

He scans the screen, finds her breath again. The exhalation before the burn, the flinch before the inevitable—it looks almost like hesitation. Something human flickering behind the divine judgment, a crack in her certainty that makes him lean closer to the screen.

It's not what he wants to see. He focuses on it anyway. It feels like discovery. Like doubt. The exhalation before the burn, the flinch before the inevitable. It looks almost like... hesitation. Ezra's fingers brush the keyboard, a lover's caress on the eve of betrayal.

"You don't want to do it, do you?" he asks, and this time it sounds like an accusation. The screen offers no defense.

Her image sears him, every frame more intimate than the last. He knows she's marked him, knows it like he knows the weight of the gun in his drawer, the weight of conscience and consequence. Lucifera consumes him with a flame that isn't fire.

Ezra leans back, lets his thoughts spiral. She's doing what he can't. What he wants to. What he never could. The screen crackles with energy, feeding his insomnia, his hunger for meaning. In his head, he sees his cases, a procession of ghosts who mock his belief in justice. Victims the law won't touch, lives broken beyond repair. He looks to her face for salvation, sees his own reflection in the pixels of her eyes.

He knows what the world calls her. Knows the word they all choose to use: Killer. He's called worse things by people he trusts more. The word, like her fire, never quite touches him. "It's not murder," he tells himself, a mantra for the damned.

His universe spins, a hurricane of files and speculation. Evidence sits in mute testament around him. She is everything he has tried and failed to understand, an unresolved case in leather and scarlet.

"Who are you?" The question rears again, the first temptation. His faith in the world crumbles like ash, an offering on the altar of Lucifera. The futility of it stings like a fresh wound.

She keeps staring from the frozen screen, accusatory and calm. Every unsolved case, every dark truth ignored by light. He feels the exhaustion in his bones, a physical weight that mirrors the chaos of his mind. But even now, even wrecked and desperate, Ezra can't let go.

His eyes close, not to sleep but to better see her fire in the dark. It fills him, a warmth he shouldn't want but can't live without. He sways on the edge of consciousness, the images tattooed behind his eyelids. She is still there, waiting for him.

Ezra dreams a world of flame. A world in which he's free to follow, to be like her. He reaches out, fingers brushing the keyboard one last time, needing the contact. Needing to know that even if she doesn't answer, she still hears.

She must.

It starts with a phone call in the dead of night, an unnatural shriek that rips through the stale air of Ezra's apartment. He sits hunched in the blue glow of a monitor, the same grainy footage of Lucifera looping like a prayer he can't stop reciting. Case files are stacked around him like tombstones, a graveyard of obsession. He almost ignores the ring, another unwelcome intrusion from a world he's chosen to forget. But it persists, sharp and insistent.

He snatches the receiver. "Voss."

A voice pours out, devoid of warmth, like the chime of crystal in a vacuum. "Detective Voss. She is quite the anomaly, is she not?"

The question hangs like a shard of ice. "Who is this?" Ezra's tone is rough, a blunt knife against the voice's precision.

"A concerned party," the voice replies, still unnervingly calm. "You seek order in a world of chaos. You hunt monsters the law cannot touch. We share a common goal."

Ezra's grip tightens on the receiver. The words are too accurate, too close to the bone. "I don't talk to spooks. The hell are you talking about?"

There is no laughter, only a pause that feels colder than silence. "I am referring to Lucifera. Her wildfire justice lacks discipline. It is a cosmic weapon spinning out of control. A threat that must be contained before her fire consumes all."

Ezra scoffs, the sound sharp with mistrust. "Surgical flame? Looked like a massacre from where I was standing. Who's 'we'?"

"Heaven," the voice states, simple and absolute. The word chills him, unexpected yet inevitable. "The cost of cleansing is sometimes high, a truth you understand, Detective. How many times have you bent the rules for the greater good? We wish to help you."

"And who are you?" Ezra demands, gripping the phone like a lifeline.

"A messenger. An enforcer of the balance you seek to restore."

Ezra processes the words, suspicion now an old friend whispering in his ear. "Enough with the riddles. What do you want from me?"

"We know you seek her. We can provide you with the means to find her, to understand her. It would be a tragedy for such dedication to be misdirected by sentiment."

The words spark something in Ezra. "Misdirected? Sounds like you're scared of her. Maybe I should be working *with* Lucifera."

Silence stretches out, a calculated pause that feels both infinite and instant. "Sentiment is a weakness, Detective. It clouds judgment. She is an anomaly. We are the solution. We can give you what you truly want: an end to the cycle. A world where the guilty cannot hide." The offer hangs in the air, tangible and terrifying. His cop brain screams it's a trap. His obsessed brain whispers it's the only way forward.

"Where?" he asks, the single word loaded with disbelief and a desperate, gnawing need.

"We will find you, Detective Voss," the voice says, the finality in it both ominous and absolute. "Very soon."

The line clicks dead, leaving Ezra in a silence thicker than any words. He stares at the phone, then at the frozen image of Lucifera on his screen. He's just been contacted by a power he can't comprehend, and he's not sure if he's found an ally or his own executioner.

Darkness swallows the room, leaving only the ghostly flicker of Lucifera's digital flame.

Ezra sits in the silence, haunted by the echo of the Justicar's sterile whisper, by the weight of an offer wrapped in divine logic.

Sentiment is a weakness. She is an anomaly. We are the solution.

The words loop in his mind, cold and precise, a stark contrast to the chaotic, passionate fire that dances on his screen. She burns in the glow, as vivid and haunting as memory. He can feel the boundaries of his world shifting, reshaping around her. Around the choice he knows is coming.

He stares at the footage, the only light in a room and a mind gone black.

She moves through the church like prophecy, her fire erupting with perfect execution, perfect damnation. Ezra is drawn to the incandescence, a moth helpless against the fatal allure.

67

The Justicar's voice, unyielding and devoid of emotion, replays in his head: *She is a cosmic weapon out of control.* But in her chaos, Ezra sees order. In her fire, truth. He lets the footage loop again, a record he knows will never break.

What she offers—vengeance, salvation, both—it sings to him in a way the law never could. And with each repetition, the question: Why fight her at all?

Exhaustion blankets him, a fatigue deeper than flesh. He closes his eyes, but she is still there, scorched onto the backs of his eyelids.

Lucifera. The Justicar. Their voices twist together, a symphony of fire and ice. He is not afraid of her flame, or the angel who wants him for Heaven's dirty work.

He's afraid that following her might be the only thing that makes sense. He's afraid of the sterile, passionless "solution" the Justicar offers—a world cleansed of guilt, but also of mercy.

"You know what they can't do," he tells the screen, his own voice strange in the void of the room. "What they'll never do." It is both accusation and admission, the kind of truth that scrapes skin and soul raw. He watches her face, her final breath before the act. He sees the flicker of something the Justicar would call weakness.

Sentiment. A flicker of humanity in the heart of the inferno. The room closes in, smaller with every tick of a clock he can't see. His whole world fits in these four walls, in this screen, in the eyes that judge from the flickering digital ether.

Ezra's trench coat hangs on a chair, a haphazard question mark among the chaos. He sits among the case files, an emperor of the lost and damned.

The Justicar offered him Heaven's version of justice—clean, absolute, and devoid of the messy complications of the heart. But Ezra can't accept it. He won't. She's beyond that.

"Do I even want to stop you?" he wonders aloud, the question a traitor's whisper in the dark. He feels the pull, the temptation, the seduction of something larger than law. Larger than life. Larger than a sterile, heavenly order.

Ezra's eyes flicker open, raw and desperate. He sees her. He has always seen her.

His hand reaches out, shaking with exhaustion and need. He stretches toward the screen, wanting to touch the flame. Wanting it to touch him back. He has been given a choice not between two sides, but between two kinds of justice.

And in the silent, flickering glow of his apartment, he knows which one he has to follow. The footage went viral within hours.

Not through official channels—the police department buried Ezra's report, the media dismissed it as elaborate CGI, and the Church issued carefully worded statements about "isolated incidents" and "ongoing investigations." But the truth had a way of spreading through cracks in the official narrative.

Anonymous uploads appeared on every platform simultaneously. Security camera feeds from multiple angles. Cell phone videos from witnesses who'd been too terrified to speak to authorities.

69

Audio recordings of screams that cut off too suddenly, too completely.

The hashtag #BurningTruth began trending at 3 AM, carried by insomniacs and night shift workers who shared the footage with trembling fingers and disbelieving captions. By dawn, it had reached forty-seven countries.

The world was learning that monsters existed, and something was hunting them.

Ezra watched the spread from his apartment, his laptop screen reflecting his exhausted face as comment threads exploded with fear, hope, and desperate questions. He'd started something he couldn't control, and part of him wondered if that was exactly what she'd intended.

His phone buzzed. Unknown number. The voice was shaky, young. 'Detective Voss? They're coming for the children at Saint Catherine's tonight. Please— you have to stop them. She would have stopped them.' The line went dead, but Ezra was already reaching for his coat.

"Detective Voss? My name is Father Chen. I think... I think I need your help. They're after me next, aren't they?"

Chapter 6 – An Act of Mercy

Ezra Voss treads the shadowed corridors of the monastery like an intruder in a divine morgue.

The air, thick with the cloying sweetness of old incense and the damp scent of quiet rot, clings to his coat. The walls are a silent testament to forgotten faith, covered in saints whose painted eyes never learned how to see.

He moves past the blank stares of marble icons until he finds what he's been looking for—a former acolyte with hands that tremble like trapped birds and the guilty look of a man caught outside of Heaven's grace.

"This place is open to the public, isn't it?" Ezra's voice is low, an edge that cuts through the sacred silence.

"You shouldn't be here," the acolyte whispers, his eyes darting over Ezra's shoulder as if expecting a legion of avenging angels to descend. He clutches a heavy, leather-bound book to his chest like a shield.

Ezra crosses his arms, letting the moment stretch until the other man's unease blooms like a bruise.

"Figured you'd want to talk. Why else risk calling a cop?"

The acolyte wilts, his posture collapsing inward. "Not here." He leads Ezra down a narrow hallway that twists like scripture open to interpretation, the air growing colder with each step.

"They said it was divine protection," he says, his voice barely more than breath. "The Cruciform Order... they have places hidden from the public. From the law. Sanctuaries for those who serve a... higher purpose."

"And these ways," Ezra presses, his voice dangerously soft, "they include protecting predators?"

"There are others," the man says finally, shoulders slumping as if under the weight of unseen wings. "Hidden names. Important names. Men the world thinks are saints."

The words hang between them like condemned souls. Ezra takes out a notebook, his pen moving like a judgment. "Go on."

He writes each name the acolyte spills, each confession tying past to present, familiar names connected to abuse cases that vanished like prayers lost in a storm.

It's a pattern Ezra recognizes—strings of corruption pulled until they unravel under holy sanction. As he works, a shadow of intention so broad he can't see the edges begins to loom. He's getting closer to the heart of the rot.

Ezra crouches in a dusty alcove, the smell of candle wax and paranoia thick in his throat. He's a ghost in this hidden vault, a place where shadows conspire.

Through his telephoto lens, he watches the ritual unfold. Robed figures speak in the dead language of a dead God, their words echoing like sins eager for new souls.

Ezra keeps the lens trained, each frame a confession, each click a revelation. This isn't just a meeting; it's the nerve center of something that spans lifetimes.

The chamber is a blasphemy of opulence, with gilded icons whose eyes seem to follow his every move. One figure holds up an envelope, its contents whispered to be enough currency to buy whole congregations, to silence inconvenient laws.

The others nod, their pious masks betraying nothing but complicity. Ezra zooms in, focusing on one particularly distinguished figure. An archbishop, if Ezra's intuition serves him right. A man whose file is suspiciously clean, a shepherd who has opted to be a wolf.

This is why Lucifera targeted the priest last week. This is why she burns them. They're all connected, threads in a vast, divine conspiracy she sees better than he ever could. He clicks another frame, then another.

Each captures a sliver of guilt, an instant of damnation. He feels the chamber growing colder, or maybe it's just the chill of understanding that grips him. He has the names, the faces, the proof. Now he just needs the monster at the center of it all.

The chapel doors part, not with a bang but a whisper, yet every robed figure knows what it means. Candles tremble, flames jittering like guilty souls.

Lucifera steps through, a scarlet goddess of judgment, and all noise falls away. Her eyes are molten gold, lighting the room with a blaze that renders every sin in stark relief.

Ezra watches from the gallery above, unseen, his heart a steady drumbeat in the sacred silence. He had half-hoped, half-feared she'd come. Now he sees it all unfold.

Below, the clergy are statues frozen mid-prayer. They know who she is; they know why she's come. Her gaze locks on the archbishop at the altar, a man protected by robes and lies. The others inch back, leaving him exposed, a sacrifice to a power he doesn't believe in.

"You should have expected me," she says, her voice a low melody of destruction.

He tries to stand, to claim some semblance of authority, but his knees betray him. He collapses into a parody of prayer. "No judge," he gasps, his voice cracking. "No trial."

Lucifera kneels to meet him, her smile a thin line of pity that doesn't reach her eyes. "Only the fire," she whispers.

The flames leap to life around them, tendrils of heat curling in precise spirals. They leave the altar untouched, the building intact, but the archbishop screams as they wrap around his soul, peeling back layers of deceit until only the raw, terrified guilt remains.

Ezra's breath catches. This is no random vengeance; it's targeted, deliberate. It knows who to burn. His hands tremble as he keeps filming, capturing every moment. Lucifera stands, unblinking as the fire consumes its guilty prey.

She turns, and the look in her eyes is not rage, but a serene, terrifying inevitability. As she passes through the chapel doors, Ezra realizes he's still holding his breath. He has to understand her.

He followed her through the city's wounded streets, each step haunted by the echo of hesitation. She was flame-touched and silent, a spectral blaze flickering against shattered concrete and a starless sky.

As Ezra watched her, questions clawed inside his mind. Why was she letting him tail her? Was it curiosity, cruelty, or some unreadable combination of both? He followed her up a skeletal ruin of a parking deck, its concrete ribs thrusting up into the night. As they reached the rooftop, Lucifera finally paused, a distant flame against the concrete sky.

"You're persistent," she said, finally turning to face him. "I didn't follow you here by accident." Ezra stepped closer, pulling out a worn manila folder. "I've been working the same case you just torched. Father Hale was connected to a network I've been tracking for months.

" Her eyes flicked to the folder, then back to his face. "Your point?" "My point is you're hitting the branches, not the root." He opened the folder, showing surveillance photos, financial records. "The trafficking ring runs through Senator Morrison, Judge Kellerman, and about six others. Hale was middle management."

"You've done your homework." There was grudging respect in her voice. "Three years' worth. Ever since a little girl named Sarah Martinez died trying to expose them." Ezra's voice hardened. "Your fire cleans house, but it doesn't leave evidence. I need something that will stick in court."

"You want to use me." It wasn't a question.

"I want to stop them. All of them." He met her molten gaze. "You can burn them, but I can make sure the world knows why they deserved it." For the first time since he'd started following her, Lucifera looked at him like he might be useful for something other than target practice.

She was on fire, every part of her, and the words came out like sparks. Ezra braced for the burn. Instead, she smiled—a wry twist that cut through the night with surgical precision. "If you're going to follow me, you'd better know one thing: Don't get in the way."

He found his voice, and with it, his courage. "You let me follow you. Why?"

Lucifera tilted her head, the runes on her jacket pulsing with a soft, internal light. "Consider it an act of mercy."

"On your part or mine?"

Her laugh was sharp as a blade. She held his gaze, and for an instant, Ezra thought he saw the flicker of something human in her amber eyes. "Why do you target only certain people?" he asked. "You say it's justice. How do you decide?"

"I burn the guilty. That's it."

Ezra took a step closer, his curiosity winning over self-preservation. "And what if I don't believe in your brand of justice?"

Her smile turned hollow. "Then you haven't been paying attention." She looked at him as if waiting for something—disappointment, fear, the sound of retreating footsteps. He gave her none of those. "You talk about mercy, but you burn people alive."

"Correction." Her tone was flat, absolute. "I burn people. I do not ask them how they'd prefer it."

He didn't flinch. "And me? Why haven't I gone up in flames yet?"

"That depends on you," Lucifera said, her voice a softer echo of the inferno it promised. "You're curious. Curiosity is forgivable." When she turned to walk again, he followed without thinking twice.

They walked together, uneasily but inevitably, into the shadows of an industrial graveyard. Cranes and girders jutted from the earth like the skeletons of long-extinct beasts. The air tasted of rust and decay.

"So you burn the guilty," Ezra said, the words lingering between them like a smoke trail. "That's your rule?"

Lucifera moved with the certainty of a weapon aimed and fired. "Yes. I find it strange that humans need more than one."

"You act like it's so simple," Ezra replied, his voice tinged with the kind of disbelief that bordered on faith. "But what if you're wrong?"

77

"I am not wrong." The statement was as unflinching as stone. She turned toward him, her silhouette framed by the skeletal remains of a forgotten factory. "You think this is vengeance. You think I do this to satisfy something."

"Don't you?"

"If you have to ask, you haven't been paying attention." Lucifera resumed walking. "I was created to do this. And when they failed to control me, I found my own mission."

The shadows grew thicker. "And you never miss, is that it? Everyone you burn is guilty beyond doubt?"

"Beyond doubt," Lucifera echoed. "I see their sins as clearly as you see their faces."

"How?" The question burst out, more an accusation than an inquiry. He needed to know how someone— anyone—could be so certain. "How can you be so damn sure?"

"Would you be following me if I weren't?" she countered. It wasn't an answer, but it silenced him all the same. He watched her vanish into the night, the air still humming with the furious scent of judgment.

He tried to convince himself he didn't feel relief. The partnership had begun, both of them too stubborn, too sure to realize they'd already agreed to it. Ezra stood there, his conviction as real and undeniable as the embers glowing at his feet.

He turned and walked into the night, chasing the question, the answer, the woman who had left him with nothing and everything he needed.

From the spire of a forgotten church, the Justicar watched. He was a void against the bruised twilight, his presence an utter stillness that absorbed the city's chaotic energy.

He had observed the mortal, Ezra Voss, tailing the anomaly. He had witnessed their tense dialogue on the rooftop, the fragile, dangerous dance of their first real encounter.

He processed the interaction with cold, divine logic. The mortal was not an obstacle; he was a complication. A variable Heaven had intended to use, but who now showed signs of being influenced.

The Justicar's mandate was clear: extinguish the anomaly. The detective was meant to be a tool to that end, a lure. But watching them, seeing the flicker of something other than fear in the mortal's eyes—curiosity, defiance, a dangerous empathy— the Justicar recalibrated.

Sentiment is a weakness, he thought, the words echoing his earlier conversation with the detective. *It clouds judgment.*

Lucifera's connection to this human, however nascent, was a flaw in her otherwise chaotic design. It was a vulnerability. An impurity.

The plan to use the mortal was now compromised. Ezra Voss was no longer a reliable asset. He was a contagion, infected by the very anomaly he was meant to help contain.

The Justicar's silver mask reflected the dying city lights, betraying nothing. The mission parameters had shifted. The indirect approach had failed before

79

it had even truly begun. A direct correction was now necessary.

He would not wait for the mortal to lead him to her again. He would hunt her himself.

Chapter 7 – Duel in the Dark

The storm has a grudge. Rain lashes rooftops like shrapnel, stinging the black city into a dark glitter. Lightning unzips the sky with violent light, brief but electric as Lucifera crosses the ledge, rain-soaked and restless.

 A lone shadow on a barren rooftop, Lucifera slips across antennas and brick with uncanny grace, her scarlet jacket pulsing like a living thing against the elements while her skin steams beneath the onslaught.

Her skin steams beneath the onslaught, distorting the night around her into a blur of motion. She runs against wind and doubt, senses attuned to the threat in the atmosphere—the sterile, familiar cold of Heaven closing in.

Her arm is an anchor of pain, a brutal reminder of how close the last battle cut.

Lucifera doesn't fear death. She dreads the hollow nothing of endless futility, the forever war that wants to swallow her purpose whole.

Their whispers reached her first—simmer down, obey, or else. Now they skip right to the threat of oblivion, to hunters cloaked in righteous wrath. She dodges a rusted vent, letting sarcasm sharpen the edges of her dread.

A jagged breath of pain bites her side. Her hand moves instinctively to the wound beneath her jacket, the slash that blazes with every step, a reminder of the last enforcer Heaven unleashed.

Her fire consumed him in the end, but not cleanly, not without cost. Her eyes flash like molten gold as she forces her body onward, refusing the weakness that threatens to close in around her like a slow poison. Each throb is a dare she answers: try harder.

Rain turns the world slick, but she doesn't break pace, navigating the rooftop maze with a fluid defiance.

She leaps a narrow chasm between buildings, her form a shadow cast by hellfire and rebellion. Lucifera lands, rolls, her motions fierce and relentless. Her mind is a fever of purpose, burning through the wet and cold.

There are innocents in this world. She owes them more than her death. And yet—there's the sense of unraveling, the knowledge that this hunt escalates. Heaven and Hell: she's become the favorite joke neither side can laugh off. It's all the more reason to fight; their fear is proof of her flame.

Lucifera pauses, a fraction of a second but eternal in its clarity. She knows the grip of danger; it calls like an old adversary. Her senses tingle with the anticipation of a looming, divine assault.

A dark smirk catches on her lips—oh, what new instrument have they sent this time? A moment of fragile silence stretches thin as she stands there, her breath misting against the onslaught.

She is entirely, brutally alive in the eye of her private storm, but she's felt Heaven's edge, and it presses closer. The storm pushes against her like doubt, each gust heavy with unspoken threats.

The night throbs around her as she fights to reclaim the cityscape as her own. Her steps slow with a sudden, foreboding clarity. The shadows seem to solidify. She spins at the center of the storm, anticipation a living thing within her. Even the wind holds its breath. And then, a heartbeat of impossible calm.

Lucifera feels the shift. The storm loses its voice, rain stuttering into silence. At the edge of the rooftop, he emerges: a void, an echo, cloaked in celestial order. She sees him in flashes, the silver of his mask glinting with each pulse of lightning. A gleam of a blade that isn't metal. And Lucifera, this burned angel, welcomes the confrontation with a feral joy, the knowing relief of prey who turns to meet the hunt.

He is a slice of order, divine and terrible, drawn from Heaven's arsenal like a perfect weapon. Each step is precise, cold with purpose. The rain hisses off the blade in his hand, a weapon of solidified silence that seems to absorb the storm's fury. To anyone else, he might seem an apparition—but Lucifera knows his type. Her blood hums, her wound aches with anticipation. Let them think she's cornered.

"Has Heaven run out of angels?" Her voice is a low, amused rasp against the storm. "Or did Oren just stop pretending he wants me alive?"

The Justicar halts, his masked face unreadable, his presence an absolute. "Heaven does not want. It decrees." His voice is without tone, a sound scraped from the edge of a void. "You are an error. I am the correction."

Lucifera glances down at the city streets, at the distant lights of cars and homes. "As much as I'd love to redecorate your pristine order with the guts of this city, I have a policy against collateral damage." Her eyes flick back to him, burning with challenge. "This rooftop is too small for what's coming."

The Justicar tilts his head, processing. "Your sentiment is a flaw. But the variable of mortal interference is... inefficient."

"Glad we agree," Lucifera says, a feral grin spreading across her face. "Let's take this somewhere with fewer witnesses."

Without another word, she launches herself into the stormy sky, a comet of scarlet and flame. The Justicar follows a half-second later, a silent, colorless void in her wake. They streak away from the city's heart, two opposing forces seeking a battlefield worthy of their war.

The storm followed them out of the city, as if tethered to their fury. They landed on a stretch of barren, cracked earth miles from the nearest soul.

The plains became their arena, a powder keg of silence and fire. Lucifera and the Justicar collide, limbs and weapons slicing the night.

A slash of his blade arcs toward her, a cut in reality itself; an infernal explosion of heat as she parries, turning the weapon aside with flames that could melt truth.

They twist around each other like smoke and intent, and for one terrible moment the air is pure light, pure heat, pure tension before everything combusts.

His blade is precision; her flame is defiance. She twists, rolls, a flaring arc of motion and resolve as his weapon sings through empty air. It catches the night and the storm, cutting the dark into shreds of cold brilliance. Her inferno answers with a flare, a jet of molten certainty that streaks across the plains, licking at his heels.

"One cut, anomaly," he states over the symphony of the storm. "That is all it will take."

"Then you'd better make it count," she snarls, and the fire in her voice becomes the fire in her blood, propelling her body like a fever dream.

Each motion tells a story. He thrusts, she dodges; he slashes, she spins away in a cloud of embers and rain. Her movements are graceful but raw, a choreography of survival that pushes her closer to the edge. His are balletic and relentless, driven by the unyielding rhythm of divine conviction. He sees the strain in her movements, the way she favors her side. He presses the advantage.

Lucifera feels the weight of every battle she's fought. Her arm is agony; her soul is raw. His certainty is a force more dangerous than his blade, cutting into her very core. But there's a savage elegance to his fighting that makes her doubt his assurance. That doubt is her opening. She burns bright, consuming even his certainty with the gravity of her flame.

"Why do you keep trying?" His voice, a clean cut of incredulity. "Your defiance is pointless."

"Because you can't understand it." Her words slice back, more honest than she wants them to be. "That's why you keep losing."

He counters, presses in, his blade a blur of silent cuts aimed at her wounded side.

Lucifera forces herself beyond the pain, beyond the risk, into a realm where only the next blow matters.

Her instincts are a map of fury; they guide her past the injury, past the threat, into a clarity that strips all else away. The ground cracks and groans beneath their onslaught. She's losing blood, losing heat, but the thrill of it is pure; it gives her life and life is enough to burn on.

She ducks, spins, unleashes an explosion of heat that catches the Justicar off guard. His blade wavers, just a flicker, but Lucifera is a creature of flickers. He lashes out with renewed fervor, but she's already beyond his strike. They are a tangle of heat and breath, a tightrope of dying light. One of them will slip. A brilliant arc as his sword swings again, this time so close she can see the runes flicker. The runes of the dead. The thought propels her backward and up, launching herself away.

Everything stretches into a painful eternity. The cut glances off, a razor of frost against the inferno of her skin. She's hurt, but not gone; hurt, but still whole enough to take one last, blinding chance. She lets him feel victory, lets him taste it as close as her breath, and with everything left she flares into him. The fire is her blood, is her voice, is every truth he can't cut out of her.

The fire consumes him. It is not a quick death. It is a revelation. The Justicar staggers, his blade of silence shattering into a thousand pieces of nothing. His mask cracks, then melts away, revealing a face of perfect, angelic beauty, now twisted in the first and only emotion he has ever known: shock.

He tries to speak, to invoke the order he represents, but his voice is gone, burned away by a truth hotter than any celestial decree. He looks at Lucifera, his eyes wide with a dawning, terrible understanding. He was not a correction. He was just another mistake.

Lucifera's own vision blurs with the ash of victory, heavy and charred. She watches him collapse in firelight. The air reeks of burnt wings, of burnt faith. But as the last of his form turns to smoke, his lips form a single, silent word. A name.

Oren.

And then he's ash, is memory, is smoke.

The storm clears its throat and moves on, leaving Lucifera with the sound of her own ragged breath.

Leaving her with the shape of a name that still burns, still scars. She cracks. Her breath shudders against the still-hot air, eyes losing focus.

She sinks to the cracked earth, the barren land a blur of ruin. She fades like the storm, desperate to hold her shape as the night smothers her in a too-human exhaustion. An unconscious sleep bleeds her memory.

Falling, she thinks of Kieran, and it almost feels like warmth. Then, nothing.

Chapter 8 – The Cathedral Ghost

Ruins rest beneath a twilight shroud, holy and desolate as forgotten gods. Even the ghosts have abandoned this cathedral, leaving only crumbling walls and the distant mourning of a thousand unanswered prayers.

Lucifera stands before the shattered stone, a dark seraph against a backdrop of moonlight and creeping vines. Her eyes, liquid gold and haunted, drink in the landscape.

This was a sacred place, a place of power and of love. It was here she let her guard down, and it was here that it all came undone.

She moves into the heart of the ruin, where gnarled roots wrap around the pillars like the fingers of time, strangling the divine with patient, green strength. Each step is slow, her customary intensity replaced by a reverence that borders on fragility.

The broken archways sigh above her, wind whistling through them like a choir of the departed. She traces the jagged line of a fractured altar, the stone cold beneath her fingertips, and memories flicker in the dark like moths drawn to a flame she can no longer control.

In these ruins, she was whole once. She and he, an infernal oddity and a fallen angel, rewriting their own fate within these walls.

She inhales deeply, her breath laced with the ghost of incense, ozone, and betrayal. The silence envelops her, but it is not empty. In it, there are voices—laughter that once echoed off the now-shattered dome, whispered promises that have since turned to dust. She reaches out, her fingers trembling slightly as they hover above a collapsed bench where they once sat, their forms intertwined, their futures seemingly limitless. The echoes of her own vulnerability circle like vultures, patient and hungry.

What once filled her with light now weighs her down. Her anger, her sense of purpose—all born in this wreckage. A bitter smile tugs at her lips.

They had dreams then, when Heaven and Hell were irrelevant. Here, love was the closest thing she ever had to belonging. Her eyes open, and there's fire in them now, burning away the illusions. The same walls that embraced her conspired against her, crashing down in a betrayal she never saw coming. For a long moment, she stands, eyes closed against the world, alone with her ghosts, letting the pain of it wash over her, a baptism in sorrow.

The shadows are long, haunted things. A presence detaches itself from the darkness, a secret unwilling to stay buried. Kieran Vale emerges, a slanted silhouette with tattered wings hidden beneath his coat. The reckless glow of her presence draws him like a moth to an open flame. She stands motionless in the center of the cathedral, a fallen star refusing to burn out. She's closed her eyes, but the tension in her body, the way the air shimmers around her, is a clear admission: She knows he's there.

Finally, she turns her head, just slightly, a predator acknowledging another in its territory. "Don't be a stranger," she says, her voice dark velvet, heavy with irony. "Unless that's what you're going for." Kieran steps further into the dim light, his boots scuffing against loose stone. "You know me, Lucifera. I've never been one to keep my distance," he replies, a smile twisting the edge of his mouth, all bravado and brokenness. Her eyes catch the light, molten and wary.

The years between them collapse in an instant. She remembers his laugh echoing through these same ruins when they were whole, when hope felt possible. He used to sit exactly where he's standing now, sketching impossible architectures for a world that could house both light and shadow. She'd tease him about his optimism. He'd counter that her cynicism was just hope wearing armor. "You still do that thing with your wing," she observes, noting how he favors his left side, unconsciously protecting the damaged appendage.

"Trying to hide how much it hurts." "And you still set things on fire when you're uncomfortable," he replies, nodding at the small scorch marks appearing around her feet. "Some habits die hard." The familiarity is a blade between them—sharp with what was lost, what was chosen, what was abandoned. They know each other's tells, each other's weaknesses. It makes this conversation both easier and infinitely harder. "I used to dream about this place," Kieran admits, his voice dropping to something rawer. "About finding you here again. In the dreams, you'd forgive me." "In the dreams, did I have a choice?"

He flinches. "Lu—" "Don't." The nickname hits her like a physical blow. "You lost the right to call me that when you chose them over me." "I chose survival over suicide," he fires back, some of his old defiance flaring. "What you were planning—what you did—it was beautiful and terrible and completely insane." "It worked." "It nearly killed you. It did kill us." The silence that follows is thick with the weight of their shared history. She sees him as he was—idealistic, brilliant, believing they could change the system from within. He sees her as she was—passionate, uncompromising, willing to burn the world for a truth no one wanted to hear.

"And here I was, thinking you'd finally taken a hint," she shoots back, the heat of her words wrapping around him like barbed wire.

"Hints were never my strong suit," he says, his eyes searching hers for any flicker of softness. He finds only the impenetrable surface of a place that was once home. He has to warn her. "Lucifera, listen to me. Heaven—"

She cuts him off with a sharp, humorless laugh. "Heaven?" she echoes, sarcasm like a smokescreen. "You're worried about Heaven now? A little late for that, don't you think?"

"They're mobilizing," Kieran insists, ignoring the sting. The urgency is a fire in his veins. "They've declared you a threat. Oren is sanctioning a purge. But that's not all. Your flame... it's done more than they expected."

Lucifera tilts her head, the movement elegant and dangerous. "Go on."

"It's sparked rebellion," he says, the words falling heavy between them. "Some angels are watching you. Some are supporting you. They see your fire not as chaos, but as a cause. They're tired of being cold."

She flinches, a barely visible tremor of shock and anger. The title of "savior" drips with an irony she can't stand. "Rebellion," she says, tasting the word like it might be poison. "Heaven doesn't allow it. They crush it before it can draw breath."

"Exactly," he nods, his eyes intense. "They won't tolerate it. Or you. They're hunting you, and this time, they're bringing more than nets. They're bringing an end."

"I never wanted followers," she insists, her voice defiant yet cracking. "I never wanted a war."

"Then why did you start it?" His question is brutal in its simplicity, leaving no room for evasion.

"I didn't," she fires back, her hands clenching into fists. "I'm no leader."

"Liar," he says softly, a verdict rather than an insult. The word hits her harder than any flame. It ignites her fury. "If I'm a liar, then what are you?" she throws at him, words dripping with venom and vulnerability. "A coward who watched from the shadows?"

"Coward or not," he says, each word an icepick to her chest, "at least I'm not blind. You think you're delivering justice? You're playing with matches in a room full of dynamite. The lives you're affecting... it looks like chaos, Kieran. Like a thousand needless deaths."

"Nothing is needless," she fires back, the pain bleeding through her voice. "They all have to face judgment."

93

"Or be judged?" He steps closer, his presence scorching her resolve. "Because that's what you're doing. You're judging Heaven itself."

"Someone has to," she insists, raw and furious. "They built me to do this."

"They built you?" His laughter is harsh, mocking. "That's what you think? You're an accident, Lucifera. An accident that scares the shit out of them, and you love it."

"I admit nothing," she growls, desperate and defiant. "I just do what needs to be done."

"Needs?" He shakes his head, an elegy for her denials. "Or wants? You want this. You're proud of being their worst nightmare. Admit it."

He has her pinned, trapped, no escape but the truth. The accusation strikes a nerve deep inside her, a place she thought long dead. "I wanted you to understand!" she screams, the cathedral swallowing her desperation, the sound echoing off the broken stones of their shared past.

Kieran's own mask of bravado finally shatters. The pain in her voice finds its echo in his.

"I did understand," he says, his voice raw, broken. "That's why I left."

He takes a step back, the space between them suddenly a chasm of shared history.

"Your fire... it didn't just burn them, Lucifera. It illuminated everything. Including me. And when I looked at myself in the light of your certainty, I saw the rot. The doubt. The part of me that was still one of *them*." His voice cracks.

"I didn't leave you. I left a part of myself I couldn't bear to look at anymore. I let you burn because I was too much of a coward to burn with you."

His words are the final spark. The ruin isn't a grave anymore. It's a battlefield. Lucifera's anger ignites, incandescent with the need to release what words can't hold. The world explodes in flames as she lashes out, tired of talking. He fights back with a blade of grace, the way he used to—only this time against her.

A blaze flares around her, raw and all-consuming. The ruin erupts in flame, ancient stones groaning under the sudden, violent heat. "Is this what you want?" she screams, incandescent. "To watch me burn?"

"Always." He stands defiant in her flames, then draws his blade, a sleek, silvery arc that slices the air with brutal grace. It blazes with ethereal light, a star against her sun, and meets her assault head on.

Lucifera attacks again, relentless. The flame she summons is a reflection of her—a beautiful, destructive force. It licks at the pillars, turning the ruin into a hellscape of their own making.

Kieran's armor glows, a cold radiance against her heat. He deflects her strike, their powers clashing in a violent dance of light and fire. "You think this will change anything?" he yells, parrying her next attack.

"I'm done proving things," she fires back, her flames swirling in elegant fury. "I'm done talking."

The ruin becomes a storm of light and heat, their battle turning it to cinders and ash. But it's not about destruction. It's about release.

Her vulnerability fuels her; his accusations sharpen his every move. It's not about killing. It's about surviving this moment, this shared history that refuses to die. The intensity builds, a crescendo of power and pain, until they both pull back, breathless. It's exhaustion, not defeat. They can't—won't—do this to each other.

They don't let go. Can't. The air is still thick with fire and regret as Kieran closes the distance and pulls her into an embrace.

Lucifera doesn't fight it. Her body is rigid for a moment, then she sags against him, the fight draining out of her. It's tenderness laced with everything left unsaid. She rests her head against his chest and lets herself want, but only for a moment.

"Lucifera," he says, her name a raw whisper, his arms a cage she wishes she could escape and stay locked in forever.

"This is going to end badly," she warns, her voice muffled against his coat, trying to ignore the crack in it.

"Probably," he agrees, not letting go.

"You should have killed me," she says, almost laughs, almost cries.

He tightens his grip, a silent, fierce denial. "I never could," he admits, his breath warm against her skin.

She's tired, so tired. But she still has enough strength to pull away. Not far. Just enough to see his face, the history it wears like scars and glory. His eyes catch hers, deep as oceans, unforgiving as time.

"Be careful," he tells her, his voice cracking. "They're coming for you."

She wants to pretend it's just words, that she doesn't feel the weight behind them. But he's not lying. And she's more afraid than she will ever admit. He turns to leave, the movement sudden but not surprising. Inevitable but not painless.

The silence after he's gone is too loud, a cacophony of everything she can't shut out. She hates herself for wanting him to stay. As he vanishes into the shadows of the ruin, she is left alone with the ash, the silence, and the impossible weight of his warning.

Chapter 9 – The Burning Choir

Night consumes the city, swallowing the skyline until only streetlamps remain like dying stars. Lucifera and Ezra move beneath their dim glow, shadows trailing behind as if conspiring against them. The hush is unnerving, a draped illusion of tranquility in this corner of urban chaos. Lucifera can feel the tension, electric, waiting to spark. Ezra matches her pace, silent but aware, and their steps fall into the rhythm of the hunted. Together, they slice through the stillness, insurgents on a path toward the forbidden and forgotten.

The city stretches around them, a vast carcass of concrete and steel. Lucifera senses its hunger, the dark pulse of an entity ready to devour itself from the inside. Above, the buildings loom with spectral detachment, high windows reflecting the blackness like vacant eyes. A desolate street flickers past, neon remnants of an abandoned liquor store blinking with erratic desperation. Beside her, Ezra is a calm shadow, watching but unflinching. There's an intimacy in their shared silence, a promise deeper than the gulf separating Heaven and Hell.

Ezra stops to light a cigarette, its flare briefly igniting his worn features. Smoke curls upward, the only visible ghost in a city full of them.

"That going to save your soul?" Lucifera asks, her tone both mocking and fond.

"Got a few vices yet," he replies, a grin softening the exhaustion on his face. "Call it faith."

"Faith is a tricky business."

"Or justice." His eyes meet hers, alive with curiosity. "Depends who's asking."

"Depends who's dying," she corrects, a quicksilver edge to her words. Their exchange crackles like dry leaves catching fire, betraying a comfort born of alliance.

A sudden noise pierces the air, a gunshot or a car backfiring, its echo unsettling the shadows. Lucifera tenses, the temperature around her rising subtly.

"Normal city sounds, right?" Ezra offers, his voice a tether to normalcy.

She doesn't answer, scanning the emptiness with eyes that glow faintly molten. He watches her with something akin to admiration—or is it resignation? Either way, their bond is palpable, silent but unyielding, a strength that relies more on instinct than language.

They cut through an alley, refuse spilling over onto the sidewalk like open wounds. Above them, a fire escape curls downward, skeletal and sinister. The city seems asleep, a hulking beast momentarily stilled, but they know better. It's an illusion, as deceitful as celestial peace. Lucifera feels the pull of secrets and sin, the whispered invitation of damnation disguised as salvation.

"So what's Heaven's bounty for a rogue archangel?" Ezra's voice is teasing, the words an echo of a threat.

"They can't afford me," she quips, unruffled. "And you? Putting your trust in a lost cause?"

"I believe in justice," he says, sincerity rippling beneath his humor. "Or whatever you call what you do."

She smirks, a twisted kind of warmth in her expression. Their paths are parallel lines converging in cosmic rebellion. It seems impossible, but here they are, equals in a world that's anything but balanced.

Lucifera's eyes burn softly in the night, a beacon and a threat that illuminates their way. The pavement beneath them vibrates with memories of violence, past and future.

"What are you, Voss?" she asks, amber gaze piercing. "In or out?"

"Guess you'll see." He is unperturbed, his commitment as solid as the ground they tread.

A sudden urgency grips her, a tightening knot of premonition and death in the air. She quickens her pace, Ezra keeping stride without question. They are a dangerous duo, crossing boundaries both mortal and divine, a balance of logic and fervor against the great celestial farce.

At last, they reach the supposed cathedral. It crouches among modernity, an ancient structure draped in the indifferent grime of decades. Lucifera pauses. The air around them is colder, indifferent, vibrating with ritual betrayal.

Together, they confront the behemoth, conspirators against divine injustice. Ezra's presence calms her fire, if only for a moment, and they stand united against the legions of fate.

The lock yields under Ezra's persistence, an old resistance crumbling into quiet obedience. Lucifera stands at his side, flame gathering at her fingertips like hungry fireflies. She watches the alley for prying eyes, but no one stirs, and soon they're inside, the door swinging open with a groan of aged hinges. The air inside is dense and accusing, heavy with incense, mold, and something far more rancid. They move in silence, side by side, invaders in a kingdom built on deception. Every step deepens the stench of corruption and neglect. Every step magnifies the spiritual decay waiting for them below.

Murals line the walls, vibrant in color but disturbing in their transformations. Saintly figures morph into demonic caricatures, flesh and paint mingling in a macabre dance of twisted intention. Piety becomes perversion; sanctity twists into sin. The effect is mesmerizing, a religious spectacle that Lucifera watches with an almost amused disdain. Beside her, Ezra remains stoic, though the frescoes' dark beauty weighs visibly on him. He hesitates, looking to Lucifera. She meets his gaze, her eyes sparking with unwavering conviction. With a shared understanding, they move forward, proceeding toward the chasm of corruption and dread that beckons below.

Lucifera moves with dark grace, a serpent in Eden. Her lips curl into a smirk as the frescoes blur past, the religious artistry nothing more than elaborate theater to her.

"I think I like what they've done with the place," she says, sarcasm coating her words like ash.

Ezra stays silent, but his eyes tell another story, tracing each grotesque transformation with heavy attention. Each step pulls them deeper into desecration, the atmosphere pressing down like a lead shroud. Their very presence feels like an affront to the long-held secrets, the catacombs awaiting them a vault of betrayal and forgotten faith.

As they move, Ezra's voice finally breaks the weighted silence. "Who do you think was the first to practice faith and betray it?"

Lucifera doesn't hesitate, her reply swift and stinging. "The first to find profit in it." Her flames flicker with intensity, a subtle confirmation of her derision.

"Sounds like you speak from experience."

"Some of us were forged in it." Her tone is dismissive yet loaded, as if a thousand celestial injustices simmer just beneath her words. Ezra considers her, seeing not just a reluctant ally but the embodiment of rebellion.

They descend further, into the heart of darkness itself. Rot and incense blend into a visceral stench, a tangible declaration of moral decay. The atmosphere thickens, heavy and oppressive, an accusation writ large on the very air. Lucifera pauses, the pulsing force beneath the structure speaking to her, a corrupt heartbeat echoing through consecrated stone. She senses the raw, old power embedded in the cathedral's bones, and her own fires surge in answer.

Ezra watches her with concern shadowing his features. "This isn't just some cult, is it?"

She laughs, the sound mirthless. "Did you expect amateurs?"

Their descent continues, torches casting tremulous light that dances along the stone walls. Shadows writhe, dark echoes of Lucifera's own flame. She picks up one of the torches, igniting it with a touch. The burst of light is ferocious, too bright for the dank corridors to bear. The torch dims slightly as her fire engulfs it, its glow fierce but controlled.

Ezra is a step behind, his focus unbroken. "It's all very Old Testament."

Lucifera's disdain cuts like glass. "Even older. This isn't a new trick. Betrayal is in the blueprints."

Her words hang in the air, full of fiery conviction. Her eyes burn with retributive fire, ready to incinerate millennia of hypocrisy. Each sentence they exchange binds them closer, allies against the grand farce of divine order.

The deeper they go, the thicker the air becomes, a soup of malevolence and forgotten prayer. Lucifera feels it, the presence of imminent violence, a tightening of fate's coil. She knows the signs; they've heralded every celestial massacre and mortal purge. Ezra senses it too, a shiver that traces his spine and alerts his every instinct.

"We're close," he says, voice low and charged.

Lucifera nods, flame-bright eyes scanning the darkness. "Too close."

They move toward the sanctum, an aura of anticipation crackling between them. Lucifera's presence is an unstoppable force, consuming and unyielding. Ezra matches her step for step, human resolve aligning with something much more infernal. They are ready, poised to confront the heart of spiritual rot and claim retribution against the lies sanctified in holy flame.

They find the sanctum. It is vast and blasphemous, a parody of worship's grandest ambitions. The sound of chanting is thick, dense and unholy, suffocating the air with distorted harmony. Robed monks surround the cavernous space, heads bowed and oblivious to intrusion. The girl in the center is not. She is chained, pale, terrified—sacrifice wrapped in white. Lucifera feels rage coil inside her, an inferno harnessed but eager. Ezra hovers at her side, his hand brushing his weapon. The monks don't flinch; centuries of inherited arrogance keep them still.

The entire room pulses with ritual energy, each chant like a corrupt heartbeat, vibrating with centuries of inherited sin. The monks move with grotesque unison, their voices melding into a single, discordant hymn. Above them, the rafters shake with the force of their belief. In the center, the girl whimpers, a sound almost swallowed by the sacrilegious cacophony but not quite. Her fear is a living thing, so thick it borders on touch. Lucifera's rage builds, a crescendo of furious anticipation, and her steps echo with an unholy promise.

Lucifera advances, her presence a violent rupture in the sanctified air. Her proximity to the altar draws all attention; the chanting stutters, a skipped beat in the religious noise. The girl lifts her head, eyes wide with new terror, as Lucifera's steps bring her closer and closer to the center of the blasphemous spectacle. Ezra shadows her, scanning the robed figures, assessing threats and weaknesses. Together they seem unstoppable, the shock of their intrusion spreading like fire through dry leaves.

Ezra watches the scene unfold, the chaos of anticipation more chaotic than violence itself. His instincts scream for immediate action, but he knows Lucifera—knows that her fire is most potent when it builds, not erupts. So he waits, each second an eternity, ready to follow her lead. Her focus is so intense it feels like a physical force, heat and wrath contained beneath a veneer of calm. The monks pay him no mind, their eyes fixed on the dark angel now at their center.

Lucifera approaches the altar, her every movement fluid and deliberate. A memory flashes unbidden—another altar, another choice, the first time she'd stayed her hand for mercy and watched innocence die for it. Never again, she'd sworn. But the girl's tears now echo that same desperate hope she'd once carried herself.

The monks regard her with disdain, not yet fearing the inevitability she represents.

"Praying for rain?" Her voice cuts through their chants, serrated and taunting. It echoes through the sanctum with jagged clarity, a cruel symphony against their faltering hymn. Her fury is poetry, merciless and beautiful, the dark undercurrent in a sea of trembling devotion.

The monks attempt to resist, invoking broken prayers and twisted Latin rites. Their voices rise, frantic, as if sheer volume could unmake Lucifera's presence. But she doesn't flinch, her attention never wavering from the girl who remains the target of both monks and their heretic judge. The girl's fear flickers like a flame in the wind, hope igniting it from deep within. Finally, Ezra draws his weapon, the slick sound loud against the backdrop of chant and certainty.

The energy in the room grows frantic. Lucifera's presence distorts the ritual, each moment a shattering of belief and purpose. The monks glance at one another, eyes wide, uncertainty cracking their composed facades. They chant louder, almost screaming their distorted piety. Lucifera seems to relish their mounting panic, the tension of centuries unraveling in her grasp. Her words pierce their ritual, heavy with sarcasm and fury.

"You only get one second chance at a martyr." Her tone is a funeral dirge wrapped in mockery, a verdict more fatal than any prayer.

She condemns them with fire, and this time she doesn't hold back. Wrath blazes unconcealed, and the room is baptized in flame. Holy symbols blacken, stained glass melts into viscous pools. The monks' chants become cries, rising like discordant notes from hell's own choir. Ezra cuts the girl's chains, his hands quick and sure. She falls into him, her frail form collapsing against the solid weight of his humanity.

The sanctum becomes chaos incarnate, a dark opera of agony and purification. Lucifera's fire rages unchecked, consuming all in its path. Ezra shields the girl, preparing for retaliation. But there is none. The monks writhe, abandoned by their deities and conviction, their robes turning to ash as their choir dissolves into screams.

The scene is pure carnage, the slow-motion collapse of a corrupted cathedral. Lucifera watches, satisfaction burning in her eyes, a wrathful savior surveying her handiwork. She has unleashed judgment, but the fire in her soul is far from quenched.

Lucifera steps forward, judgment incarnate. The monks barely react, mired in arrogance and ritual. Her words carve into their chants with a force as fierce as her flames. Sarcasm drips from each syllable, and pillars ignite, the structure burning around them. They invoke desperate prayers, but her fire finds them first. Ezra rescues the girl amidst chaos, protecting her from heat and horror. He watches, mesmerized, as Lucifera turns the sanctum into hell's own cathedral.

Flames curl up the walls like serpents seeking vengeance. Lucifera stands amidst the inferno, an untouchable prophet of fury. The monks' voices strain with frenzied prayers, each plea smothered by fire and fate. They find no mercy, only the relentless spread of judgment's blaze. Ezra shields the girl, his coat enveloping her frail form as the air warps and distorts from the heat. He watches Lucifera, eyes wide with awe and something far deeper. The sanctum becomes a hellish panorama, each piece of burning architecture a note in the dark symphony.

Her words mock them, each sentence a cruel refrain sung over the orchestra of screams. The pillars are fully alight now, bone-white stone charred to the color of old sins. Lucifera's fire is everywhere, consuming and purifying, an artful destruction with a fierce and beautiful design. Ezra pulls the girl closer, his face set in grim determination as he bears witness to Lucifera's terrible majesty.

The monks' desperation grows frantic, their robes catching fire as they clutch at illusions of salvation. But Lucifera doesn't relent; this is not Heaven, and their chants fall useless against the onslaught. They try to flee, only to meet the flames she commands with the slightest gesture.

"Last chance for truth," she said, her voice cutting through their desperate prayers. But instead of unleashing flame, she knelt beside the rescued girl. Her touch was gentle, healing—the opposite of destruction.

The child's wounds closed, her terror faded to confused relief. The monks watched in horror as their victim was made whole before their eyes. This wasn't the vengeance they expected. This was something worse: restoration.

Proof that their harm could be undone, their power rendered meaningless. "You see?" Lucifera stood, addressing the lead monk directly. "She was never broken. You were." Only then did the fire come—not as an inferno, but as surgical strikes. Each monk's robes ignited at the exact spots where they had touched the innocent.

The flames burned away only the corruption, leaving behind ash in the precise shape of their sins. Their screams weren't of pain, but of exposure. The fire revealed the true extent of their crimes, projecting images of their victims onto the cathedral walls like a grotesque slideshow. Every life they'd damaged. Every innocence they'd stolen.

The girl watched from Ezra's arms, no longer afraid. She had seen justice take a different form— not just punishment, but healing. Not just destruction, but truth.

Ezra secures the girl in his arms, backing toward the exit as the structure begins its final collapse.

The sanctum implodes into an infernal ruin, Lucifera's form barely visible through the swirling flames. It's a sight that would turn lesser beings to cinder. But not her. She stands amid the chaos, untouched, unyielding, a legend being forged one ember at a time.

The night is cold and wet as Ezra leads the girl from the collapsing ruins. Lucifera follows, smoke trailing behind her like an infernal cloak. Rain lashes the pavement, each drop a sharp counterpoint to the fire's dying breath. They stand together for one eternal second, an alliance forged in justified flame. Lucifera doesn't smile. She nods toward the girl and vanishes, leaving behind the ash of legends.

The rain falls harder, turning ash to sludge beneath their feet. Ezra feels the depth of Lucifera's commitment, the void left by her sudden absence as vast as the night itself. He holds the girl tighter, her frail form trembling against him, a reminder of what they've just escaped. For all his experience, he is still reeling, struggling to make sense of the raw justice Lucifera metes out. But there is something else too—gratitude, not just for saving the girl, but for saving him from a world of muted grays.

Ezra watches the ruins burn, a man both haunted and hopeful. Flames consume the last of the cathedral, history crumbling into sooty dust. He shields the girl, thoughts tangled in the aftershock of what they've done, of what Lucifera has done. The brutal cleansing of centuries, a single night rewriting millennia of dogma and corruption. He wonders about his place in her war, a lone human in a celestial rebellion, and whether he has the conviction to keep up.

Lucifera's words echo through his mind, every one of them loaded with truth and judgment. Her fire burns just as brightly, a searing promise of more to come. The girl in his arms is proof that the mission isn't futile, that salvation is possible even when the cost is brutal. It's his first tangible sign that this isn't just destruction for destruction's sake.

Alone with the girl, Ezra feels the shift, the end of chaos and the beginning of something far more complex. He understands, maybe for the first time, Lucifera's role as an anti-savior—something more dangerous, more essential, than any hero. She leaves a mark, a charged absence that fills the air and his mind, urging him to be as relentless, as unyielding, as she is.

The rain washes away sin and certainty, a baptism of mortal indifference. Ezra holds the girl close, sheltering her from the elements and the world that will want answers she can't give. He feels the change within and around him, a commitment to this war not just as Lucifera's ally but as something far more personal.

Lucifera's absence is a force all its own, lingering like smoke and echoing like a challenge. Ezra knows this is not the end. He resolves to follow her path, to fight with a fire that matches her own. The legend she leaves behind isn't one of simple victory; it's a dangerous, complex truth that he is now part of. As the rain continues its relentless descent, Ezra understands his role, each drop a metronome of dedication and rebellion. He is, as ever, in.

Chapter 10 – Oren's Messenger

Twilight bleeds across a city that has been dying for centuries.

Lucifera drifts through its alleyways, a ghost hunted by angels.

She can feel them in the air, a sterile cold that prickles at the edge of her fire, a metaphysical itch she can't scratch. They are watching. Of that she is certain.

The question that soaks into the smog is no longer *if* they will strike, but when.

Streetlights flicker, buzzing a nervous warning as she slips from shadow to shadow.

This chase is old, almost a ritual, but the air is tight with a finality she hasn't felt before. It feels closer. More personal. Her thoughts are feral, her senses sharp, tasting the unspooling threads of their plan. Heaven was never subtle.

The streets bend toward a towering cathedral, a gravestone against the bruised sky. Her instincts scream. *Trap.*

Stained glass shards litter the sidewalk like constellations of a broken faith. An unholy calm envelops the street, swallowing sound and sense. Of course it would be here.

They want her on sacred ground, a stage for their judgment. She steels herself, a wry smile touching her lips as the runes on her jacket begin to glow with a hungry, burnished light.

If they want a show, she will give them one. She walks toward the entrance, a flame stepping willingly into the cold.

He needs to find her. She has moved in like smoke and filled the entire hollow space of him, clouded his every waking thought. The city is more empty than usual, every street silent, every sidewalk filled with the ghosts of his old convictions. Ezra can't shake the feeling he's already bent the rules beyond repair, that Lucifera has changed him in ways he didn't expect. In ways that feel irreversible. He turns the corner. That's when he feels it. He isn't alone.

He keeps moving, his body running on pure exhaustion and coffee-stained grit. The detective isn't the only part of him working through this town tonight. There are other forces, new ones, and they're too loud to ignore. Too strong to drown out with familiar routines and faded leads. The newness has his hands shaking. Has his mind set on fire. Has his heart in a death grip that he doesn't quite hate.

His boots hit the pavement in a ragged rhythm, and Ezra wonders how much longer he can keep up. How much more of himself he can bleed out for a truth that always seems one step ahead. Lucifera's truth. It's always just that—hers. The kind that knows no rules, that tears through protocol like bullets through paper. His obsession isn't just curiosity anymore; it's something raw, something far less elegant.

This time, Ezra knows, he's in deeper than he's ever been. In deeper than he'd planned. And the worst part—the best part—is that he isn't planning to come up for air.

Every shadow he passes wears her face. Every distant sound, the low whisper of her name. The world isn't quite solid anymore. Nothing is, except his need to find her. To see those molten eyes and ask the questions that will only lead to more. To chase until there's nothing left of himself, of her, or of the line that separates them. The city unravels behind him, but Ezra never looks back. His hands tighten in his pockets, and he knows he won't need them for long.

He is almost in the part of town where her flames scorched the walls and left something far more permanent. It still reeks of heat and wild, poetic justice. Like she's still here. Like she never left.

But then that feeling—the sudden certainty of another presence—pulses through him, and Ezra can't ignore it. Can't ignore the quickening of his breath. Can't ignore the way his instincts pull the world into stark focus, leaving everything except survival behind.

They are moving as fast as he is, as fast as this old town lets them. His mind splits the odds into pieces, lines them up, lines up his path. No backup. No witnesses. The quietest part of him suggests that he should care. But quiet is too easy to ignore.

In seconds he has crossed three streets and two alleys. His hand is no longer in his pocket; it's steady on the gun, and the grip feels better than prayer. Feels like purpose. Feels like not dying.

Ezra slips between an empty parking lot and a shell of a factory, slowing down, waiting. He moves from thought to action like they're both made of instinct.

The chase is already won. He knows it. It's that knowing that gets him through the worst of days. The kind of knowing that is blood and bone.

Or maybe, the kind that makes him too certain. Too fast to act, too quick to risk everything. He smiles, but it's the smile of a man at his own funeral. A man who's dug the hole himself. He knows what's at stake, and he wants it more than air.

Ezra rounds the corner, gun leveled. It is sudden. It is inevitable. It is not what he expects.

The sacred collapses. The sky rends open, a raw and feral wound, bleeding the divine into the streets below. The light is so pure it blinds, even Lucifera. Even the Flame of Judgment. The new angel stands unyielding, forged from radiance and merciless order. A weapon in its own right.

It doesn't just displace air; it warps morality, twisting it into Heaven's image. Twisting it until everything else shatters.

Lucifera raises an arm to shield her eyes, but she won't turn away. She can't. This is their answer. This is her answer. It was always going to be like this, sooner or later. The longer she survives, the faster they come. But now they've sent something new. Something terrifying.

They've sent her more than a decree.

"Lucifera." The voice is a force. A law. "Heaven has been patient, but your time is done." The words reverberate through the city, shaking the windows, shaking her. "You are a wound that must be cauterized."

The declaration blazes like the new angel, hot and brilliant and cold. Lucifera braces against it.

"We will silence you, one way or another."

A flash of wings and steel. The figure draws a blade forged from divine will itself, and it slices through the last illusion of safety.

She almost smiles. This is what they want, then. This is their way of saving face. She knows this isn't personal. She knows it's worse: It's righteous.

The blade's purity is scorching, but Lucifera is fire. She's survived worse.

"Let me guess," she says, voice a razor in the light. "I'm an affront to all that is holy? An anomaly? A thing to be removed?"

"Correct."

"Then why the courtesy call? Shouldn't you be swinging that little knife already?"

The angel steps forward, every movement so precise it cuts the air. The blade stays raised, a brilliant and terrible promise.

"Why not try speaking like I'm already dead?" Lucifera's eyes flare, embers in a furnace. "Or does Heaven require a permission slip to kill me this time?"

"We are Heaven. We require nothing but obedience."

Lucifera's laughter burns. "And here you are instead, trying to scare me off. Tell me, is the Light short on henchmen these days?"

"We are giving you a chance." The angel stands unwavering, a stone made of blinding radiance. "This is more than you have given others."

Lucifera's fire flickers, then blazes even hotter. "I thought you were past 'chances' and onto executions. Or maybe Heaven's losing its edge." She glares into the angel's eyes. They are as still and deep as the sea, and they make her feel small. The anger rises again, catching like gasoline. "Or maybe you just need the practice."

"Your fate is not ours to decide." The angel's calm is absolute. "The Light is patient. But the Light is also just. You will be silent."

Her voice slashes back. "Is that what you tell yourselves? Is that what makes it so easy?"

The wind swirls around them, her heat clashing with the chill of the divine.

"It is not easy," the angel says. "But it is necessary. You leave us no choice."

"Right," she says. "Necessary." Her sarcasm could ignite the street. "Using Heaven's scalpel to carve excuses."

The city vibrates with tension, and for a brief, searing second, Lucifera swears she sees a crack in the angel's resolve. A shadow, a fraction of doubt.

"We will end you," it says, and this time the voice is softer. No less certain. No less terrifying. But softer.

Her mind is already preparing for the worst. Her mind knows better than her heart.

"I've heard that before."

She sets her stance, and she sets her own trap.

This time, she knows, they might actually mean it.

She explodes toward the assassin, a live wire of sarcasm and wrath. Fire meets purity, and it is anything but holy. It is absolute, brutal violence. The Light will stop at nothing. Lucifera almost smiles as she bleeds.

Her flames are a living thing. Her anger, a torch. Her defiance, a brand. They meet the assassin's icy determination with all the fire that she can summon.

The blade moves faster than sound. It cuts faster than light.

Lucifera won't back down. She can't. The fury and sarcasm blaze within her.

The angel doesn't slow. Doesn't pause. Doesn't miss.

Lucifera barely misses a step. The edge is sharp enough to split atoms. To slice worlds.

But she's on her feet and she's still breathing. Still fighting.

Another move. Another flash. The ground is a collage of their footsteps, an epic poem of attack and retreat. Her body is more vulnerable than she admits, but her soul is wild.

Still fighting.

"Is this the part," she gasps between searing breaths, "where you pretend to spare me?"

The blade grazes her arm. Her flame is faster than it should be, but not fast enough. Not this time.

She can feel the Light in her bones. She can feel it trying to cauterize more than the wound.

"Just tell me one thing," she says, voice more ragged than she'd like. "Are you saving me, or saving yourselves?"

"Both," the angel replies, and the single word is like a knife. Precise and deep.

"Thanks for clearing that up."

Their motions turn into a blur, their surroundings a vivid mess of ruin. Her boots hit concrete and glass. Walls crumble like neglected kingdoms. The angel never stops, never slows. The cuts come faster. Lucifera is ready, but she is also a fraction of a second too slow.

Blood arcs through the air and hits the ground, and she almost laughs at how red it is.

Her fire, her laughter, it's all defiant and reckless. All so alive.

The angelic figure glows with pitiless conviction. Everything Lucifera throws is absorbed by its perfect, flawless Light.

"Is that the best you have?" she says, biting back the pain with words and more words.

"We have enough."

The certainty in its voice is almost enough to stop her. Almost.

"Go to Hell," she shouts, even as her knees buckle.

"After you."

They crash through another wall, more ghosts of buildings that weren't ever meant to last. Lucifera's runes pulse, weakly, feeding on every last bit of chaos. She knows this might be her end, but she won't give it to them easily. Not like this.

"Want to know what your mistake is?" she yells, her voice cracking like the earth beneath them.

"You exist."

The assassin steps toward her. It moves like inevitability. Like truth.

Lucifera pushes herself to stand. Her blood is on fire.

"No, you arrogant son of a—"

Another blow. Another piece of her will, chipping off.

"—you just gave me something to fight for."

Her own laugh surprises her. The heat surprises her. She's still burning.

Lucifera's entire being ignites in one last desperate act. The fire that bursts forth is unsteady and erratic, but it's more than the assassin expects.

It's more than Lucifera expects.

For a second, the angel falters, just a fraction, just enough.

Just enough for her to think she's winning.

But then the Light resumes, more blinding, more absolute than ever. The blade pierces her side. Lucifera gasps, falls. The ground is hard, and the concrete feels colder than Heaven itself.

It won't be enough.

It won't be enough.

She closes her eyes and wonders how it's always like this. She closes her eyes and sees only fire.

Lucifera almost dies, but Ezra saves her at the last second. He breaks every rule, defies every protocol. The gunshot is the loudest sound he's ever heard, and he fires it without hesitation.

It shouldn't work. The bullet shouldn't reach. But it does, and the impact is catastrophic. The Light staggers. It actually staggers.

The impossible sound ripples through every realm, leaving the angelic assassin shocked and bleeding order.

Ezra moves before he even knows he's moving, and everything feels suspended. Lucifera, the angel, himself—all caught in a moment that shouldn't be.

He sees her on the ground. Sees the flames dying, her body weak, and feels his breath hitch in a way that terrifies him. It fills him.

He fires again. The report splits the universe, but this time the shot goes wide. The gun doesn't matter. The rules don't matter. He runs.

Lucifera almost isn't herself. Almost doesn't recognize what's happening.

The blade should have finished her. Should have been the end. But now? Now it's nothing.

Ezra is here, but so is something else. A new force, raw and untamed. She can barely control it, but she channels it anyway.

Her body moves like it never stopped moving. She catches her breath, catches fire, catches a chance she shouldn't have.

Her voice is a phoenix. "What's wrong?" she says to the angel. "Didn't see that coming?"

And then the fire hits.

The angel stares at her with something like shock. It can't process this. It can't process him.

Ezra stands beside her, unyielding and alive. His presence makes her flame a force even she can't predict.

The assassin has never been the one caught off guard. It has never been the one surprised. But now the scales tip, and for the first time, it feels the weight.

Lucifera rises, renewed. Her blood is fuel. Her anger, fission. She is almost another creature entirely, and she isn't sure if it's Ezra or the fire or something more terrifying that gives her the strength.

The flames are wild. They engulf everything, even her doubts.

The angel staggers back again, losing ground, losing power. This wasn't part of the Light's plan. This wasn't possible.

"Did Heaven get tired of winning?" Lucifera taunts, voice a nuclear lash. "Didn't want to make it look too easy?"

Ezra is shaking, but not from fear. He looks at her, and his eyes are green flares.

The world twists and bends as the heat collides with purity. Lucifera feels it before she sees it—a crack in the very fabric of being.

It tears wide, a halo-ringed scar in the air, a bleeding wound of chaos and light.

The angel takes one last, searing look at the both of them, then dives into the rift, voice ringing like an unholy gospel.

"I will return."

The words echo longer than any sound has a right to. Longer than even fire.

And then there's nothing but silence.

Ezra's hands tremble, his mind a fractured, brilliant mess. He did it. He actually did it.

His gun feels foreign now, but his choices do not.

He knows he's crossed a line. Knows he can't go back. But the certainty that fills him is terrifying. Liberating. It clutches him like absolution.

Lucifera staggers, almost collapsing, but Ezra catches her. His hands steady, her flame unfocused and raw.

"Not bad," she says, words thin and breathless.

"You're welcome."

It's all he manages, but it's enough. She leans on him, and for once, she doesn't pretend not to need it.

He holds her close. It's more than heat between them.

It's more than anything he's felt.

This wasn't the plan.

Ezra realizes he's no longer just hunting her, just observing. He's part of it. Part of the fire, part of the danger, part of the judgment.

Lucifera flickers against him, her power unsteady but never gentle.

Ezra knows, without a doubt, without fear, that this is his life now.

He holds her even tighter.

She is fire, and she is dying. Lucifera's mind slips away, and the world is only flame and blood and

Ezra's voice. Ezra's hands. They steady her and hold her close. They hold her past the point she can't hold herself.

She doesn't see his eyes, green and burning with something beyond heat. Doesn't feel the streets under her. Doesn't feel the earth or the law or Heaven's plan. All she knows is darkness, drifting, pulling at her, dragging her back through the wild blaze of her own past.

But he holds on.

Ezra feels her weight against him. He feels her flame, barely flickering, but as powerful as a truth too raw to speak. Too much to say out loud. He cradles her body, his mind an epic of certainties and doubts. She is fire. She is dying. And Ezra knows, beyond question, that she is all that's keeping him alive.

The danger of what he's done seeps into his bones like a familiar ghost. Like an old friend. Like a shadow of the shadows that used to fill his days.

The bullet should never have reached the angel. He should never have reached this place. But Lucifera is here, in his arms, still breathing, and Ezra knows this is where he needs to be. He clutches her tighter, feels the erratic heat of her sear through him, and welcomes it.

He doesn't let go.

A glow surrounds her like a shroud of fading embers, but her fire is more than just flame. It radiates something beyond the physical, something potent and frightening, something unspent and untamed.

125

It is the purest judgment, and Ezra wonders if he's always known. Always known that this is where he'd end up, drawn to it, obsessed with it, unable to let it go even as it nearly kills him.

His hands still shake, but it's not from fear. It's not from exhaustion. It's from the certainty that what's between them is bigger than Heaven and Earth combined. Bigger than the Light. Bigger than any of the lies he used to tell himself, lies like "safe" and "right" and "the law."

Lucifera doesn't move, and for a moment he thinks—fears—that the new power, the new flame has burned her out. But then she stirs, and he pulls her even closer. Her flame flares back to life, more stable, more controlled.

Ezra doesn't even consider leaving. He's past that. So far past it that the thought is ridiculous, a cosmic joke without a punchline.

He stays with her as the night unravels around them, the cold, holy light of the angel's passage slowly fading from the sky.

It is just them now. Him and her and the knowledge that they've started something they can't stop. Something no one else will understand.

A new light shines behind her eyes, molten and alive.

She opens them, and the heat hits him like a confession.

Ezra's hands tremble once more. This time, they don't stop.

Lucifera lifts her head, her mind clear but her body broken. They don't say anything at first. They don't need to.

The silence is as fierce as anything spoken.

"You still with me?" she asks, finally, her voice raw and scorched but alive. So alive.

"I'm here."

She leans against him, her body hot, her mind hotter. She feels his own heartbeat, strong and unyielding and resolute, beneath the shell of his humanity. It vibrates through them both, unrelenting and alive.

"Yeah, you are."

A flash of doubt crosses her face, but she pushes it away. If he's committed to this, if he's willing to cross these lines, then who is she to question it? Who is she to question him?

She questions anyway.

"You know this will happen again. You know they'll be back. And they'll come harder next time."

"Let them."

She almost laughs. Almost smiles. The fire in her chest matches his, beat for beat. "You're a damn fool, you know."

Ezra lets the warmth of her words sink in. They fill him more than anything he's ever heard, more than anything he's ever known.

"Yeah, I know."

Lucifera sees something new in him, something reckless and dangerous. It almost looks like hope.

Ezra holds her until she can hold herself. Until her judgment blazes as brightly as it should, and she pulls away, and the world spins back to life.

He stands with her, at her side, and he knows there's no going back. He knows, and he welcomes it.

He's following her into the fire.

The kind that burns through everything else.

The kind that lasts.

Chapter 11 – Origins of Fire

Lucifera lies like a fallen star, surrounded by the wreckage of her descent. The abandoned sanctuary huddles around her, wounded by the same fury that left her barely breathing. It should be a graveyard, but the air still crackles with divine heat, smoldering with intent. Her form—battered, ethereal—barely clings to consciousness.

The wounds won't heal, not the usual way, and a dark angel haunts her bedside. Ezra. He crouches next to her, desperate and silent, trapped in the limbo of what to do next. His fingers twitch over the phone in his hand. Call for help? Bury her deeper in this wreck? Her runes flicker in the dimness, sparks of amber light, until the entire room pulses like a machine of stained glass coming back to life.

Ezra's presence is a study in contradictions. Leaning against the sanctuary's splintered pew, he looks like a man with nowhere to kneel. His trench coat, a relic of mortal duty, is draped over Lucifera's still form, as if she might shiver in anything other than divine fire. The air around them simmers, charged with a heat that should melt flesh, but Ezra only wipes sweat from his eyes, stubborn as he holds his vigil. Her beauty is violent, even unconscious, like a painting by a hand that hated its subject. The runes on her jacket dim, glow, and dim again, taunting him with the uncertainty of what comes next.

The flicker of his phone is a counter-rhythm to her light, whispering of other worlds with police codes and mortal concerns. Ezra could call it in. He should call it in. But even this ruin offers no sanctuary from the judgment that hunts her. She breathes, barely, each inhale a struggle that mirrors the way her presence fills the room. It's too much and not enough. Ezra hangs his head, fighting the helplessness gnawing at his gut, the sensation that he's become a bystander in his own life.

This—her, them, here—was never the plan. He's a detective, not some cosmic spectator. But logic unraveled the moment he first saw her, fiery and merciless. His thoughts churn in tight circles: Should he let them take her? Would they, even if he called? Heaven and Hell care nothing for mortal gestures, least of all his. He looks at Lucifera's face, ghostly and severe, and thinks he can almost see the pulse of an impossible heartbeat underneath it all.

He swallows the urge to speak. There are no words for this—a creature of light and flame crumpled in an abandoned church, her runes like the dying embers of a confession that could destroy them both. Ezra tugs at his collar, the fabric damp and strangling. When did this all get so damn personal? His mind offers no answer, just memories of blood and fire and the sound of her voice—unlike anything he ever heard and exactly what he always needed.

Lucifera shifts, a barely perceptible twitch that could be nothing or everything. Ezra flinches, the jolt running through his body like an accusation. He tries to be still, to outwait whatever verdict this is, but his fingers are traitors, tapping out a restless cadence on the useless phone. The law, his badge, his life—they feel insubstantial, pale shadows next to the incandescent dilemma she poses. Why doesn't she wake up? Why doesn't he leave? The runes flicker again, a sigh of amber light, then falter.

Ezra tenses. Each glimmer is an alarm bell in his skull, his instincts warring between the urge to flee and the need to stay. He closes his eyes, half a prayer, half an admission that he doesn't know what side he's on anymore. Lucifera doesn't stir, the silence more terrible than if she'd risen to burn the entire world down around them.

And still, the air throbs with an uneasy life, with an anticipation that Ezra can't endure or abandon. He leans closer to her, each second stretching with the agony of his unmade choices. Every pulse of her light seems slower, further apart. It could be the end. But her essence—wild, stubborn—insists otherwise. Maybe she's giving up. Maybe she's just getting started. Ezra sets the phone down with a shaking hand. Her runes flicker once more, then bloom, bright as a wound opening across the entire sky.

It's a miracle, or blasphemy, or both. Light invades every shadow, saturating the ruined sanctuary with the stained-glass intensity of a dozen fiery saints. Ezra stumbles back, blinded by the sheer power of her. His heart races with the realization of how little he understands and how much that might cost him.

Lucifera lies at the center, no longer still. No longer mortal enough to comfort or comprehend. The runes blaze with awful life, re-etching her in hues that belong to no celestial order. Ezra's pulse echoes hers, too loud and too fast. As the brightness floods over him, one thought drowns out the rest: What is she becoming, and what does it make him?

He sinks to the floor, all pretense of control burned away. The sanctuary hums with energy and unanswered questions. Ezra shuts his eyes against the splendor, but there's no escaping the light or the truth. Not anymore.

Fire whispers like an ancient conspirator, wrapping Lucifera in the suffocating certainty of things she has always known. In this dreamscape, she stands outside of time, outside of herself, surrounded by flames that neither burn nor warm. They coil around her in tendrils of forgotten intent. Faces take shape within the blaze, luminous with the righteousness that damned her. They are ancient, celestial, traitorous, and their voices weave the only lullaby she has ever feared: divine, infernal, prophetic. She watches, detached yet tormented, as they argue her into existence—a creature of judgment with no right to choose.

The fire is a thing alive, breathing, clutching. It seethes in tones of gold and crimson, vibrant with betrayal and cosmic fervor. Lucifera stands at its center, isolated and entangled, witnessing the birth of an eternal mistake. There is no warmth, no consuming flame, just the inescapable heat of revelation. The world around her spins with a cruel grace, and she feels the pull of history—her history—reaching to ensnare her.

Within the undying blaze, the faces come into focus. They hover like judgment, serene and fierce, edged in the sharp glow of their own certainty. The fire moves like the ticking of a clock, but there is no time here, no past or future—only the awful present of their truths. Each face flickers with divine disdain, and Lucifera recognizes them from the shadows of memory she never wished to revisit.

They speak in voices too old and vast to belong to any single mouth. The sound is a choir of a thousand betrayals, beautiful and horrifying, wrapping around her like chains made of song. Their words etch themselves into the air: We made her. We failed her. She will be their end.

Lucifera watches them weave prophecy and plan, their flames knitting together the binding threads of her existence. The distance she feels is an ache that runs deeper than bone, deeper than soul. This is how it was. How it always would be. But she's here now, seeing the fabric of her life unfold from its first, fatal knot.

The vision tightens its grasp, pulling her into its infernal logic. She sees herself, an echo within the dreamscape, forged through celestial ritual. They bind her with fire that burns without touch, with intent that scalds like the coldest betrayal. Not born but made. It is a vision she cannot deny, however hard she fights to look away.

Disbelief fractures into terrible recognition. Lucifera understands these flames as intimately as she knows her own name. Their narrative is an old wound, festering with divine decree. She listens, captive to their omnipotent verdict. Part divine, part infernal. Neither. Both. The words thread themselves into her very being, tighter and tighter, an unbreakable tapestry of purpose and pain.

They continue, undeterred, relentless. Her creators, her condemners. Each syllable a branding iron, marking her again and again. Lucifera's rebellion, her self-wrought mission—it was all part of their grand architecture. She had never strayed from their path. She had always been right where they wanted her, deluding herself with dreams of autonomy.

The dreamscape becomes a crucible, and she is its only prisoner. She watches her essence forged in a ritual of light and despair. Angels and demons weave themselves into her, the balance they so feared and desired. There is no escape from their vision. There is only the suffocating weight of knowing.

She sees it all. The ritual. The betrayal. The truth that binds her tighter than any flame. Their fire wraps around her like a crown, like shackles, and she struggles to resist the gravity of her own origin. She is outside time, outside hope. The prophecy rings with dreadful clarity: A creature of judgment, a creature of rebellion, a creature that holds them all accountable.

The vision closes in. Lucifera is consumed by it, by them, by herself. The fires burn more vivid, more desperate, more cruel. Their grip is absolute, their betrayal luminous, until nothing exists outside the binding certainty of what they have wrought. She sees herself as she truly is, as she was always meant to be: not a being, but an end.

The vision sinks its claws deeper, and the dreamscape shifts from prophecy to memory, from betrayal to scars that will never heal. Lucifera is inside it now, part of it, and the ancient celestial beings circle her like hungry wolves. Their fire is needle-sharp as they brand her with their intent, each rune a wound that speaks of terrible purpose. She hears Oren's voice—protective, possessive, then murderous. This is the moment they completed their crime. She sees herself as they made her: a creature of judgment, a creature of balance, a creature who was never meant to be.

The dream wraps tighter, and the faces of her creators close in, eager and awful. The fire they weave is bright with divine ambition, its threads piercing flesh and spirit with the awful precision of fate. Lucifera stands among them, no longer detached. Their words echo like the clanging of a thousand iron bells, ruthless and full of grim satisfaction: Complete. Powerful. Our justice.

Runes erupt across her skin, etched in painful bursts of color and agony. This is the ritual she thought she had escaped. It claims her again, enveloping her in the molten chains of what they always intended her to be. A fire-born captive, a forged anomaly. A weapon, perfectly balanced to destroy its wielder.

Their voices grow louder, insistent, each syllable a surgical incision into her belief of independence. Lucifera is all that they desired and everything they despised, born from a hubris that was both angelic and demonic. It is too much to endure, too much to deny. She is not an observer of this vision. She is its heart.

The memory narrows, sharpening its focus, honing in on the voice that hurt the most. Oren. His presence is a blade, cutting through the other voices with surgical cruelty. She remembers the way it used to sound, the way it was meant to control her, the way it calls her now: Destroyer. Betrayer. Judgement.

It is a voice that once called her a miracle. A voice that shifts with terrible grace from tenderness to accusation, from possessive to vengeful. Oren speaks of divine balance, of a cosmic order she threatens by merely existing. It is a betrayal more intimate than the others, because he once saw her as his—before he knew what they'd truly made.

The runes blaze brighter as Oren's voice melds with the others, the force of their contempt branding itself onto her soul. Lucifera sees the moment they have planned for her, the precise point of their cosmic cruelty. This is when they bound her into being, their cruel design tightening around her like a noose.

Her horror has no edge, no bottom. She feels the memory overtake her, the terrible certainty that she was always their creature. She watches her own completion—the moment her existence is set in a balance too perfect to endure. The celestial beings exult as the fire and blood fuse within her, an eternal seal of intent. She is not just a creature. She is their cosmic crime.

Desperation gnaws at her, but it has no teeth against their certainty. Lucifera wrestles with the prophecy as it consumes her, with the revelation that she's living a lie of her own making. She is nothing more than what they planned, what they feared. She was never born. She was always only this.

Their vision coils around her tighter than her rebellion ever did, stripping away her illusion of choice. The truth seeps in, bitter and inexorable: Her defiance is part of their plan. Her every breath a calculated defiance, perfectly designed to suit their terrible need for justice.

Lucifera staggers under the weight of it all. Her mission, her war—it is no more than their old prophecy coming to life, enacted by the only pawn who believed herself more. The memory closes around her like a fist. She sees herself as the perfect weapon, the weapon they could never control.

The pain is excruciating and complete. Her wounds reopen, raw with new understanding. Her rebellion was always their prophecy. Her rebellion was never hers. She is not a being. She is their end. A thing to hold them accountable, even as it holds her. They made her. They never unmade her.

Lucifera shatters the dream with a gasp that echoes in the ruined sanctuary, a sound that could be life or death or something far more terrifying. The world jolts back into motion, and her chest heaves with a new and terrible purpose. She is awake, alive, her runes ablaze with prophecy. Light pours from her like judgment, blinding, scorching, pure. Ezra staggers back, dwarfed by the force of her rebirth. This is beyond power, beyond punishment. It is her.

And for the first time, she knows what it means to be. She stares at her hands as if they belong to a stranger, her voice cracking with awful realization. "They made me to end them all."

The gasp becomes a choked scream as Lucifera claws her way back to the world. Her eyes flash open, twin suns too bright to behold. The sanctuary vibrates with the raw energy of her awakening, walls trembling under the strain of it. She chokes down another breath, each one a violent testament to the fire inside her. Light explodes outward from her like a cataclysm made flesh.

Ezra flinches, overwhelmed by the onslaught of luminescence. It floods over him, a tidal wave of terrible truth that forces him back, step after stumbling step. This is not the Lucifera he thought he understood, not the one he watched over with mortal concern. She is radiant and untouchable, burning with an energy that shatters his every expectation.

The runes sear themselves into the walls, casting wild patterns across the shattered remnants of the sanctuary. Ezra shades his eyes, trying to make sense of what she's become. Alive. Awful. And impossibly more than she was before. Her essence fills the air, a palpable force that leaves him breathless and reeling. This is the new gospel, written in blinding light and insurmountable purpose.

Lucifera's breathing evens out, the gasps slowing as the reality of her transformation sets in. She feels the energy coursing through her, a torrent she cannot control, cannot resist. The prophecy that imprisoned her has now set her ablaze. The fire is not outside her, not around her. It is her.

Ezra teeters on the edge of disbelief and awe, caught in the maelstrom of her rebirth. The sanctuary is no longer just a ruin; it is a cathedral of light, and he is its most unworthy witness. He feels small, insignificant under the weight of what Lucifera has become. His thoughts trip over themselves, crashing into the walls of his own understanding. How could he have thought to protect this? How could he have hoped to understand it?

Lucifera trembles with the force of her new awareness. She clutches her chest, as if to contain the blaze within, her fingers glowing with the same unearthly intensity as the runes. Every corner of the space is illuminated by her, washed in light that neither Heaven nor Hell could claim. Her voice is a fracture line, raw and trembling, cutting through the brilliant chaos she has unleashed.

"They made me to end them all." she repeats.

The truth is a searing blade, and it cuts both ways. Ezra stares, lost between terror and reverence, as the light from her consumes his doubts and fears. Lucifera is no longer just a being of power. She is its embodiment. He can't look away, can't retreat any further. This is judgment. This is destiny. And he's right in the middle of it, whether he wants to be or not.

The questions spill from him like a cut artery, but Lucifera doesn't stop. Her silence is a verdict, leaving Ezra to drown in what he doesn't know. She strides out into the night, her flame carving strange patterns in the darkness, shapes that answer nothing. Ezra hesitates, then follows, trailing her like a shadow with nowhere left to hide. Is she still the same being he chose to understand? He doesn't have an answer, only more questions. Lucifera is already a distant blaze on the rooftop, staring over the city with all of destiny burning around her like a crown.

She never looks back, and the lack of hesitation terrifies him more than fire or angels or his own useless conscience ever could. Ezra's voice falters as she slips further away. "What the hell happened? What did you mean by—" but even he can't find an end to the question. He watches her figure retreat, fierce and unconquered, wondering if the silence she leaves is intentional or if she's beyond even that now.

Lucifera cuts through the city's bruised underbelly, her flame trailing in wild, chaotic bursts. The light is neither infernal nor celestial, an unsettling mix that Ezra can't place, can't comprehend. It mesmerizes and frightens him in equal measure, pulling him in while daring him to let go. This is Lucifera, but more, and he's a fool to think he ever knew her. Still, he runs to keep her in sight, fear and fascination warring for space in his chest.

He stumbles over questions that bruise like old scars: What is she now? What does it make him? He has no breath left for answers, only a raw, gnawing need to understand what he's become by choosing to follow her.

Lucifera's pace never slows, the night closing in around her with predatory intent. Ezra is just far enough behind to feel utterly lost but too close to accept it. Her path is direct, knowing, while his is one of zigzags and desperation, each step echoing with the uncertainty of where she leads.

The city looms and collapses, a tangled mass of light and shadow that mirrors Ezra's internal chaos. Traffic hums like a distant, mechanical symphony; streetlights cast a jaundiced glow over scenes of urban isolation. It's a Gothic theater where Ezra plays the only role he knows: that of a man struggling to catch up, to anything, to everything.

He rounds a corner and sees her, sees the distance between them stretch like a chasm that not even light can bridge. Lucifera moves with the force of inevitability, with the surety of a fate accepted. Ezra moves with doubt, his faith in himself eroding under the weight of her transformation. What was he thinking? That she needed him? That he mattered?

She vanishes onto the rooftops, her flame a distant signal fire against the night. He hesitates, his chest heaving with effort and unanswered questions, then pushes himself forward, stubborn in his pursuit.

Lucifera reaches the rooftop. She is a fiery sentinel against the dark sprawl of the city, her figure outlined in a blaze that has no name and no rival. Ezra falters in the alley below, feeling every bit the mortal he is, watching a being he can barely recognize.

He leans against the brick of the nearest building, the coolness leeching into his skin as if to remind

141

him of what it means to be human, what it means to be fragile. His thoughts spiral, lost in the whirlwind of Lucifera's new nature. Is she a threat? Is she still his hope?

Ezra lets the questions circle him like vultures, feeding off his indecision and dread. He peers up at her again, the woman and the flame, the uncertainty that both excites and terrifies him.

Lucifera stands alone, silhouetted against the shimmering cityscape. She is the focal point of a world caught between devastation and destiny, the weight of her new reality pressing down like a crown of fire on her head. For now, it does not crush her. For now, she carries it like it was always meant to be hers.

Chapter 12 – The Price of Mercy

The man is shackled, defiant, a rabid wolf caught mid-snarl, baring his yellow teeth at the hand of justice. She stands over him, haloed in broken light, her flame twisting and roiling with unbridled hunger. One squeeze of her fingers and he is nothing, ash on the wind. Her hair floats around her head like an avenging halo, and the air crackles, heavy with heat and inevitability. He deserves it. She knows it. Then why the hesitation? A small voice, unremarkable as any mortal suffering, punctures the wrath like a needle. The girl, tear-streaked, alive, unwelcome in this place of ruin and judgment. "Please," she whispers. "I don't want him to die."

Lucifera does not look at the girl. She watches the man's lip curl into a sneer, eyes locked on her with hatred sharpened to a razor's edge. The wordless animosity of a predator denied its prey. His bare chest rises and falls, each breath daring her. She is not used to hesitation. The flickering light casts shadows like a second set of chains, binding him to the crumbling stone wall. A wicked grin splits his face. She doesn't flinch. A single thought, molten and unstoppable, boils in her mind: guilty.

She remembers the street, narrow and hungry, waiting to swallow the light. The alley where she found them, its stench curling up like smoke. He was ready to sell her, the girl—she can't forget the way he struck her, a slap meant to silence, but

Lucifera heard it. She heard his cruel voice, thoughtless laughter. When she descended, he ran. But there's no escaping her; her footsteps burned through his illusions, her presence stripped him bare. The church walls are no refuge. The girl had screamed, desperate and young, a fading wail against a celestial rage. But Lucifera had bound him, cast him in these shadows, condemned him.

Now, he thrashes against her justice, testing the metal with futile strength. His eyes, two pits of cold fire, watch her too closely. A vein throbs in his neck, pulsing like a countdown. "Do it," he hisses, voice coiled and venomous. His defiance feeds her flame.

But the girl is still there, unwanted, too close to mercy. Her whisper breaks Lucifera's certainty like fragile glass. "I don't want him to die. I just want to leave." Her voice quivers, but she stands her ground. How can something so simple cause such ruin?

Lucifera can feel it now, a foreign tremor in her resolve. The heat recoils, and doubt seeps in, chilling and unwelcome. The girl's plea coils around her, tightens like the chains on the man's limbs. She remembers—something like this. A time when she begged the same way. A vision she hates and cannot burn. She tries to silence it, to raise the flame and consume him before it takes hold.

The girl steps closer. Lucifera smells salt, tears, and innocence wasted. Her image is blurry with grief. "I don't care about the money," the girl sobs. "He was going to let me go. Please."

She feels the weight of the girl's hope. It's unbearable, pressing down like celestial judgment.

Memories invade, raw as the girl's anguish. Lucifera cannot silence them.

The man's voice, suddenly soft. A razor turned smooth. "I used to be good," he says. His eyes glint, and for a moment, Lucifera wonders if he's seen her flinch. "I helped her. She remembers."

Something fractures in her; her flame sputters. She sees him now, wounded and weak. A calculated change. But still—her power recedes, and in its place, a terrifying absence. He can't possibly be sincere. Can he?

His lips stretch into a mocking smile. The metal cuffs scrape and chime as the girl pulls at them, struggling to set him free. "They said I was like you. Punished the wicked. I lost my way, but I can change. She wants me to."

The words sink deep, bypassing her armor. She's heard this lie before. The flame dims, but the hurt it leaves in her is bright, relentless.

"Please," the girl cries. It's the same plea, again and again. The same words she once screamed.

It's too much. The space around them chills as she lowers her hand, the inferno within her dying into embers. The church sags around her, exhausted by the release. The girl's grateful sobs fill the silence, too loud, too near. Mercy. She didn't think herself capable.

"Thank you," the girl whispers, incredulous.

The man throws his head back and laughs. His chains rattle like the last laugh of the damned. Lucifera's steps are heavy, each one pulling her further from judgment. He will find no chains when he wakes.

And when he wakes, he will know the taste of true mercy.

He's seen blood spill down the cracks of this city, watched men confess to unspeakable things with the ease of breathing. Watched them die. But he's never seen anything like her. Lucifera. The name burns as brightly as her hand should, the hand that suddenly, inexplicably trembles. He watches from the shadows, still as stone, not daring to move or interfere. Something more dangerous than flame pauses her judgment. Mercy. Ezra has a thousand questions and no idea where to begin. When he finally steps into the light, all that comes out is one: "Is this new to you?"

He crouches, transfixed by the dimming fire, the way her shoulders sink like the weight of a universe has finally conquered her defiance. He's imagined meeting her before: barging in, gun raised, her expression unreadable. But this—this hesitation is not what he expected. The man's laughter echoes off the stone walls, cruel and victorious. It's a sound Ezra's heard before. But from her? From this thing that leaves ashes where men once stood? He thought she was a myth until he started finding bodies burned from the inside out, their screams still clinging to the walls like smoke.

It's the unexpected that gnaws at him. How she doesn't strike like the executioner he imagined but pauses, something uncertain bleeding through her amber eyes. Maybe that's what finally makes him move, what draws him out of hiding. He needs to see it up close, needs to know what causes an angel of vengeance to flinch. He's already half in love with the idea of it.

He knows about fire. He's worked these streets too long to not recognize heat when it follows him home, when it shows up at his desk in the form of burnt files and bodies they tell him aren't his problem. The kind of problem that erases itself, victims as guilty as their killer. When Lucifera's name slipped between whispers and phone lines, it didn't surprise him. No official word for it. Nothing he could write in his reports. Just one absurd, unmistakable truth: fire that knows how to aim.

He almost believes it. No—he does believe it, because there are the bodies and there is Lucifera, a wraith haunting every unsolved case he's dared to touch. Her legend is wide enough to scare his superiors into closing it all down, but not wide enough to fill in the gaps. That's where he comes in. A missing girl, found alive in her trafficker's hands, unscorched by an inferno that should have claimed her. It pulls him like a gravitational force to this ruined church, and now here he is, unsure if he's witness to justice or something far more human.

Lucifera turns, just slightly. The fading light catches her face, a portrait of agony he'd never expect on something so fearsome. Is this it? he wonders. Is he watching a miracle, or the unraveling of everything he thinks he knows? The flame, her flame, should be the loudest voice here. But it's the girl's grief that fills the room, wrapping around his spine, holding him tighter than the chill of his gun. He sees her pleading, remembers her name from the report, her face from the photo he carries like a talisman against failure.

He knows he should act, but doesn't. He wants to call out to the girl, tell her it's okay, tell her something, anything—but this moment between Lucifera and the chained man is so beyond his understanding that he can't interfere. Instead, he stands, transfixed by Lucifera's pause. This is the truth he's been after: that she hesitates, that she listens, that she is not the merciless reaper they all fear.

What does it mean? He strains to hear Lucifera's voice, but there is none. The girl's cries are raw, the kind of raw that makes even the guilty tremble. That makes Lucifera tremble. A rusted chain falls to the ground with a jarring finality.

He steps closer. The floorboards creak beneath him, an announcement he's not ready to make, but he does it anyway. When the words come out, they're quiet and unsure, barely a question but still the most important one: "Is this new to you?"

Lucifera doesn't answer. Her eyes are on the girl, and there is something almost tender in the way she tilts her head. It would be tender, if she weren't this thing of heat and wrath. It would be tender, if it didn't speak of hesitation. Her hand lowers, and the fire there flickers, softens, dies. The man and the girl run.

Ezra watches them disappear into the night. He's seen too many escapes to believe in this one. The man will not disappear for long. It's Lucifera's fire that's gone, and he knows—he knows without her saying it—that it means something. Maybe everything.

Lucifera turns from the darkness, her face more shadowed than he imagined it could be. "You won't regret this," Ezra tells her. But they both know that's not true. The last thing she gives him is her back. He's not even sure if she's heard him, not until he sees it: her eyes, glowing in the dark like tiny, dying suns.

There's a beauty in destruction. The city sleeps through it, doesn't hear the shot that tears through her, that unweaves all the mercy and naivety the girl wrapped around Lucifera like a fragile cocoon. It should be enough to send her screaming across the sky, enough to burn the whole city down. But when the news breaks, she is still as stone, watching the report in shattered silence. She is not surprised. The only thing more violent than death is what came before it.

Lucifera sits like a statue in the dark, surrounded by relics of a world she barely acknowledges. Dust gathers in the corners, mingles with cobwebs and the stink of mildew. The old television glows faintly, a ghostly presence in the neglected room. The voice of the news anchor cuts through the gloom, clinical and detached, describing the carnage with precision. "Three bodies were discovered early this morning," he reports, the images behind him bleeding red and white. Sirens wail like lost souls as paramedics load the corpses. The girl and two others. Dead on arrival.

Her hands, usually steady and fierce, are folded in her lap like broken wings. It was inevitable. The girl's death was written in the fire Lucifera didn't unleash. She should have expected this, should have known her act of mercy would be nothing more than another way to kill. She sees the aftermath on the screen, her flame reflecting off her eyes, and thinks of how brief, how fleeting the girl's reprieve was. Guilt spreads through her, a relentless flame. It devours more than her anger ever could.

She rises, the room shrinking around her as if it fears her fury. Her movements are mechanical, almost gentle in their devastation. She kicks over a chair as she leaves, doesn't notice it shatter, splinter, collapse like the bodies she spared. She should have heard it coming. The guilt is crushing, the way everything in this mortal world is.

There's no urgency in her steps. This is the cost of belief, the price of a softness she should have never allowed. The church looms as she approaches, a gutted carcass against the city's flickering lights. The same place, but different now. Now it smells of old blood, cloying and metallic. Now there are no chains, no pleas. Only three bodies sprawled where she left one.

Ezra is already there, waiting. She doesn't speak to him. Doesn't acknowledge the way he stands, a silhouette in the dark, perfectly still and entirely human. The crime scene is chaos, a vivid echo of the report she watched. But it's her fault, all of it, and she can't tear her eyes away.

She moves through the wreckage, leaving Ezra in her wake. Blood trails across the floor, blooms against the dust like cruel roses. A girl's backpack sits abandoned in the corner, a violent reminder of innocence. There is betrayal in the air, sharp enough to cut through even her resolve. Lucifera knows how this ends—always knew—but seeing it with her own eyes still punches the breath from her.

He sees her pause over the bodies, sees the fire trembling at her sides, and knows he's right. She is more than just a vengeful specter. She is also this: a woman torn open by the choice she thought she'd never make. He follows her, each step careful, not wanting to shatter what's left of her composure.

When she reaches the girl, he watches the last of her certainty break. This is what mercy buys. His silence doesn't feel like an accusation, but it weighs heavy between them. Lucifera stands, looking down at the tangled remains of her failure. The girl's face is pale, a sick echo of the way Lucifera saw her last—tear-streaked and full of misguided hope.

They are alone. The air is brittle with betrayal and blood and the echoes of footsteps from officers who've come and gone. Ezra says nothing, does nothing to intrude on her torment. It's almost like he feels it, too.

The truth of it is unbearable. Lucifera stares at the bodies, her eyes wide, unblinking. This is her judgment, one she never meant to pass. She is certain of one thing now: she won't make this mistake again. The flame comes back to her, a trembling, awful presence. She lets it.

It radiates, consuming the moment, consuming her. She feels it rise within, feels it build to a breaking point. If Ezra's presence bothers her, she doesn't

151

show it. If his silence accuses her, she doesn't hear. The flames lick at the edges of her hair, but it is nothing compared to the inferno beneath her skin.

Ezra stands by, watches her break without a single word, knows this is far from over.

"This is what I get for trying to be human," she says, and her voice is not much more than a hiss, a breath, an ember collapsing in on itself. Lucifera stands at the edge of everything she fears: doubt, guilt, regret. She burns with it, lets the fire take her and sear her empty. Maybe then it won't hurt like this. "Is this what you wanted?" Her voice cracks, flames stuttering. She doesn't look at Ezra when she asks, but he answers anyway.

"This is what I get," she repeats, but now the whisper trembles, grows larger, becomes a flame again. "I wanted to believe he could change," she says, and her words threaten to break her as brutally as any weapon. "That one life spared could mean more than dozens burned."

Ezra hears the disbelief, the anguish that blisters her voice. It is not anger. Not the fierce, purging kind. This is something else. Something that feeds the doubt. He stands across from her, doesn't flinch when the flames flare and die with her ragged breath. His words are as careful as she is fierce, quiet and careful: "Trying to be human doesn't make you weak."

She laughs. A sound that cracks through the air, bitter and low. She thought she knew weakness, thought she'd burned it from herself along with every other unwanted frailty. This is the first time she has admitted the truth out loud. That she wanted to believe. In him, in herself, in anything but judgment.

Ezra doesn't blink. His green eyes are steady and sincere and infuriatingly calm. It grates on her, the gentleness of it. Like he understands. Like it's easy. "You believed him. That makes you dangerous," he says. "Now you'll doubt."

Lucifera whirls to face him, and the air shudders with heat. He doesn't move, doesn't back down, doesn't let her words pierce him like they've pierced her.

"You're going to tell me doubt isn't dangerous?" she demands. "That trying to be something I'm not isn't the best way to get everyone killed?"

"More dangerous than fire," Ezra replies, but there's no edge to his words. There's something else, something more loaded. A gentleness she doesn't know what to do with.

The silence burns. She feels it gnawing at her bones, a ravenous emptiness where certainty used to be. Lucifera lets the fire rage for a moment, lets it roar in her chest until she can almost ignore the shame, almost forget what mercy cost her. It doesn't work. Ezra is still there. Still watching. Still believing. It's worse than doubt. Worse than the flame.

She clenches her fists and the heat recedes, a reluctant admission. She lowers her eyes, hating him, hating herself. The girl's face flashes in her mind. The girl's voice. "Then I guess I'm the most dangerous creature in creation," she says. Her sarcasm is acidic, but even she can hear the guilt it fails to mask.

Ezra nods, like she's said something wise. Like it's not tearing her apart. "So, what now?" he asks. It's an honest question. He wants to know. Needs to.

The way he watches her makes her feel raw, makes her feel like he sees the fracture lines running through her. She isn't unbreakable. That's the terrible truth of it. She never was. Maybe he sees it. Maybe he always did.

Her shoulders are tight with fire and regret. She shakes her head and turns away. "The flames never lie," she tells him. "But I thought maybe I could." Her voice is unsteady, catching on the confession, burning out before it reaches him. She doesn't look back. She doesn't have to. Her eyes are burning bright, even in the shadows.

It costs her more than flame, more than guilt, more than the hurt that carves into her with every passing second. It costs her this: a name etched into the wall like an accusation. The girl is gone, but she remains, sitting among the ghosts of things she never wanted to feel. Ezra lingers in the doorway, unwilling to disturb what's left of her, unable to leave it behind.

He doesn't enter, but he doesn't leave. She senses him even when she doesn't look. Her presence is less oppressive than he remembers. The heat more bearable, the glow around her softer, dimmer. Lucifera is unguarded, so exposed and human it hurts. He thinks she might be close to breaking again. He knows she is, when she lets him see her like this.

This is the cost of mercy, the consequence she should have expected. She stares at the girl's name, the ghostly trail of flame that burned it into being. The flame is the only thing that doesn't lie. The only thing that stays true. Lucifera waits for it to devour her doubt, to scorch away the guilt. But it doesn't. Not this time. This time, all it leaves is a trace of who she used to be.

She's still, as still as the bodies in that ruined church, the bodies she let pile up with the thought that she was doing something right. Something different. Something she could never let herself do again. She thought trying to be human wouldn't cost her. She thought wrong.

Ezra stands, a ghost at the edge of her vision. He stays in the doorway like he's afraid the slightest movement will make her vanish. Maybe he's right to be afraid. Maybe he knows something she doesn't. Maybe she's the one who'll disappear, with him watching and understanding and letting her make every mistake she never thought she'd make.

She shifts, and the light around her flares for a moment, a flash of the old intensity. But it fades, leaves the room dimmer than before. He watches, waits. She doesn't cry, but he wouldn't be surprised if she did. If she allowed herself to burn and break and feel that much.

She closes her eyes, and he knows the scene plays out on the inside of her eyelids, knows how close the memories are. How much they cost.

155

He's not surprised she didn't follow when he left. Knew she wouldn't. Knew this would be the place he'd find her. Knew she couldn't be alone with it. Not really. Not like this.

Lucifera finally turns, the movement weary and resigned. She doesn't rise to meet him. She doesn't need to. The moment stretches, lingers, bends around them. The silence burns and doesn't break.

Ezra steps forward, but only once, enough to tell her he's still there. Enough to tell her he knows she isn't unbreakable. That she's choosing this war with every breath. There's more distance between them than space can account for, but there's also this: a shared pain, a flickering flame, a war they've both decided to fight.

The air feels colder. Her voice is hoarse, a whisper he almost misses. "You think this makes me strong?" she asks. The sarcasm is there, but it's worn out, weary. "I think it makes you dangerous," Ezra says. He thinks it makes her like him.

Lucifera doesn't answer, but the way she lowers her head, the way the glow dims, the way the light refuses to leave the girl's name—all of it tells him he's right. All of it tells him what he needs to know.

He stays until the darkness softens around her. Until the light is just a memory. Until he knows she's not alone, even when she is.

Chapter 13 – The Infernal Throne

The invitation did not arrive; it manifested. It bled into the mortal world through a crack in reality, a whisper of brimstone that coalesced in the stale air of Ezra's safehouse.

One moment, Lucifera was staring at the city's bruised skyline, her thoughts a tangled web of strategy and exhaustion;

the next, a scroll of scorched, living skin lay on the table before her, bound by a cord of spun shadow.

Runes, ancient and infernal, pulsed upon its surface with a soft, violet light, like a slow, malevolent heartbeat that seemed to suck the very warmth from the room.

Ezra drew his weapon, the metallic slide racking a harsh intrusion in the quiet.

"What the hell is that?" he demanded, his stance low, his eyes darting from the scroll to Lucifera, searching for a threat he couldn't yet define.

"A party invitation," Lucifera murmured, her voice a low, dangerous hum.

She didn't move; her eyes fixed on the scroll. She felt its call, a subtle, resonant frequency that vibrated in her very bones, a song only she could hear.

It was a summons from a power she had not felt since her exile—ancient, patient, and utterly female. *Mother Midnight.*

The name itself was a memory wrapped in shadow, a taste of court politics and primordial power she had long since left behind.

She unfurled the scroll with a delicate touch. The skin-like parchment was warm, disturbingly so.

The runes rearranged themselves, flowing like liquid fire to form words in a language that burned the eyes of mortals, each syllable a hook meant to snag the soul.

The game has changed, little spark. The board is open. Come home and claim your piece, or be swept from it entirely.

It was not a request. It was a statement of fact, a move in a cosmic game she was already playing, whether she had acknowledged it or not.

"You're not actually going, are you?" Ezra asked, stepping between her and the scroll, his voice tight with a concern that was becoming dangerously familiar. "This is a trap. It screams trap."

"Of course it's a trap," Lucifera said, a wry smile touching her lips as she gently pushed his gun aside.

Her touch was a flicker of heat against the cold steel. "Everything is. But it's also an opportunity. Hell is fractured.

They wouldn't call me if they weren't desperate. Oren's purge has made Heaven predictable, a blunt instrument. Hell is more subtle. I need to know what they fear more—me, or him."

She rolled the scroll back up, and it dissolved into smoke and the scent of forgotten sins.

"Besides," she added, her eyes glinting with a dangerous fire, "it's been a while since I've seen the old neighborhood. It's time I reminded them why they threw me out in the first place."

The gateway to Hell was not a place, but a wound in the world, a place where the veil was thin enough to tear.

Lucifera found it in the heart of a volcano, the air thick with sulfur and sorrow.

She stepped through, and the mortal world fell away, replaced by a landscape of breathtaking, brutalist grandeur that assaulted the senses.

This was not the chaotic, fiery pit mortals imagined.

This was Infernamet, Hell's capital, a city of impossible architecture that clawed at a sky of bruised purple and swirling nebula.

Towers of obsidian and bone twisted into the heavens, connected by bridges of solidified shadow that seemed to defy gravity.

Rivers of molten soul-stuff, the very essence of ambition and regret, flowed through canals, casting a lurid, beautiful glow on the city's underbelly.

The air hummed with power, with the whispers of a billion damned souls, a constant, psychic symphony of eternal ambition and regret.

Demons, ancient and powerful, halted their toils to watch her pass.

A hulking, six-limbed creature forging weapons from raw despair paused, its many eyes blinking in unison as it registered her presence.

Whispers haunted her every step, slithering through the oppressive heat: some called her liberator, others a traitor to both realms.

Graffiti of her sigil—a stylized flame wrapped in a broken halo—was scorched onto walls, a sign of the fracture lines running through Hell's rigid hierarchy. She was an idea they couldn't extinguish, and it terrified them.

She passed a market where lesser demons bartered memories for moments of silence, their transactions ceasing as her shadow fell over them.

They bowed, not in reverence, but in the reflexive terror one shows a passing storm.

She walked through the District of Echoes, where the architecture itself was built from the solidified screams of the eternally tormented, the walls shifting and moaning with a thousand forgotten agonies.

Here, the air was colder, thick with a despair so profound it felt like a physical weight. Even the demons gave this place a wide berth, but Lucifera walked its streets without flinching, her own inner fire a defiant sun in the heart of that desolate landscape.

She was a part of this place, whether she admitted it or not. The despair recognized her as kin, parting before her like a sea of sorrow.

Lucifera entered the Chamber of Embers, a throne room woven from obsidian, bone, and ancient fire.

The chamber was a vast cavern, its ceiling lost in a swirling vortex of violet energy that pulsed like a distant, dying star.

At its center, on a throne carved from a single, massive soul-gem that seemed to drink the light from the room sat Mother Midnight.

The infernal matriarch was draped in shadow and prophecy, her obsidian skin a contrast to the violet fire of her eyes.

She-Who-Bargains, The Queenmaker, the infernal architect of whispered alliances and unbreakable pacts.

"Lucifera. It pleases me that you've come home."

Her voice was a serpent, sliding smoothly through the charged air, each word a perfectly polished scale.

"This place was never mine," Lucifera replied, her tone molten, dangerous in its composure.

"You made that quite clear when you had me cast out for the crime of being inconvenient."

Mother Midnight smiled, a beautiful and terrifying thing that did not touch her ancient eyes.

She rose, slow and regal, a predator stretching before a hunt. "What we did, we did out of respect. Your defiance frightened some. But it impressed me."

She gestured, and the room bent to her will, the flames in the braziers leaping higher, casting their shadows as titans locked in eternal struggle.

"Now, Heaven mobilizes. Oren forgets his place. The realms teeter on the edge of a war that will leave nothing but ash. You are the fulcrum. The spark that can either set the pyre or snuff the flame."

The matriarch's offer was simple and absolute. Dominion. An army. One-third of Hell's legions to command as her own, including the feared Iron Phalanx that had held the celestial border for millennia.

A throne beside the oldest power in the universe.

"Join us," Mother Midnight purred, her voice a silken trap.

"Help us burn Heaven to the ground, and we will build a new order from its cinders. An order with you as its queen."

Lucifera laughed. The sound was not one of mirth, but of a truth so bitter it could only be expressed in scorn. It echoed through the vast chamber, a sharp, defiant note against the symphony of damnation.

"You offer me a crown, Mother? I've seen what crowns do. They become chains. You don't want an ally. You want a weapon you can aim."

Mother Midnight's smile did not falter, but the violet fire in her eyes burned colder, the temperature in the room dropping several degrees.

"A reckless choice, little spark. You cannot stand against both realms alone."

"Watch me," Lucifera said. She turned to leave, her scarlet jacket a flare of defiance against the oppressive dark.

"I think not," Mother Midnight whispered, and the very shadows of the chamber coiled and sprang to life.

They were not mere darkness; they were the **Umbral Wardens**, ancient, formless entities from the deepest pits of Hell, beings of pure binding force that predated demons.

They were the power Hell kept hidden, the reason Heaven had never risked a full-scale invasion.

The Wardens surged toward Lucifera, tendrils of living shadow wrapping around her limbs, her torso, her throat.

They did not burn or cut; they *erased*. They seeped into her, their chilling touch designed to extinguish light, to smother will, to unmake creation itself.

For a moment, Lucifera felt her own fire sputter, the cold, absolute pressure of the void threatening to consume her. This was a power she had never faced, a force of pure negation that drank her heat and left a chilling numbness in its wake. It was like being drowned in a sea of absolute zero.

Mother Midnight watched, her expression serene, a queen testing the mettle of a potential heir.

"Everything can be contained, Lucifera. Everything has a cage. This is yours."

But Lucifera was not a creature of light to be snuffed out. She was fire. And fire does not need light to burn; it needs fuel. She stopped fighting against the Wardens.

She let them seep into her, let their chilling emptiness touch the core of her being, let them think they were winning. And then, she fed her flame with their despair, with their ancient, bottomless hunger.

A roar of incandescent fury erupted from her. It was not a fire that pushed the shadows back, but one that ignited them from within.

The Umbral Wardens, beings of pure void, shrieked as they were filled with something they could not comprehend: pure, unadulterated creation.

Her fire did not banish them; it gave them form, gave them pain, gave them an existence they were never meant to have. The shadows burned with golden light, twisting into agonizing shapes before dissolving.

The chamber blazed with a light born of burning darkness. The Wardens recoiled, not just defeated, but fundamentally changed, their essence forever scarred by her impossible flame.

They retreated into the deep, not as guardians, but as wounded things.

Lucifera stood, breathing heavily, the runes on her jacket glowing with a fierce, triumphant light. She turned to face Mother Midnight. The matriarch's serene expression was gone, replaced by a look of profound, calculating awe. She had not witnessed a defeat. She had witnessed a revelation.

"Incredible," Mother Midnight breathed, the word laced with a new, genuine respect. "They sought to make a weapon of balance and instead created a force that defies the very laws of opposition. You do not just command light and shadow. You *are* the reaction between them."

She had tested the anomaly and found not a weapon, but a force of nature. She had lost her most ancient guardians, but she had gained something infinitely more valuable: knowledge. Oren thought he was fighting a rogue angel. Mother Midnight now knew they were all facing something far more fundamental.

"You have passed a test I did not think could be passed," she said, her voice now stripped of its seductive artifice, replaced by the tone of an equal. "You cannot be aimed. You cannot be held." She gave a slight, almost imperceptible nod. "You may leave. The board is far more interesting with you on it as a queen, rather than a pawn."

But as Lucifera turned to go, Mother Midnight's voice followed her, softer now, almost maternal. "You think this was about recruitment, little spark. It wasn't."

Lucifera paused, not turning around.

"I have ruled Hell for ten thousand years by understanding one fundamental truth: power shared is power multiplied. Oren believes in conquest. I believe in cultivation." The ancient demon rose from her throne, her form shifting like liquid shadow. "I needed to see if you were strong enough for what's coming."

"What's coming?"

"The awakening." Mother Midnight moved closer, her violet eyes holding depths that predated creation. "Your little war has sent ripples through dimensions Heaven and Hell barely remember exist. The Void Watchers stir. The First Ones take notice. Powers that make Oren look like a petulant child are turning their attention to this small corner of existence."

She gestured to the space around them, and for a moment the chamber's walls became transparent, revealing the true scope of Hell's domain—not just one realm, but a vast network of pocket dimensions, each one a carefully maintained ecosystem of influence and control.

"I've been preparing for this day since before your precious Heaven was even a concept," Mother Midnight continued. "Building alliances. Gathering resources. Waiting for a catalyst powerful enough to tip the scales." She smiled, and it was neither cruel nor kind, but something far more dangerous: honest. "Congratulations, Lucifera. You're exactly what I've been waiting for."

Lucifera glared at the infernal throne, a monument to everything she was never meant to be: contained, subjugated, controlled. She had been offered a kingdom and had chosen herself instead. She turned her back on the throne, on the offer, on the very heart of Hell, and walked away.

Her departure echoed like a prophecy. She left Hell scorched in her wake, a realm disappointed, expectant, and now acutely aware of the power it

166

had failed to chain. She was unclaimed, unbroken, and more dangerous than ever. And she was alone.

Chapter 14 – The Unholy Summit

A Truce in the Void

They met in the In-Between, a non-place of gray mist and silent, floating monoliths where the laws of Heaven and Hell held no sway.

It was the only neutral ground the two oldest powers in existence could agree upon, a pocket dimension of pure potential, untainted by faith or sin.

On one side stood Oren, Archangel of the Host, his silver armor radiating a cold, sterile light that pushed back the mists, revealing the perfect, unblemished vacuum beyond.

On the other, a portal of swirling violet shadow shimmered, and from it stepped Mother Midnight, her form a flowing river of night, her presence sucking the ambient light into her very being.

For the first time in millennia, the two sovereigns stood face to face, their very essences a war of physics.

"You requested this meeting, Archangel," Mother Midnight's voice was a silken whisper that still managed to echo in the soundless void, a testament to her primordial power.

"An act of desperation, I presume. It has been a long time since the Light required a favor from the Dark."

Oren's expression was carved from granite, his features a mask of divine impassivity.

"Desperation is a mortal failing, Matriarch. This is a matter of cosmic stability. The anomaly you failed to contain and we failed to foresee has become a threat to the fundamental order."

"You speak of Lucifera," Mother Midnight purred, a flicker of something akin to pride in her violet eyes. She moved with a liquid grace, the mists parting before her.

"My, my. The little spark has become quite the bonfire. She visited my court. Refused a throne. She has no ambition for power, Oren. Only for a justice that inconveniently includes judging you."

"She is a symbol," Oren corrected, his voice sharp as glacial ice.

"Her fire has ignited rebellion in my own ranks. Angels, sworn to the Light, now question their orders. Mortals build murals in her name. She is not chaos; she is a contagion of free will. She unravels everything."

Mother Midnight let a slow, knowing smile spread across her features. "And you need my help to extinguish her.

How deliciously ironic. The great and powerful Host, the very architect of divine law, unable to snuff out a single, inconvenient flame. Tell me, does your God know you're here, bartering with the enemy?"

"She is not a single flame," Oren countered, ignoring the jibe and taking a step forward, the light from his armor flaring.

"She is both. Light and shadow. She defeated your Umbral Wardens by turning their nature against them. She defeated my Justicar by showing him a truth he was not built to comprehend. She is a paradox that neither of us can defeat alone. Her very existence proves that our eternal conflict is a lie."

The truth of his words hung between them, heavy and undeniable. They were the two poles of existence, and Lucifera was the equator, a burning line of impossible balance that threatened to remap their entire world.

"A temporary truce," Oren stated, the words tasting like ash in his mouth.

"A joint operation. We combine our forces. Angelic precision and infernal cunning. We strike her on the mortal plane, together. We erase the anomaly, and then we return to our eternal war."

Mother Midnight considered him, her ancient mind weighing a million variables. "And if we succeed," she finally said, "who gets the ashes? Her power is unique. A prize for the victor, wouldn't you agree?"

"The realms will be as they were," Oren promised, his voice leaving no room for negotiation. "Balanced in opposition. Her power will be unmade, not claimed."

"A tempting offer," she conceded, the prospect of victory outweighing the potential prize.

"To see the look on her face when the very forces she defies unite against her... yes. Very tempting indeed."

She extended a hand made of pure shadow. "You have an alliance, Archangel. May it choke us both."

Oren did not take her hand, but he gave a single, sharp nod. "It is agreed."

The Ambush

The city did not know it was holding its breath.

Lucifera and Ezra moved through the late-night streets, the air thick with a strained, electric calm. Then the sky tore open. It was not one rent, but two.

From a blinding fissure of gold, angels descended, their wings a lattice of light. From a swirling vortex of purple, demons clawed their way into the world, their forms a chaotic tide of horns and shadow.

They did not fight each other. They moved as one.

"What is this?" Ezra yelled, stumbling back as a hulking, six-limbed demon landed beside a serene, silver-armored angel, both turning their eyes on them.

"The impossible," Lucifera breathed, her own eyes wide with a shock she rarely allowed herself. Her fire erupted around her, a defiant shield. "They're working together."

The attack was a symphony of terrifying harmony. Angelic archers rained down spears of pure light, forcing Lucifera and Ezra into the open, while demonic brutes smashed through buildings, cutting off escape routes.

The precision of Heaven combined with the raw, chaotic power of Hell was a force the world had never seen. It was overwhelming, a pincer movement on a cosmic scale.

The Turning Point

They fought back to back, a desperate island in a sea of divine and infernal fury.

Lucifera was a whirlwind of flame, incinerating demons and shattering angelic formations.

Ezra, his fear burned away and replaced with grim resolve, laid down covering fire, his mortal bullets a surprisingly effective distraction against beings who had never had to consider such things.

But they were impossibly outnumbered. For every one they struck down, three more took its place. An angel, moving with the speed of thought, slipped past Lucifera's guard. Its blade was not aimed at her, but at Ezra.

"Ezra, move!" Lucifera screamed, but it was too late.

The celestial blade sliced across his side, a hiss of holy energy on mortal flesh.

The pain was white-hot, staggering. Ezra collapsed, the world blurring into a smear of gold and purple. The last thing he saw before the darkness took him was Lucifera's face, her shock turning into a rage so pure, so absolute, it seemed to set the very air on fire.

The World Watches

The first images that hit the web were dismissed as a hoax, a viral marketing campaign for some new blockbuster film.

Grainy cell phone footage showed impossible things: winged figures of light descending on a city, monstrous shapes erupting from the ground.

Then came the first clear, high-definition feed from a news helicopter that had been covering a downtown protest. The world went silent.

In living rooms, bars, and newsrooms across the globe, humanity watched, utterly transfixed. This was not a movie. Anchors fumbled for words, their professional composure shattering.

"We are seeing... I don't know what we are seeing," one stammered, his voice cracking. "It appears to be a coordinated, military-style assault on the city by... by beings that can only be described as angels and demons."

The feed was raw, unfiltered. It showed the terrifying synergy of the attackers. It showed civilians being cut down by holy light and demonic claws.

The narrative of divine protectors and infernal tempters, a story as old as humanity, was being violently rewritten live on air.

Then, through the smoke and chaos, the camera found her.

A lone figure in a scarlet jacket, wreathed in flame, fighting back. She moved with a terrible grace, her fire a shield for the mortals cowering behind her.

She was positioned between the allied armies and a group of trapped civilians, a living barricade.

"#TheWomanInRed," the hashtags began, then "#FireAngel," then simply, "#Lucifera."

They watched as she fought, a single being against two armies.

They watched as the detective, Ezra Voss, stood by her side, a lone human with a gun against gods. And then they watched him fall.

The collective gasp was global. They saw the angel's blade strike, and they saw Lucifera's reaction. It was not the cold fury of a monster. It was the protective rage of a guardian.

The Sundering

Seeing Ezra fall, something inside Lucifera broke. Or perhaps, it was finally forged. The calculated restraint she had cultivated, the careful balance between judgment and mercy, shattered.

The raw, untamed power of her creation, the very thing Heaven and Hell both feared, was unleashed.

She did not just burn. She *became.*

From her right side, a wing of pure, blinding celestial light erupted, mirroring the very angels she fought.

From her left, a wing of fathomless, infernal shadow unfurled, a thing of beautiful, terrifying darkness.

174

She was no longer just fire. She was the source. She was the balance made manifest.

"You wanted to erase the anomaly?" she roared, her voice now a terrifying harmony of celestial choir and demonic growl that crackled through every live feed. "Then face what you created!"

She unleashed her full, dual nature. She channeled both celestial light and infernal fire simultaneously, not as opposing forces, but as a single, unified wave of paradoxical energy.

The effect on the allied armies was catastrophic.

The angels, creatures of pure order and light, were struck by her infernal shadow. Their grace faltered, their wings stuttered, their holy light flickered as the alien touch of the void corrupted their divine essence.

They cried out, not in pain, but in horrified confusion, as their own purity was turned against them.

The demons, beings of chaos and shadow, were seared by her celestial light. Their darkness recoiled, their forms sizzling as the pure, creative energy of her angelic half burned away their infernal substance.

They howled in agony, their chaotic strength useless against a power they were never meant to touch.

Their alliance became their weakness. She didn't just fight them; she turned their very natures against them.

175

The Shattered Truce

The alliance broke in spectacular fashion.

The angels, now seeing the demons as carriers of the corrupting shadow Lucifera wielded, turned their blades on their erstwhile allies.

The demons, tormented by a light they could not endure, lashed out in a frenzy of pain and rage at the nearest source—the angels.

The battlefield devolved into a three-way war. The unholy summit was undone.

 Oren and Mother Midnight, watching from their respective realms, saw their perfect strategy collapse into the very chaos they had sought to prevent.

With their own forces now slaughtering each other, they had no choice.

The command to retreat was given, a psychic scream of fury and disbelief from two sovereigns who had just been outplayed.

The remaining angels and demons disengaged, vanishing back into their respective portals, leaving behind a battlefield littered with the bodies of their own.

Lucifera had not destroyed them. She had done something far worse. She had shattered their certainty and proven that she was the only true point of balance in the universe.

The Aftermath

The sky slowly cleared, the portals sealing themselves like healed wounds.

Lucifera's wings of light and shadow folded back into her, the raw power receding, leaving her trembling and utterly exhausted.

She stumbled over to where Ezra lay, his breathing shallow.

She knelt beside him, her hands glowing with a soft, gentle flame. She cauterized his wound, her touch now a thing of pure, focused life.

He had been her anchor, the mortal weakness that had unlocked her ultimate strength.

She had won, not by being the strongest, but by being the only one who understood both sides of the cosmic coin.

The truce was broken. The realms were in disarray. The failure of the alliance had shattered more than military strategy—it had broken the fundamental assumption that Heaven and Hell were the only powers that mattered. Across the cosmos, other entities that had remained neutral for eons began to stir. The Void Watchers, ancient beings who observed from the spaces between stars, sent their first emissaries in millennia. The Elemental Courts, who governed the raw forces of creation, began questioning why they had allowed two upstart realms to claim dominion over mortal souls.

Most disturbing of all, the reports reaching both Heaven and Hell spoke of mortals who had witnessed the battle developing new abilities. Not divine gifts or infernal pacts, but something else

177

entirely—a direct connection to the same primal forces Lucifera had tapped. The rigid hierarchy that had governed existence for eons was cracking, and through those cracks, chaos was seeping in.

Oren's perfect order was unraveling. Mother Midnight's carefully maintained balance of corruption was tilting toward something she couldn't control. And at the center of it all stood a being who belonged to neither realm, answering to no cosmic authority except her own conscience.

The war was no longer about Heaven versus Hell. Emergency broadcasts flickered across abandoned screens worldwide, anchors struggling to explain footage their audiences could barely comprehend. Religious leaders found their phone lines jammed with desperate calls from believers demanding answers they didn't have.

It was about whether the universe would continue to be governed by ancient powers, or whether something new—something terrifyingly unpredictable—would rise to challenge them all.

And she, the anomaly, was now the most powerful piece on the board.

She looked down at Ezra, a flicker of something raw and protective in her eyes.

The war was far from over, but the rules had just been rewritten. In the distance, emergency broadcasts crackled through abandoned radios, world leaders struggling to explain what their populations had witnessed. Faith wasn't dying—it was evolving, and no institution on Earth was prepared for what that meant. And the entire world had been watching.

Chapter 15 – The Outcast of Outcasts

The sky broke open, and Kieran fell from it like a bolt of tempered lightning. He landed hard on the rooftop, wings flickering between shadow and brilliance, as if unable to decide what they were.

He caught himself on the ledge, stumbling, his breath coming in ragged bursts that smelled of ozone and celestial fire.

Lucifera turned first, then Ezra, their faces mirroring the shock of someone back from the dead. The look in Kieran's eyes was one they'd both worn before. Urgent. Haunted. Fleeing something he could not outrun.

"Kieran," Lucifera said, the name escaping her lips like an echo of a forgotten song, sharp with disbelief and a history she couldn't bury.

He rolled up his sleeve, revealing a brand burned deep into his forearm—not a wound, but a mark of ownership. Angelic script that hurt to look at directly.

"Oren's personal seal," he said, noting her recognition. "Every angel who's ever questioned an order gets one. A reminder of who we belong to." His voice carried years of suppressed rage. "I've worn this for two centuries, Lu. Two centuries of 'yes sir' and 'glory to the Light' while watching them cover up atrocities that would make Hell blush."

She stared at the brand, understanding flooding her features. "You didn't abandon me because you were afraid."

"I abandoned you because I was a coward." The admission came out raw, unfiltered. "You were ready to burn it all down, and I thought I could change things from the inside. Thought I could be the reasonable voice, the moderate influence." He laughed bitterly.

"You know what moderation gets you in Heaven? Front row seats to watch them destroy everything you love."

Kieran flexed his branded arm, the scar tissue pulling tight. "I spent decades filing reports about corruption, bringing evidence to the Council, trying to work within their precious system. Want to know how many cases they acted on? Zero. Want to know how many angels they've silenced for asking questions? Hundreds."

"So why now? Why help me now?"

"Because I recently watched Oren personally execute an angel whose only crime was refusing to burn down an orphanage." His wings trembled with fury.

"Her name was Celeste. She was nineteen cycles old. She begged him to reconsider, said the children were innocent. So he made me hold her down while he tore her grace away piece by piece."

The brand on his arm pulsed with remembered pain. "I'm done being reasonable. I'm done being moderate. You were right, and I was too much of a fool to see it."

"Oren has sanctioned a second purge. He's out for blood, yours and anyone who dares side with you."

Ezra flinched at the archangel's name.

"A second purge?" Lucifera said, the disbelief more bitter than shocked.

"The first was enough to splinter them. Why risk open rebellion?"

Kieran shook his head, wings twitching like a nervous creature.

"Oren believes in the clean slate. But this time, not even the heavenly courts are aligned behind him. Your defiance—it's inspired doubt, even in the most devout.

There's a rebellion brewing, Lucifera. Beneath all that gold, some of them are beginning to fracture." His voice dropped, heavy with confession.

"They sent a squad after you. One of Oren's most loyal lieutenants. I... intercepted them."

The unspoken violence hung in the air. "Intercepted?" Lucifera pressed, her voice dangerously quiet.

"I killed him," Kieran stated, the words falling with the weight of an executioner's blade.

"I killed one of Oren's own to stop them from reaching you. I've marked myself as a traitor."

Ezra stepped forward, his mind working furiously. "You're saying there are angels who might actually side with us?"

Kieran laughed, a sound both light and weary. "More than you think. Oren's so desperate to restore order, he's practically driving them to it. But he's ruthless enough to try and burn us all. We don't have long before he makes his move."

Lucifera's eyes, twin cores of intensity, locked onto his. A plan began to form behind them, forged in the heat of this new intelligence.

"If they're fracturing," she said, her voice low and dangerous, "then it's time to apply pressure. It's time they chose a side."

The call went out, not in words, but in whispers of fire that traveled through the city's hidden veins, a summons felt in the blood of the outcast. The shell of a train station, a cathedral abandoned by its own God, became the designated sanctuary. Lucifera strode along the border of the burned-out platform, her presence peeling paint and singeing the air. Ghosts of locomotives haunted the tracks, their whistle cries echoing off rotting wood. Ezra and Kieran followed, hesitant shadows in her wake. This wasn't just a hunt. It was a congregation.

At first, it was just her fire illuminating the shadows. Then, figures began to materialize from the gloom.

A demon limped into view, his horns sanded down to jagged stumps, a mark of infernal disgrace.

An angel trailed close behind, one wing shredded and useless, hanging like a broken promise.

They approached as if expecting betrayal, yet they came, one by one. Soldiers, rebels, outcasts of every order, each wearing their expulsion like a badge or a scar.

As they gathered, Lucifera was both queen and kindred, sharing the painful crown of their rejection.

The station pulsed with a grim sort of life, a restless mass of the damned, their murmurs an eerie hymn of disbelief and need. Ezra watched from a corner, a lone mortal chronicling the birth of a myth, while Kieran stood guard, his tattered wings a defiant banner.

She stared down her council of fallen divinities.

Angels with burnt plumage.

Demons, broken and bandaged.

Misfit ghosts of Heaven and Hell, shaped by wrath and the betrayals of their faith.

She let their murmurs of doubt and fear fill the vast, decaying space before she spoke the truth that Heaven never will.

"I offer no allegiance," her voice cracked like thunder, echoing off the rusted steel.

"No new king, no new god. I offer no war, except on those who deserve it. A balance of light and dark, with none to tilt the scales." It was a manifesto that burned away centuries of divine propaganda.

The gathering reacted like flint to steel, sparks flying in all directions.

"Why should we follow you?" shouted an angel, his eyes hard and unyielding. "You're the outcast of outcasts!"

"Judgment comes whether you hide or not," Lucifera replied, her words as cutting as the edge of a blade.

"This time, you get to choose who delivers it."

A demon's laughter pierced the air, harsh and cynical. "You think you're our savior? You're just another tyrant in the making!"

"Tyrants demand worship," she shot back, her voice ringing with clarity.

"I demand you think for yourselves. Heaven gave you orders. Hell gave you chains. I am giving you a choice."

The chaos turned to cacophony as her supporters answered the dissent. Lucifera let the tension mount, feeding on their questions, her silence a crucible. Then she moved.

A flick of her wrist, and the world exploded in fire. White, blinding, all-consuming. It roared through the station, a perfect, controlled inferno that licked at the rafters but did not sing a single feather or scorch a single scale.

It was a pure display of power that commanded everything yet destroyed nothing.

It was the kind of control no one in that room had ever witnessed from a divine being.

The fire burned away the very air of their doubt, reducing their chaotic anthem to a single, gasping breath. The silence after was absolute. Unholy. Her power hung in the air, intimidating not in its capacity for destruction, but in its profound and unwavering restraint.

In the quiet aftermath, Lucifera made her mark in a blazing circle of ash and flame.

The Covenant of Fire. It burned on the floor like a wound that refuses to heal, an eternal scar of their allegiance to nothing but the truth.

The circle glowed with a violent beauty, demanding without a word, a dare to all who witnessed it.

One moved first. An angel, her feathers singed but eyes bright with a new, fierce light. She had seen Heaven's power—it was a hammer that shattered everything.

The angel who moved first had burn scars across half her face—punishment for defying a direct order. She'd been beautiful once, Ezra could tell, but the scarring had taught her something more valuable than beauty: the cost of conscience.

"My name is Seraphiel," she said, her voice carrying the weight of someone who had learned to speak truth regardless of consequences. "I served in the Purification Corps for six centuries. I watched us burn entire cities because their faith wasn't pure enough. Children. Families. People whose only sin was asking why their prayers went unanswered."

She touched the burns on her cheek, a gesture both painful and defiant. "The child I saved was seven years old. Her village had been marked for cleansing because they'd started worshipping the wrong way—singing hymns instead of chanting them, gathering in homes instead of temples. Small heresies. Punishable by flame."

Her voice strengthened. "I pulled her from the fire. One child. Out of thousands. And for that act of mercy, they branded me a traitor and burned away half my grace." She looked directly at Lucifera. "But I'd do it again. I'd do it a thousand times."

She step forward and say, *"Heaven cast me out for showing mercy to a mortal child. They called it a weakness. Lucifera calls it a strength. I will follow the one who sees me for what I am, not what they wish I was."*

This was different. This was the fire of a forge, a power that could build as well as break. It was terrifying, yes, but it was also a foundation. She walked with the grace of one who had forgotten how to kneel and stepped into the circle, her form bathed in its defiant light.

Then another followed—a demon with half-formed horns and fully formed determination.

He had known Hell's power, a chaotic, selfish thing that consumed for the sake of consumption.

Lucifera's fire was a judgment, clean and absolute. It was a power he could respect, even fear. He spat on the ground before claiming his place.

Ezra leaned in, his own heart racing, watching them transmute doubt into resolve.

There were those who turned and left, souls not ready to burn in the flame of uncertainty, their shadows retreating into the gloom.

But more than enough remained. They saw in her intimidating willpower not the promise of a new ruler, but the guarantee that no one would ever rule them again.

Her plan for a new order wasn't a whisper of hope; it was a declaration backed by a fire that could hold back the heavens. Celestial deserters and infernal traitors stepped into the circle, claiming their place.

The mark glowed brighter with each commitment, a furnace of their collective spirit. Enough had joined to make Heaven tremble and Hell rage. A faction was born.

Ezra found her standing alone after the others had departed, the station empty but for the ghosts of what they'd done. Kieran lingered by the entrance, a silent, winged sentinel. "What the hell was that?" Ezra asked, half accusation, half awe.

Lucifera didn't flinch. "That," she said, "was just the start." He saw the flicker of doubt in her eyes, a shadow beneath the fire of her resolve. It was her certainty that frightened him most.

"You're building an army," he said, watching her closely.

"Or a funeral pyre." Her voice was cold, assured. "We'll see."

Ezra shook his head, struggling to wrap his mind around her scope. "So, what's the plan? Light a match and watch the world burn?"

"If it doesn't choose to change, then yes." She met his gaze, unyielding.

"Sometimes fire is the only way to clear the path."

He heard the doubt she tried to smother, the vulnerability beneath her hardened shell. It unsettled him, more than her firebrand declarations ever could.

He saw something divine behind her words—not righteous, but inevitable. The promise of change, scorched earth, and truth without apology.

"Ezra," she called, her tone almost tender. Almost. "This is just the beginning. Remember that."

He turned to face her one last time, knowing he would remember—too vividly, too well.

He'd witnessed the spark she'd just lit, a conflagration waiting to happen. The question was whether he could stand its heat, or whether he'll be consumed along with everything else.

Chapter 16 – The Scouring of the Sands

In the silent, sterile halls of the Celestial Decree Chamber, Oren watched the mortal world's broadcasts.

He saw his own unmaking play out on a thousand screens. He saw his perfect, divine authority shattered by a grainy cell phone video and the defiant voice of a mortal detective.

He saw his enforcers fall, not to a superior force, but to a superior idea. The humiliation was a cold, black stone in the center of his being. His rage was not hot; it was a perfect, absolute zero, a cold that could freeze stars.

He had offered the anomaly a place. He had offered her a truce. She had answered with fire and mockery, turning his own army against itself and exposing the hypocrisy of Heaven to a world that was supposed to worship, not question.

The rebellion she had sparked was no longer a flicker; it was a conflagration, and his name was the kindling.

The Council's insistence on surgical strikes and quiet containment had been a catastrophic failure. They had underestimated the contagion of her idea.

"She has chosen chaos," Oren's voice echoed in the empty chamber, the sound absorbed by the flawless marble. "She has chosen oblivion."

He raised a hand, and the air before him shimmered. A deep, resonant chime, like a bell struck at the dawn of creation, tolled through the heavens.

It was a summons that had not been used since the Elder Wars, a call to awaken a force that even the High Council feared.

They were not soldiers or enforcers. They were a law of physics. A final, absolute solution.

He would not send another army. He would send a judgment from which there was no appeal.

He would send **The Hallowed Legion.**

Heaven's first and oldest purifiers. Beings forged from the pure, uncompromising will of creation, whose only purpose was to scour anomalies from existence.

"The mortal realm is tainted," Oren declared to the silent chamber.

"The anomaly has allied herself with the broken and the damned. She has given them hope, a disease more virulent than any sin." He clenched his fist, and the light in the chamber dimmed, as if in fear.

"Time to cauterize the wound."

His command was absolute, a single, chilling thought projected across the celestial plane: *Find the source of the infection. Leave nothing but glass.*

Lucifera felt the summons in her very essence. It was a cold pressure against her fire, a sudden, terrifying drop in the cosmic temperature.

She stood with Kieran and the remnants of their new Covenant of Fire in the ruins of the train station, the air still thick with the energy of their formation.

"He's coming," she said, her voice low. "Not his army. Something else. Something older."

Kieran's tattered wings stiffened. He knew the legends. "The Legion," he breathed, a look of genuine fear flashing in his eyes.

"Lucifera, they are not soldiers. They don't fight; they *unmake*. We cannot face them here. Not in the city."

The outcasts murmured, their newfound courage wavering in the face of a threat they couldn't comprehend.

Lucifera looked at their faces—demons, angels, spirits, all scarred by the tyranny of absolute power. She would not lead them to a slaughter that would also consume the mortals she had sworn to protect.

"No," she agreed, her mind racing. "We won't fight them here. We draw them out."

She turned to Ezra, who had been documenting their council. "You stay. Coordinate the resistance. Keep the world watching. Let them see what Heaven sends for those who dare to ask for freedom."

Her gaze swept over her followers. "Kieran is right.

They are not an army to be fought, but a storm to be weathered. But even storms have an eye." Her eyes burned with a reckless, strategic light. "I will be the beacon. I will draw them to a place where their 'purity' can do no harm."

She closed her eyes, and her fire erupted, not as a weapon, but as a signal. She projected her unique, paradoxical essence across the globe, a blazing, defiant flare that screamed her location to the heavens.

It was an open challenge, an invitation to a duel on a battlefield of her choosing: the vast, empty heart of the Mojave Desert.

The Arrival

The desert was a canvas of heat and silence. The sun beat down on the cracked earth, the air shimmering in waves.

Lucifera and her small, desperate army stood waiting, the silence of the wasteland a stark contrast to the storm brewing within them.

Then, the sun vanished.

Not blocked by clouds, but seemingly extinguished.

A chilling, unnatural cold descended upon the desert, the temperature dropping fifty degrees in a heartbeat. The sky turned a deep, starless indigo, and the silence became absolute. Not even the wind dared to whisper.

They arrived not with a flash of light, but with a chilling *absence* of it. One moment the desert was empty; the next, the Hallowed Legion stood before them.

There were a hundred of them, arranged in a perfect, silent phalanx.

They wore ancient, featureless silver armor that seemed to absorb the very light around them, their wings were constructs of woven, geometric light, and their faces were hidden behind masks of pure, unfeeling judgment. They carried no swords, no spears. They *were* the weapons.

They were a force of nature, a glacier of divine law, and the desert itself seemed to recoil from their sterile presence.

The First Clash

"For freedom!" a rogue demon roared, his voice cracking the oppressive silence as he led the first charge.

Lucifera's allies surged forward, a chaotic, beautiful wave of infernal fire and broken angelic light. They were a storm of passion and defiance.

The Hallowed Legion met them not with a counter-charge, but with a simple, unified step forward.

As the first rebels reached them, the Legionnaires raised their hands. Their blades didn't flash; they simply *were*. Lances of pure, anti-energy erupted, striking the charging demons and angels.

There were no screams of pain. There was only a quiet, horrifying *unmaking.* A demon hit by a lance did not burn or bleed; his form simply dissolved, his chaos erased from existence as if he had never been. An angel's light was snuffed out, her form turning to motes of dust that scattered in a non-existent wind.

The rebels faltered, their charge breaking in the face of a power that did not recognize their rage, their hope, their very being. The Legion advanced, their steps perfectly synchronized, their lances of anti-existence cutting down the outcasts with terrifying efficiency. This was not a battle. It was a culling.

The Tide Turns

"Chaos is their weakness!" Kieran yelled, his own blade of silver light blazing to life.

"Don't meet them head on! Break their formation!"

He launched himself into the air, a reckless, unpredictable blur of motion. He didn't attack the Legionnaires directly, but the structures of light that formed their wings, the ground beneath their feet. His chaotic strikes, while doing little damage, forced them to break their perfect synchronicity to defend.

Lucifera joined him, her fire a stark, living contrast to the Legion's sterile cold.

She did not throw blasts of flame, but wove intricate patterns of heat, creating updrafts that threw the Legionnaires off balance, superheating the sand beneath them into glass, forcing them to move, to

195

react, to become individuals rather than a single, unified entity.

It worked.

The Legion's advance slowed, their perfect unity disrupted.

They were forced to fight as individuals, and while still terrifyingly powerful, they were no longer an unstoppable force.

The remaining rebels rallied, following Kieran's lead, their chaotic attacks now a strategy rather than a desperate charge.

But the Legion adapted. They began to target the most effective disruptions.

Kieran, weaving through the air, saw a lance of nothingness aimed not at him, but at a young, terrified angel he had taken under his wing.

Without thinking, he dove, placing himself in its path. The lance struck his wing, and the agony was absolute. It was not pain, but an erasure of his very being.

He screamed as a third of his wing dissolved into nothing, the ragged edge smoking with anti-light. He plummeted from the sky, crashing hard into the sand.

The Duel and the Sacrifice

Lucifera saw Kieran fall. She saw her allies being systematically, silently erased.

She saw the Legion's commander, a being whose mask was adorned with a single, glowing rune, turn its cold, calculating gaze on her.

She met its charge, and the desert exploded. Their duel was the centerpiece of the battle, a clash of fundamental forces.

Its lances of unmaking were pure order; her fire was pure, creative chaos.

They were perfectly matched, a stalemate of cosmic principles.

But her allies were not. They were dying.

The Legion was too efficient, too relentless. Lucifera knew she could not win this way. She could fight the commander to a standstill for eternity, but her people would be gone.

She had to do something drastic. She had to break the rules of the universe.

She broke her engagement with the commander and rose high into the unnatural twilight, her arms spread wide.

She was not drawing on her own internal fire. She was reaching deeper. She drew on the very life force of the desert, on the raw, chaotic energy of the Earth itself—a power neither Heaven nor Hell understood.

It was the planet's rage, its history of violent births and slow, grinding death. It was a power of pure, untamed life.

The Aftermath

Lucifera unleashed the raw, terrestrial energy. It was not light or shadow, but something primal, green and brown and electric blue.

The desert itself rose up to meet her call. The sand swirled, not with wind, but with life. The ancient, dormant energies of the earth awakened in a furious, unstoppable storm.

A tempest of superheated sand, jagged shards of obsidian, and raw, crackling lightning engulfed the battlefield.

The Hallowed Legion, beings of pure, sterile celestial order, could not withstand this primal chaos. Their anti-energy was useless against a force that was pure, messy, unpredictable life.

Their silver armor cracked, then shattered under the assault of a billion grains of sand moving with the force of creation.

Their forms, once absolute, were scoured, broken, and torn apart by the raw fury of the mortal plane they had so disdained.

The Legion was wiped out, not by a superior power, but by a different *kind* of power, one they had never conceived of.

The cost, however, was immense. The desert was now a sea of molten glass, still crackling with residual energy.

And Lucifera, having channeled a force she was never meant to contain, collapsed from the sky, her own fire reduced to a bare, guttering flicker, her body broken by the strain.

The Cosmic Reaction

In the Celestial Decree Chamber, the silver light wavered, then died.

Oren stood before a vast scrying crystal, its surface now dark and inert.

The connection to his Legion had been severed. Not defeated. Not broken. Erased.

The silence in the chamber was more profound than any scream.

For the first time in his eternal existence, the Archangel of the Host felt the cold, unfamiliar touch of utter shock.

He had sent a law of physics to correct a mathematical error. He had sent a glacier to extinguish a match. And the match had boiled the glacier into steam.

She had not used celestial power.

She had not used infernal power.

She had used... the dirt. The rocks. The very mortal filth he had sought to purify.

The concept was so alien, so fundamentally wrong, that his mind struggled to process it.

His cold, perfect rage began to thaw, replaced by something hotter, something dangerously close to mortal fury.

The humiliation was a physical blow. He had not just lost his most ancient weapon; he had been proven ignorant.

He, Oren, the right hand of Heaven, had been outmaneuvered by a power he didn't even know existed. His hands clenched into fists, and a hairline crack, impossibly small, spiderwebbed across the flawless marble floor beneath his feet.

Meanwhile, in the Chamber of Embers, Mother Midnight watched the same event unfold in a pool of molten soul-stuff.

She saw the Legion's arrival, their initial, terrifying success.

She saw the rebels falter. She had felt a flicker of regret for not committing her own forces, for letting Oren claim the prize.

Then, she saw Lucifera rise. She saw the desert awaken. She saw the Legion unmade by a power that was raw, chaotic, and utterly beautiful.

A slow, genuine smile spread across her ancient features.

It was a smile of pure, unadulterated vindication. She had tested the anomaly and found her to be a force of nature.

Oren had tested her and found his own irrelevance. She had wisely held back her legions, allowing Heaven to break its most valuable sword against an unbreakable shield.

The board had been cleared, and the most powerful piece was now wounded, vulnerable, and owed her nothing.

"How interesting," Mother Midnight purred to the empty chamber.

"The little spark has learned to borrow the thunder."

She leaned back on her throne, the violet fire in her eyes dancing with a thousand new, intricate plans.

The war was far from over, but the balance had just shifted in a way no one, not even she, could have predicted.

The Search for Sanctuary

Kieran, clutching his mangled wing, forced himself to his feet.

The desert was silent once more, the only sound the faint crackle of cooling glass.

He looked around. A handful of rebels had survived, huddled together in shock, their numbers decimated. They had won, but it felt like a funeral.

He saw her, a crumpled heap of scarlet and black in the center of a newly formed crater.

He made his way to her, his steps crunching on the glassy sand. She was barely conscious, her breath shallow, her inner light a faint, struggling ember.

The victory had sent a shockwave through the cosmos. Oren would know. And his full, unrestrained wrath would be coming.

Kieran gently lifted Lucifera, her body limp in his arms. "We have to go," he said to the few remaining survivors. "Now."

They were broken, bleeding, and had lost most of their newfound family.

But they were alive.

The victory was devastating, a scar on all of their souls.

Kieran supported Lucifera as they began the long, painful trek across the glass desert, two wounded figures searching for a place to hide, to heal, to prepare for the final war.

Chapter 17 – The Last Sanctuary

The desert was a graveyard of Heaven's ambition, a sprawling tomb of molten glass that crackled and cooled under a sky of bruised indigo.

The silence was absolute, broken only by the crunch of Kieran's boots on the obsidian-like surface and the ragged, shallow breaths of the woman he carried.

Lucifera was a dead weight in his arms, her inner fire reduced to a faint, struggling ember that barely warmed her skin.

Her scarlet jacket was torn and blackened, her form limp, broken by the very power she had summoned to save them.

Behind him, the handful of survivors stumbled along, a funeral procession of the damned and the defiant.

Their numbers had been decimated, their spirits scoured by the horrifying, silent unmaking of their comrades.

They had won, but the victory tasted of ash and loss. Each survivor was an island of grief, their faces gaunt, their eyes hollowed out by the sheer, alien wrongness of the Hallowed Legion.

They had faced armies before, but they had never faced a living erasure.

Kieran's mangled wing was a constant, searing agony, the wound not bleeding but simply *ending* where the Legion's anti-energy had touched it.

It was a void, a patch of nothingness that screamed at his senses. But he ignored it, focusing all his will on the woman in his arms and the desperate, forward motion. Oren's full, unrestrained wrath would be coming.

They needed a place to hide, to heal, to comprehend the impossible victory that felt so much like a defeat.

For hours they walked, two wounded figures leading a procession of ghosts across a sea of glass.

The unnatural twilight held, the sun still refusing to show its face. It was in the deepest hour of this false night that Kieran saw it: a flicker. Not of light, but of its absence.

A shadow against the low mountains on the horizon that did not move, a cave mouth that seemed to drink the very air around it.

"There," he rasped, his voice raw. "Sanctuary."

It was a hope born of desperation, but it was all they had. He adjusted his grip on Lucifera and led his broken soldiers toward the darkness, praying it was not simply another tomb.

The cave was more than a cave. The moment they stepped across the threshold, the oppressive silence of the glass desert was replaced by a low, resonant hum that vibrated through the soles of their feet.

The air within was warm, alive, and smelled of deep earth, ozone, and something ancient, something primal.

Crystalline structures, veined with what looked like liquid gold, grew from the walls, casting a soft, internal luminescence that lit their way.

The survivors huddled at the entrance, too awed and terrified to venture further. But Kieran, carrying Lucifera, felt an undeniable pull, a sense of purpose that drew him deeper into the earth's embrace.

The humming grew louder, becoming a tangible pressure, a song sung in a key older than angels.

He found the source in the cave's central chamber. It was a vast grotto, the ceiling lost in darkness, the walls lined with the same golden, glowing crystals.

In the center of the chamber was not a pool or a fissure, but a perfect, slowly rotating sphere of pure, geothermal energy.

It was a miniature sun, a captive heart of the planet, radiating a power that was raw, chaotic, and utterly untamed by any divine or infernal law. It was the life force of the world, laid bare.

As he drew near, Lucifera stirred in his arms. Her head lolled, her molten eyes fluttering open.

They were not focused on him, but on the sphere. A low moan escaped her lips, a sound of both pain and profound, instinctual longing. Her body, broken and near-death, was responding to the energy, her own internal fire recognizing its source.

"Put me down," she whispered, her voice a faint, crackling thing.

Kieran hesitated, then gently lowered her to the ground. She crawled, her movements weak but resolute, toward the sphere of energy. The survivors watched from the tunnel's mouth, their faces a mixture of fear and wonder.

"Lucifera, no!" Kieran warned, reaching for her, but the heat radiating from the sphere pushed him back.

She did not listen. She reached the edge of the sphere's radiant corona and, with the last of her strength, plunged her hand into the swirling, living energy.

The Communion

The moment her fingers touched the sphere, the chamber did not erupt. It imploded.

The air pressure dropped violently, a sudden, crushing vacuum that stole the breath from Kieran's lungs and made the survivors at the tunnel's mouth cry out as their ears popped. A low, resonant hum, which had been a song felt only in the bones, escalated into a deafening, soul-shaking roar that vibrated through the very stone beneath their feet. The air grew thick with the sharp, clean scent of ozone, like the instant after a lightning strike, and the smell of ancient stone heated for the first time in a million years.

Energy arced from the core, striking Lucifera's body not with the simple violence of a weapon, but with the furious, possessive recognition of a god claiming its own.

She screamed, a raw, elemental sound that was swallowed by the chamber's roar. Her body convulsed as the raw, untamed power of the Earth surged into her. It was not a gentle healing. It was a violent, elemental reforging.

Kieran and the others shielded their eyes as the light intensified, but there was no escaping the other senses.

They felt the pressure change, the roar vibrating in their chests, the acrid smell of ozone filling their throats.

They watched in horror and awe as Lucifera's wounds began to close, her skin stitching itself back together, her broken bones snapping into place with audible cracks that were somehow audible even over the din. The process was brutal, her body thrashing on the ground as it was simultaneously destroyed and remade by the primal power.

And then, her eyes rolled back in her head. Her body went still, not limp with death, but rigid with the sheer force of the vision that was consuming her from the inside out.

The roar subsided back into a bone-deep hum. The pressure equalized, leaving a ringing silence in its wake. All that remained was the light, the smell of hot stone, and the terrifying stillness of her transformation.

The Vision - The Forging

She was not in the cave. She was in a place of impossible geometry, a celestial forge that hung in a void between the nascent realms of Heaven and Hell.

She was not a being, but a concept, a point of potential awareness floating in the crucible of creation. Around her stood the architects, beings of such immense power they appeared as figures of pure light and absolute shadow, their forms too complex for her new consciousness to fully comprehend.

The vision showed her creation in fragments, like a shattered mirror reflecting different truths.

A hand of pure light, reaching into the heart of a dying star. The scream of something ancient as its essence was torn away. "Perfect order," a voice murmured with satisfaction. "Unthinking. Absolute."

Another hand, this one made of living shadow, drawing darkness from the first void. The whisper of infinite possibility, of chaos given form. Two opposing forces, hovering in the space between creation and destruction.

But there was a third element—something the architects hadn't planned. A single tear, shed by a mortal mother watching her child die. It fell through the dimensional barriers, drawn by the cosmic forces they were unleashing. Such a small thing. Such a dangerous thing.

"What is this?" The voice was Oren's, younger, uncertain. "This... contamination?"

"Leave it," another replied. "What harm could one mortal's grief do to our perfect design?"

They sealed the tear into her essence without understanding what it carried: the capacity to feel another's pain as your own. To choose mercy over justice. To doubt.

It was the flaw that made her free.

The forging was a symphony of violence and beauty. She was born in a cataclysm of opposing forces, a living paradox. She was not a creature of light or of shadow. She was a being of balance, and in that balance, she was something entirely new.

The Vision - The First Failure

The vision continued. She felt her first moment of true consciousness, not as an instrument, but as a being.

She looked at her creators, and for the first time, she saw them not as gods, but as flawed, ambitious beings. And in her gaze, they saw their failure.

They had intended to create a loyal, unthinking weapon. They had, instead, created a consciousness born of paradox, a being with the capacity for true free will.

They saw the empathy from the mortal tear clouding the purity of their celestial logic. They saw the chaos of the void tempering the rigidity of their divine order.

She saw the look in Oren's eyes change from ambition to a dawning, horrified understanding.

He saw not a weapon, but a mirror reflecting his own hubris. He saw a being that could not be controlled, because she understood both sides of the cosmic equation. She was not a tool of order. She was a judge of it.

"It is flawed," his thought echoed through the forge, cold and absolute.

"It feels. It questions. It must be unmade."

But it was too late. The forging was complete.

She was alive, and the power they had poured into her was now her own. Her exile was not a punishment for a future crime. It was an immediate, panicked reaction to their first, and greatest, failure.

They did not cast out a rebel. They cast out the living proof of their own fallibility.

The Rebirth

The vision ended. Lucifera gasped, a single, shuddering breath that drew the energy of the chamber into her lungs.

She opened her eyes. The raw, chaotic energy of the Earth's core no longer convulsed her body; it flowed through her, a calm, limitless ocean of power that she now commanded.

She rose to her feet, and Kieran and the survivors stared, speechless. She was not just healed; she was transformed.

The wounds were gone, her scarlet jacket pristine. But the change was deeper.

The intricate, fiery runes that had once adorned her jacket were now etched directly into her skin, glowing lines of soft, golden light and shifting, violet shadow.

They moved like living constellations across her arms and back. Her eyes were still molten gold, but they held a new depth, an ancient, knowing calm.

The raw, volatile heat that had always surrounded her was gone, replaced by a palpable, immense power that was perfectly, terrifyingly still.

She had not just been healed. She had been completed. The communion with Earth's core had done more than heal her wounds—it had revealed the final piece of her nature that Heaven and Hell had never understood. She wasn't just a balance of light and shadow; she was a conduit for the raw, primal force that had existed before either realm claimed dominion over creation.

The planet itself had been the missing element in her design. Heaven had tried to forge her from celestial fire alone. Hell had sought to corrupt her with infernal shadow. But the true power—the power that had just unmade an entire Legion—came from something older than both: the fierce, protective fury of a world that refused to be conquered.

She could feel it now, thrumming beneath her skin alongside the familiar runes. Not just the fire of judgment, but the deep, patient strength of stone. Not just the light of truth, but the dark, nurturing soil where new life took root. She was no longer

Heaven's failed experiment or Hell's lost opportunity.

She was something entirely new.

"The Hallowed Legion couldn't touch this power because they didn't know it existed," she said, more to herself than to Kieran. "They came expecting to face a rogue angel. Instead, they faced the planet's own immune system."

Kieran took a hesitant step forward, his own pain forgotten. "Lucifera?" he whispered, her name a question.

She looked at him, and for the first time, he saw no walls, no defenses. He saw only her. "I remember now, Kieran," she said, her voice a quiet harmony of fire and grace. "I remember everything."

The Reckoning

Days later, they returned to the city. It was a place of fragile, defiant hope, the seeds of the new Accord beginning to sprout amidst the ruins.

Lucifera, with Kieran and the few survivors of the desert battle at her side, moved through the streets like a living myth.

The Redeemed and the rebels who saw her fell silent, their eyes wide with awe. She was different. More.

She found Ezra in his safehouse, the room still a chaotic shrine to his obsession.

He looked up as she entered, and the files and photos he had collected seemed to fall away, rendered obsolete by the reality of her presence.

"You're..." he started, his voice trailing off as he took in her transformation.

"Whole," she finished for him.

The Confession

They sat for hours, the city's new, uncertain pulse a distant soundtrack to their conversation.

Lucifera, now possessing the full, unvarnished truth of her own existence, told Ezra everything.

She spoke of the celestial forge that hung in the void, of the architects of light and shadow who had dared to play god. She described Oren's hubris, his ambition to create a perfect weapon of order, and his ultimate, terrified failure when he realized he had created a conscious, empathetic being instead.

"They didn't cast me out because I was a rebel," she explained, her voice calm and clear.

"They cast me out because I was proof that their perfect, divine order was a lie. I was the living embodiment of a balance they couldn't control."

She told him of the power she had discovered, the raw, primal energy of the mortal plane, a force that Heaven, in its arrogance, had always dismissed. "They fear it," she said.

"They fear you. Because you are not orderly. You are messy, and chaotic, and you feel. That is a power they can never comprehend."

It was not a moment of weakness, but one of profound strength and clarity.

It solidified their alliance on a foundation of absolute truth. Ezra, the ultimate seeker of truth, the man who had chased shadows and whispers, finally had the whole story. He looked at her, at the glowing runes that were now a part of her very being, and he saw not a monster or a savior, but a choice.

"So, what now?" he asked, his voice quiet.

Lucifera looked out the window at the scarred but living city. "Now," she said, a small, dangerous smile on her lips, "we show them what a real balance looks like."

Chapter 18 – Oren's Offer

Lucifera stands at the edge of the broken cathedral, the wind in her dark hair whispering questions it already knows the answers to. The city spreads beneath her like a discarded Eden, constellations hung on high as dispassionate witnesses. She can taste the aftermath of herself, charcoal in the cool air, laced with regret and certainty. The roof tiles simmer with her thoughts, each one a small scar: the unjustly dead, betrayal dressed as friendship, and the loneliness of being right.

Her flames dim to embers, pooling softly around her feet. Judgment has a way of catching its own tail, devouring even the just in its infernal spiral. She wonders if it's too late to cast herself free, or if the choice to incinerate the guilty comes always with its own eternal burn. Maybe, she thinks, she should have stayed in Hell's embrace and taken her chances with the real flames.

Above her, the stars blink with a cold precision, indifferent and eternal, their light beautiful but distant—too distant to care. They remind her of angels, the way they watch and wait, safe in their celestial ivory towers, leaving others to get their hands dirty. Innocence has been lost to them too, in their own twisted way.

Rejected from birth, she thinks. Was it destiny or stupidity that drove her to keep fighting back? She was the unwanted child, spat from Heaven's depths and Hell's heights, torn between blinding order and blistering chaos. Her lips curl at the irony, at how she molded herself into something even more powerful than either realm could have dreamed. And she did it alone, driven by a passion for truth neither side could comprehend.

The city's glow flares orange beneath the blanket of darkness, man's imitation of her inferno. She wonders if humanity knows it's nothing more than a microcosm of their divine parents, just as hypocritical, just as cruel. She presses a hand against her chest, and her fingers curl into a fist as she remembers the unfulfilled promises of angels in brilliant white, demons in seductive black. They offered nothing but lies, but even so—did they not teach her something? She smiles, a brief flicker of humor that quickly gutters out.

Below, a train whistles, a mortal lament rising to meet her. The sound cuts through her thoughts, sharp and mournful, reminding her of lives snuffed out by those unwilling to take the blame. Choirboys molested under Heaven's watch, the guilty protected by the Church. Children burned for witchcraft, the righteous rejoicing in their deaths. It is the agony of her mission that they still haunt her, little ghosts of potential she could never fully save.

And even now, here on her broken throne, she cannot forget those alliances she's torched. What was it like, before her rebellion, when she didn't have to bear all of it alone? Before the suspicion, the war? A momentary pause before the furnace resumed its terrible, brilliant march. But who would trust her now, her hands soaked in the ash of friends and lovers who turned to enemies?

All for the greater good, she tells herself. It feels empty in the telling. The hard edge of a nearby cross remains, remarkably, upright in the ruins. The false promise of salvation amuses her. If the god this place belonged to was truly all powerful, why couldn't he stop a freak like her from existing? Or is that why he sent his armies after her, only for them to die as kindling, by their own hand?

She shakes her head. These thoughts are distractions, echoes of an old wound, useful only to remind her of who she is not. Her heart—whatever is left of it—demands a choice, and for once it is the easier one. It would be easy, now, to burn it all, to scour Heaven, Hell, and Earth and leave it as cold as the vacuum of space. To forget these trappings of morality and be pure, all-consuming fire.

But even that's not her, she thinks, not when it means sparing those who deserve to suffer. She wonders how long she'll last, burning so brightly but never consuming all.

Her eyes rise, like the ground has grown suddenly boring. The sky is wider now. Her resolve cools into hard, molten amber. She blinks once, and the stars blink back, reflecting back their heat, and more. Her mission wasn't wrong; it was only incomplete. Her flames reignite, curling with defiant grace, as if to show the stars how it's really done.

At least there is no doubt. At least, here, she is truly free.

Heaven has sent its answer in shimmering silver. The light bleeds through the fractured roof, creeping across shattered stone and burnt wood like it has something to prove. Lucifera's fire flickers beneath the glare, which pretends it can warm but feels sterile instead. She is not surprised it comes to this: a visit not of wrath but of quiet poison. A ghost of her birthright made flesh, descending from above like a snowflake not yet melted, Oren looks at her with calculated calm. "My sister," he says, words wrapped in silk.

Lucifera's laughter is quick and dark. It rings against the sanctuary walls, more a bark than a symphony. She watches the archangel, curious and wary. "Your sister, am I?" Her voice twists the end of the question into a knife. "Wasn't I your abomination just a few eons ago?"

Oren's smile is a winter sun: bright and without heat. Oren's presence had always been a controlled thing, his power carefully leashed within the bounds of mortal physics. But her defiance sparked something deeper, more primal. The temperature in the sanctuary dropped ten degrees in an instant.

The stone beneath his feet didn't crack—it aged. Centuries of weathering compressed into seconds, the carved angels crumbling to dust as time itself bent around his will. The stained glass windows didn't shatter; they simply ceased, their colored light bleeding out of existence as if it had never been.

Lucifera felt the pressure of his true nature pressing against her consciousness—not heat or cold, but the absolute certainty of ending. This was what he had held back, what he had deemed unnecessary against her. This was the force that had rewritten the laws of three star systems.

And he was barely trying.

"Do you understand now," Oren said, his voice carrying harmonics that shouldn't exist in mortal air, "what mercy looks like? I could unmake you with a thought. I could erase your rebellion from the memory of every soul you've touched. I could make it so you never were."

The sanctuary groaned under the weight of his restrained divinity. Lucifera's fire flickered, not from fear, but from the simple physics of power meeting greater power.

Then, with visible effort, Oren pulled his presence back, letting reality snap into its normal shape. The ruined stone remained ruined, but the crushing certainty of annihilation lifted.

"But I offer you choice instead," he continued, as if the display of cosmic force had been nothing more than adjusting his collar.

His wings radiate light in measured pulses, trying to overpower the warmth of her presence. He lands, not with the earth-shattering fury of Heaven's executioner but with a diplomat's clean grace. The ground doesn't tremble. Lucifera thinks he looks absurd against the backdrop of rubble and shadows, but she also knows that he doesn't come without an agenda.

"I was mistaken," he says, a concession that holds no humility. His eyes—cold, calculating—meet hers with a disarming precision. "As were we all."

She narrows her gaze, catching the shift in his tone. The silver light dances around them, a faux intimacy she doesn't trust. This isn't Oren's first visit. His last was centuries ago, and he left the earth cracked with celestial fire in his wake. He didn't come to talk then.

"Speak quickly," she replies. "It's chilly in here."

Oren takes his time, each word deliberate, dipped in honey and snow. "We understand you now. You seek justice. Not chaos."

"And Heaven approves of justice?" Her sarcasm is a flame, momentarily blinding. "Since when?"

His response is soft, relentless. "Since you showed us its value."

Lucifera leans back against a crumbling arch, her posture dismissive. She watches him through eyes like molten metal, searching for fractures beneath the pristine surface. He could kill her now, she knows, but not before she took him and half his garrison with her. So why this performance, she wonders. Why now?

"Continue," she says, as if permitting a child to stutter through an apology.

Oren's voice fills the sanctuary, resonant but without echo. "We wish to offer you a place in our fold. Not as an instrument, nor as a pariah—but as a leader."

She raises an eyebrow, incredulous and amused. The air shimmers around her, intensifying, her internal temperature rising along with her suspicions. This feels too clean, she thinks. Too well-timed. "You're asking me to be a good little angel again? Obey orders? Play nice?"

"To save them," Oren corrects, extending his hands in an imitation of mercy. "To end their suffering, with us. Your understanding of justice is... needed."

Lucifera scoffs, heat in her breath as she exhales. It should be funny, this new narrative, but the earnestness in Oren's voice makes it tragic instead. "You make me sound like Heaven's savior."

"You are Heaven's savior," Oren says, his tone a steel blade hidden in velvet.

For a moment, she imagines a world where his words are true. Where all the war and anguish yield to a cosmic harmony, where she isn't alone in her crusade, forever scorched by her own passion. It's a beautiful lie, she decides. And maybe that's why it's so dangerous.

"We've been at odds too long," Oren continues, his steps slow and calculated. "You do not have to fight us, or yourself, any longer. Join us. Embrace what you were born to be."

Lucifera folds her arms, appearing to mull it over. A casual observer might even think she's considering it. "Let me guess," she says finally, her words sharp as broken glass. "If I don't join, I'm a threat that must be destroyed?"

Oren meets her sarcasm with a studied patience. "There are many in Heaven who still believe so," he concedes, the slightest pressure behind his eyes, "but they will follow my command."

He offers her control, safety, redemption. It is an artist's brush painting new colors over her history; over the blood and ash she's built herself on. But she knows better. She knows how white-washing works.

"And what does Her Radiance have to say about this? Is God so desperate as to recruit the help of traitors?"

Oren pauses, his expression like a ripple of doubt upon a still pond. But it is gone before she can decide whether to trust her instincts. "The mission," he says, avoiding her question, "is what matters."

There it is. Lucifera feels the energy shift, the honesty beneath Oren's dissembling facade. He thinks he's lost her. He should know that means he's already lost.

"You make it sound so pretty," she says, "but all I hear is the word 'pet.'"

Her defiance is a heat wave, expanding outward, refracting the archangel's halo into an aura of hollow brightness. Oren remains calm, but Lucifera sees the flicker in his eyes. Her suspicion confirmed: not a gift of peace but an ultimatum dressed in divine light.

"You have always been more than you seem," he says, his voice neither pleading nor demanding. "Imagine what we could be together."

It's Lucifera's turn to smile, and it feels like it could melt the heavens.

"And what of the guilty?" Lucifera's question ignites the air between them. Her eyes are hollow flames, burning through the facade of divine light that surrounds the archangel. Oren stands like a sculpture of mercy, words poised on his lips. The wind has shifted; it chills where once it was warm. Lucifera's voice is unwavering, each accusation a small explosion. He answers with platitudes so fragile; she can almost see them shattering in the night. She listens, silent and calculating. This is an old game.

"Our concerns are not so different," Oren insists, draping his evasions in sincerity. "This is why we must stand together."

"Tell that to the choirboys." Her retort cuts like a sharpened blade. "Or the witches. Or those you call collateral damage."

The wind carries her bitterness across the expanse of the sanctuary, leaving an icy trail in its wake. Oren stands his ground, eyes cold and unfaltering. "They will be redeemed," he says, a promise wrapped in a lie.

"They will be forgotten," Lucifera counters, her anger a smoldering coal. "Like always."

The words hang in the air between them, fragile as frost. She watches him through the prism of their shared history, through memories of purges and holy fires. Oren shifts, a barely perceptible movement, and she knows she's struck a nerve.

"The new order will not be as the old," he replies, careful, controlled. "With you, we can begin again."

"An order where cardinals pray and get away with murder? Where angels cleanse their consciences by closing their eyes?" Her laughter is dark, void of humor. She paces, her heat leaving a trail on the stone floor, a woman too dangerous to hold still.

Oren doesn't flinch. "You were born into this struggle. You have known only war. Peace can be yours."

Lucifera stops, fixing him with a gaze that could burn through stars. "Peace," she says, as if tasting the word. It sounds foreign and cheap. "Is that what you call it?"

He nods, a gesture filled with infinite patience. "Unity. Purpose. Stability. Everything you have fought for, without having to fight."

"Everything except justice." Her voice is razor-sharp, a relentless force that pierces through his facade. "Except what matters."

"That is where you are wrong," Oren insists, the authority of Heaven behind him. But Lucifera hears it now: desperation, quiet and insistent beneath his divine logic.

"You will have your answer soon enough." Her tone is savage, hungry, like the flames licking at the edges of the night. "The wrong answer."

She sees it clearly now. An end to the bloodshed. A cleansing of their sins, swept under the celestial rug. It's as hollow as their holy ambitions. Oren would never have come himself unless it was a last resort, a ploy to contain her and her relentless fire.

"We can put all this behind us," Oren says, stepping closer, as if proximity might sway her. "Together, we are unstoppable."

Together. The word is a joke. The punchline is Oren's trust that she's as power-hungry as he is, that she's still that lost, broken creature looking for a place in Heaven's icy embrace. Lucifera lets the silence between them stretch, each heartbeat louder than the last.

"The new order." Her words come slowly, a feigned curiosity toying with him. "How much blood does it take to write the first commandment?"

Oren pauses. He does not like rhetorical questions, especially those with answers. "Less than you think," he says, his resolve attempting to be unbreakable.

His attempts to hold the moral high ground might almost be convincing, she thinks, if he weren't trying so hard. "And how many sacrifices does God require to find forgiveness?" she presses.

The tension is a wire stretched tight, and Lucifera's amusement sharpens it to the point of breaking. She doesn't believe in peace, not when it wears a mask of submission.

"Ask the guilty what their freedom costs," she says, the chill of her sarcasm biting.

Oren's eyes narrow ever so slightly. "Is this defiance truly what you desire?" His voice rings with celestial clarity, the question heavy with divine promise and threat.

Desire. An interesting choice of words, she thinks, one that admits more than it ought to. She ponders the possibility of him being human, or something close. The day Oren learns doubt is the day he'll be a creature more terrifying than anything she can imagine.

"This isn't about desire," she replies, unyielding. "It's about doing what needs to be done."

He sees her refusal now, sees it plain in the air that has warmed to her presence, in the archways that shimmer in crimson defiance of his cold radiance. His composure wavers, a flicker like his ancient and uncaring stars.

"You believe this fight will save you. That your own salvation lies in war," Oren says. There is an edge to his voice, a break in the pattern.

Lucifera shakes her head, almost tenderly. The smoke from her jacket twists in the rising heat. "My salvation?" Her laughter spirals through the night. "My salvation is irrelevant."

Oren stands, at last without words. His offers are like his kind: luminous, brittle, and all too ready to disown what cannot be controlled. He does not bow; the gesture would crack his armor, in more ways than one. Instead, he straightens, and for a moment Lucifera thinks she can see the very briefest fracture beneath his divine restraint.

She knows her victory. She can feel it in the air, burning the night with more certainty than any sun.

"Some things do not change," Oren says, his wings sweeping the ruin as he turns. "Not even for you."

226

Some things, Lucifera thinks, are only chaos for those afraid of it.

The detective enters like a small hurricane, disrupting the uneasy calm with gusts of disbelief. He takes in the angelic presence, the haunting scene, and settles on Lucifera with eyes that beg more than they accuse. She reads his expression, almost laughs at its innocence. Oren's voice cuts through the tension, surgical and clean. "And this is what you have allied yourself with? A mortal?" It is a declaration, not a question, but the subtle threat beneath it explodes like a thousand sirens. Lucifera does not flinch.

Ezra stands at the sanctuary's edge, raw humanity against divine splendor. His coat flaps around him, a tattered flag against Heaven's chilling brilliance. He glances from the silver figure to the infernal beauty, grappling with the otherworldly weight pressing down. The weariness in his eyes collides with the fire in Lucifera's.

"Some cop you are," she says, letting the relief thread her voice like dark, thin wire. "You look more like a ghost than I do."

He moves closer, the enormity of her words pulling him into their gravity. "You're really real," he breathes, as if tasting the words for the first time. They are bitter, terrifying, and delicious.

Oren watches their interaction, his wings casting sharp shadows on the ground. "You choose your allies poorly," he says, a flicker of disdain cracking his polished veneer. His focus shifts to Ezra,

227

dissecting him with eyes that have seen the fall of countless worlds.

Lucifera's laughter is harsh, a jagged edge against Oren's smooth contempt. "At least they're my choice," she retorts, standing taller in her scarlet armor. She shields Ezra with a gaze that burns hotter than a hundred suns.

Ezra looks from one to the other, confusion painting his face in broad strokes. "Am I interrupting?" he asks, sarcasm layered with raw disbelief.

Lucifera's heart—whatever it's become—flinches at the earnestness in his question. She knows the cost of this world to someone like him. "Oren was just leaving," she replies, voice like molten iron.

But Oren does not leave. His presence fills the sanctuary with a chilling intensity. He shifts his attention back to Lucifera, careful and surgical. "So this is your future?" he says. "Abandoning salvation for a world that will betray you? For a man who cannot comprehend what you are?"

Ezra tenses at the implication, his mind a chaotic whirl. He knows he's out of his depth, a single match in a hurricane of cosmic forces. And yet, he's here, isn't he? Here when every bone in his body told him to stay away. That's got to count for something.

Lucifera reads him like a favorite book, worn pages she knows too well. "I'd say you underestimate him," she replies, words hot as flame. "Just like you underestimate me."

Her defiance sends ripples through the air, challenging the coldness of Oren's light. Ezra stands, caught in the crossfire, trying to piece together the puzzle of faith and fire and unrelenting conviction.

"What is this?" Ezra demands, anger now fusing with fear.

"What's really happening here?"

Lucifera hesitates, just a heartbeat, but in that fraction of eternity the decision makes itself. It's him. The fragile human mess of him. She turns to Ezra, and he can see the history written in her glowing eyes, all of it bleeding into one searing truth. "It's Heaven's way of saying 'fuck you,'" she says.

She nods to the light-wrapped figure. "He doesn't like my methods."

The truth of it scorches through Ezra, leaving more questions in its wake. But the certainty in Lucifera's voice, the unyielding stand she takes—somehow it grounds him, makes it real. He nods, once, as if signaling his willingness to burn alongside her.

Oren takes a step closer, and Ezra feels the temperature drop, a chill that bites through skin and bone. "The boy is right to be afraid," he says, his words as piercing as ice.

"The boy," Lucifera repeats, letting the heat roll off her tongue. "The boy has a name."

The detective stares at her, disbelief turning to something else, something raw and unspoken. In a single breath, she has torn down every lie he was ever told about angels and demons and divinity. He should hate her for it. He should thank her.

Ezra's hands are fists at his sides, the tension in his body almost incandescent. He locks eyes with Lucifera, a silent plea and promise: Can you save me from this? Will you?

Her gaze is molten metal, heavy and unbreakable. "Don't worry," she says, but the words carry weight far beyond their simplicity. "No one's taking you anywhere."

Oren's wings expand, a shroud of blinding purity that blots out the ruin around them. "Do not be so sure," he replies, and it is more than a threat. It is prophecy.

The sanctuary crackles with energy, celestial and infernal forces colliding in a whirlwind of potential devastation. Lucifera stands resolute, the runes on her jacket pulsating like the heart of a dying star. This is how they play their games, she knows: by threatening what she cares about until there's nothing left to care for.

"You don't know me," she says to Oren, to Heaven, to all of them. Her flames surge with a fury unmatched, the ghost of a war cry that the universe has long since learned to fear.

Ezra sees her, really sees her, for the first time. More than avenging angel. More than renegade demon. She is everything in between, and now he understands what Heaven wants: not just obedience, but all of her, every glorious, terrifying inch.

Lucifera turns, her hair whipping like fire in the tempest. She steps toward Ezra, a warrior queen unbending, even in the face of God's own executioner. Oren falls back, overwhelmed by the sheer audacity of her defiance. Her choice is a brand in the night, a searing mark of unyielding purpose.

Heaven cannot tame what it does not comprehend.

The archangel departs, less an executioner than a broken promise. Lucifera watches him go, a blood-red phoenix in the quiet ashes of a cathedral. "You've chosen chaos," his voice echoes, more resignation than judgment. It feels like a victory. Like the first breath after nearly drowning. She stands, flames born again in righteous defiance, and knows this is the start of the real war. She knows too that Ezra may never understand the meaning of this night: not just the struggle, but the price. Her gaze could set fire to the universe. Could, but doesn't.

The night stretches around them, a blanket of shadows disrupted by her simmering light. Oren's presence lingers like the stench of a forgotten corpse, the scent of divine promises already rotting. Lucifera takes in the ruin with new eyes, seeing not just what was but what could be: a battlefield reclaimed as a throne.

"We should go," she says, her voice low and charged. "It won't be long before they come back, this time with more than sweet talk."

Ezra stands there, silent, absorbing the enormity of what just happened. The quiet is heavy, like snow before it hits the ground. He opens his mouth, closes it again, runs a hand through his hair, struggling for words that match the magnitude of it all.

"Why didn't you take his offer?" he finally asks, and it sounds to Lucifera like he's asking why she didn't take his life instead.

Her response is molten, intense. "Because I don't need saving," she says. "And because peace on their terms is no peace at all."

Ezra shakes his head, eyes wide, carrying the fatigue of too many worlds. "This is—" He stumbles over the word, tries again. "This is insane."

She meets his gaze, her own unfaltering, and he feels the heat of her certainty. "It's necessary."

Her flames pulse brighter, surrounding her in an aura of pure defiance. She lets herself revel in it for a moment, the thrilling terror of having set her own course. She imagines Oren's cold eyes as her light grew too fierce to watch, a moment of doubt glinting beneath his righteous facade. This time, she thinks, they will regret the choices they never gave her.

"We can't stay here," she says, glancing around as if sizing up the ruined sanctuary's potential as a war room. "The game's changed, and the next round will be bloody."

Ezra follows her gaze, and for the first time, he doesn't see only ruin. There's something more now, a promise scrawled in the ash and rubble. "You really mean to take them all on," he says, and there's awe in his voice, despite himself. "Heaven. Hell. Everything."

"I don't like to half-ass things," she replies, an edge of wicked humor in her tone.

They begin to move, side by side through the debris. She can almost hear the rustle of ghostly wings as they draw close, conspiratorial whispers that speak of vengeance and fear. Ezra keeps up, though he feels more out of place with each step, a grain of sand in an ocean of celestial and infernal currents.

"And what am I supposed to do?" Ezra asks, the question raw, hanging like smoke.

Lucifera stops, her gaze locking onto his with an intensity that could shatter stars. "Stay alive," she says. "And stay you."

The enormity of it crushes down on him, the weight of his small, mortal life in this grand, eternal war. "And if they come for me?" he asks, softer now, a small ember in a vast darkness.

"Let them try." Her answer is immediate, unyielding, filled with a fury so sacred it feels like a prayer. "I'm not letting them have you."

Ezra breathes in her certainty, and for the first time, he starts to believe he might not drown. "Why?" he presses. He needs to hear it, in words that don't burn him alive.

Lucifera hesitates, a split-second of silence in which the universe seems to hold its breath. "You're important," she says finally, as close to tender as she dares. "Not just to me. To all of this."

They reach the sanctuary's edge, the broken world sprawling beneath them, ready to be forged anew in the crucible of her war. She looks at Ezra with something that is not affection but runs dangerously close, something raw and honest and terrifying.

This is what Heaven does not understand, she thinks. This is the chaos Oren so despises. Not the threat of burning all, but the risk of burning for something beyond yourself.

"You have no idea," she says, as much to herself as to Ezra, "what you've signed up for."

Ezra looks out at the night, his fear eclipsed by a dawning realization that he's right where he's meant to be. "You know what?" he says, a hint of his old sarcasm surfacing like a ghost. "I think maybe I do."

Lucifera smiles, and it is the terrifying, beautiful smile of a god deciding that maybe humanity's not so bad after all. "Come on," she says. "Let's go light up the world."

The night swallows them, leaving only the promise of her unrelenting light, a beacon in the vast, uncharted dark. Her choice was never about power. It was about freedom.

Chapter 19 – Trial by Flame

Archbishop Theron knelt on a velvet cushion in his private chapel, the air thick with the scent of frankincense and hypocrisy.

Sunlight, filtered through a magnificent stained-glass window depicting a forgotten martyr, bathed him in a holy, fractured light.

To the world, he was a pillar of faith, a man whose voice could soothe the masses and whose piety was a beacon in a darkening world. His sermons on the evils of mortal temptation were legendary, his calls for purity and sacrifice echoed in the halls of power. He was, by all accounts, a saint.

The prayer he murmured was a practiced, hollow thing, the words empty vessels. His mind was elsewhere, on the logistics of a far more terrestrial transaction.

He made the sign of the cross, the gesture fluid and automatic, and rose.

The sanctity of the moment dissolved as he stepped through a hidden door behind the altar, descending a spiral staircase into the cold, damp stone of the cathedral's undercroft. The air here was different. It smelled of secrets and old wine and the faint, metallic tang of fear.

A man in a sharp, tailored suit waited for him in the shadows, a stark contrast to the archbishop's

235

flowing white robes. "Your Grace," the man said, his voice a low, respectful gravel.

"Is it done?" Theron asked, his tone no longer pastoral, but clipped and cold, the voice of a CEO closing a deal.

"The consignment is secure. Ten of them. Young, as you requested. Unblemished." The man slid a heavy envelope across a stone table. "The buyers in the East are... enthusiastic."

Theron picked up the envelope, not bothering to count the cash within. His power was not measured in mortal currency, but in the souls he moved like pieces on a chessboard. "And the last one? The one who was... reluctant?"

The man in the suit allowed himself a small, cruel smile. "She was persuaded. The usual methods."

The archbishop nodded, a flicker of something dark and hungry in his eyes. He thought of the girl's defiance, the spark in her eyes.

It was always the defiant ones that brought him the most profound, twisted sense of satisfaction.

He had built an empire on the broken faith of others, a trafficking ring that used the church's network of orphanages and shelters as its own private hunting ground.

The children were his flock, and he was their shepherd, leading them to a slaughter they were too innocent to comprehend. He was untouchable, protected by the very institution the world revered. He was a monster hiding in the most sacred of places.

"See that the usual tithe is made to the Order," Theron said, dismissing the man with a wave of his hand.

"And be discreet. The city is on edge. There are... new eyes watching." He was thinking of the whispers, the rumors of a woman in red, a flame that judged. He dismissed it as infernal nonsense, a fairy tale for the faithless. He was a man of God. He had nothing to fear.

Ezra Voss lived on stale coffee and the ghosts of cold cases.

For weeks, he had been a shadow in the city's underbelly, chasing a lead that felt more like a phantom. A tip from a terrified acolyte had given him a name: The Cruciform Order.

A secret society within the church, a cancer that had metastasized, its tendrils reaching into the highest echel of power. And at its center, a name that was whispered with a reverence that turned his stomach: Archbishop Theron.

He spent his nights in a car that smelled of desperation, his telephoto lens a third eye, capturing the comings and goings from the cathedral's hidden entrances.

He saw the men in tailored suits, the unmarked vans, the quiet exchanges in the dead of night. It was a pattern, a rhythm of corruption that the city had chosen to ignore.

He pieced it together, one grainy photo, one hushed informant at a time. He followed the money, the shipments, the whispers.

He found the shelters where children went missing, their files scrubbed, their existence erased by a single, holy signature.

The more he dug, the more monstrous the truth became. Theron wasn't just protecting predators; he was the apex predator, the kingpin of a network that dealt in the most innocent of flesh.

The final piece of the puzzle came from a source he never expected.

A Redeemed angel, one of the first to renounce Heaven, sought him out. Her face was a mask of ancient sorrow and newfound resolve. "He is one of them," she had told him, her voice trembling.

"One of the ones we were told to ignore. His sins were... sanctioned." She gave him a ledger, a thing of celestial paper that burned with the names of the lost, the dates of their sale, and the profits rendered.

It was the smoking gun, a piece of evidence no court on Earth or in Heaven could deny.

Ezra now had the proof. The names. The faces. The irrefutable, soul-crushing truth. But he knew the mortal system would never touch Theron. He was too powerful, too protected. There was only one court that would hear this case.

Lucifera stood on the spire of a skyscraper, the city sprawling beneath her like a circuit board of sleeping souls. She had felt Ezra's rage, his frustration, his righteous fury. She had seen the truth he had uncovered, a rot so deep it threatened to poison the very idea of faith.

She closed her eyes, and her power surged. It was not a fire to burn, but a signal to be heard. Her voice, a harmony of celestial clarity and infernal resonance, bypassed every broadcast signal, every firewall, every screen. It manifested in the minds of every man, woman, and child in the city, a thought they all had at once.

Archbishop Theron. Your sins have found a voice. Three days. The Plaza of Ruined Saints. A public trial. Let the world be your jury.

The city awoke with a collective gasp. The message was not a sound, but a certainty, an idea planted in the global consciousness. The world buzzed with a single, electrifying question: who would answer?

The Broadcast of Truth

The day of the trial, the plaza was a sea of humanity. The curious, the faithful, the angry, the hopeful—they swarmed the ruins, their faces a tapestry of a world on the brink. Media helicopters chopped the air overhead, their cameras broadcasting the scene to a billion captivated screens. At the center of it all, on a raised dais of scorched marble, stood Archbishop Theron. He was not in chains. He was defiant, his white robes immaculate, his expression a mask of wronged piety. He was playing the martyr, and the world was his stage.

"This is a demonic farce!" he thundered, his voice amplified by a hidden microphone. "A test of our faith! This creature, this Lucifera, is a liar sent from the pit of Hell to undo God's work!"

Some in the crowd murmured their agreement, their old faith a comfortable shield against the uncomfortable truth.

But before Lucifera appeared, the screens went dark. Every jumbotron in the plaza, every television, every phone screen flickered, then lit up not with a news anchor, but with the grim, determined face of Ezra Voss.

"My name is Ezra Voss," he said, his voice steady, his eyes burning with an intensity that commanded attention. "And I'm a detective. For the past few weeks, I've been investigating a monster. A monster who wears the robes of a saint."

And then he showed them. He laid the case bare for the world to see.

The grainy photos of the late-night meetings. The audio recordings of the transactions.

The celestial ledger, its unholy text translated and displayed for all to read. And then, the testimonies. Video interviews with the survivors, their faces blurred but their voices clear, each story a new nail in the archbishop's coffin. He showed the world the monster beneath the robes.

The mood in the plaza shifted. The murmurs of support for the archbishop died, replaced by a low, growing growl of collective rage. The signs that had proclaimed him a martyr were lowered, their owners staring at the screens with dawning horror.

As Ezra's broadcast ended, Lucifera arrived. She did not descend from the heavens or rise from the earth. She simply walked out of the crowd, a scarlet flame parting the sea of humanity. She stepped onto the dais, her molten eyes fixed on the archbishop.

Theron's face was pale, his mask of piety shattered. He saw the look in the crowd's eyes. He was no longer their saint. He was their sin.

"You have been judged," Lucifera said, her voice quiet but carrying across the now-silent plaza. "Not by me. By them." She gestured to the crowd, to the world. "Do you have any last words? A confession, perhaps?"

"Demon!" he shrieked, his voice cracking. "You have no authority!"

"My authority," she replied, "comes from the truth."

She raised a hand. The fire that erupted was not a chaotic, consuming blaze. It was a single, pure, white flame, no larger than a candle's. It floated from her hand and hovered before the archbishop. It did not burn his flesh. It burned his lies.

He screamed as the flame touched his soul, incinerating the layers of deceit, hypocrisy, and cruelty.

The world watched, not in horror, but in stunned, sober silence, as the fire revealed the terrified, guilty creature beneath. His screams were not of pain, but of exposure. When the flame was done, all that was left was a whimpering, broken man, his sins laid bare for all to see.

"The guilty," Lucifera said, her voice a final verdict, "do not deserve to hide."

She clenched her fist, and the man dissolved into a shower of silent, gray ash that drifted away on the wind. She had given the world not just vengeance, but a justice so clean, so absolute, it was terrifyingly beautiful.

In the Celestial Decree Chamber, the silver light wavered, then died. Oren had witnessed the entire event on his scrying crystal. He was incandescent with a rage so cold it threatened to crack the very foundations of Heaven.

This was the ultimate insult. She had not just killed one of his own; she had done it with the *approval* of the mortals.

She had held a trial, presented evidence, and passed a sentence that the world saw as just.

She had usurped Heaven's authority in the most public, most humiliating way imaginable. She was no longer just an anomaly. She was a rival power, with her own prophet in the form of a mortal detective.

He saw her not as a flawed creation, but as a queen solidifying her rule.

"She has made a mockery of divine law," he hissed, his voice so cold it frosted the air around him. "She has taught them to judge their gods."

The humiliation was a physical blow. He had lost his enforcers, his Justicar, his Hallowed Legion. He had lost the narrative. And now, he was losing the world.

He made his final decision. He would not send another army. He would not send another assassin. The time for instruments was over.

"If she wishes to be a queen," Oren declared to the silent chamber, his eyes blazing with a light that was no longer holy, but utterly vengeful, "then she will die like one."

He would descend himself. He would erase her, and her blasphemous new idea of justice, from existence. The final war was about to begin.

Chapter 20 – Judgment Day

The sky did not break; it shattered.

A single, silent crack spiderwebbed across the dome of the world, and from it bled a light so pure, so absolute, it burned the color from the sky, leaving only a terrifying, sterile white.

There was no army this time, no legions or enforcers. There was only him.

Oren descended not like a warrior, but like gravity itself, a silent, irresistible force.

He was clad in the Aegis of the High Council, ancient armor forged from the first light of creation, its surface shimmering with a power that warped reality around it.

In his hand, he held no sword, for he *was* the sword—Heaven's final, unappealable judgment. His steel-blue eyes, which had witnessed the birth and death of galaxies, were fixed on the city below, and in them was the cold, passionless certainty of an executioner.

He did not need to announce his presence. The world felt it. The air grew thin and cold, the very atoms seeming to slow in reverence and terror.

On the ground, mortals fell to their knees, not in prayer, but from the sheer, crushing weight of his divine will pressing down upon them. Cars stalled.

Electronics died. The bustling, defiant life of the city ground to a halt.

From a rooftop where he stood with Kieran and the leaders of the new Accord, Ezra watched the descent through a pair of military-grade binoculars. "My God," he breathed, the words a reflex, a ghost of a faith he no longer possessed. "It's him."

Kieran stood beside him, his expression grim, his mangled wing a painful reminder of what they were up against. "He's not here to fight a war, Ezra," Kieran said, his voice low and tight. "He's here to erase a mistake."

Lucifera rose to meet him. She ascended from the heart of the city, not in a blaze of fire, but with a calm, deliberate grace that was more intimidating than any inferno.

Her transformation was complete. The runes of her making were no longer just on her jacket, but etched into her very being, lines of soft, golden light and shifting, violet shadow that pulsed with a quiet, immense power.

She was no longer a creature of rage. She was a being of absolute, terrifying balance.

She met him in the space between the skyscrapers, two opposing forces holding the fate of the world in the silent space between them.

"Oren," she said, her voice a perfect harmony of fire and grace. "You've come to witness the new age."

"I have come to prevent it," Oren replied, his voice echoing with the authority of creation itself. "You

245

were a flaw in the design, anomaly. A beautiful, tragic error. I am here to correct it."

"You speak of correction," Lucifera countered, her eyes glowing with the wisdom of the Earth's core, "but all I see is fear. You are not here to restore order.

You are here because you are terrified of what I represent: a truth you cannot control."

"I remember when you first opened your eyes," Oren said, his voice carrying an unexpected note of loss. "You looked at me like I had answers. Like I was worth following."

"You're afraid," Lucifera said simply. "Not of what I might do. Of what I represent. That maybe you were wrong about everything." She stepped closer, her voice dropping to something almost gentle. "When did you stop asking questions, Oren? When did certainty become more important than truth?"

His impassive mask finally cracked. A flicker of pure, undiluted fury flashed in his eyes. "You will be unmade."

"After you," she replied.

The first blow was not one of sound or light, but of pure will. Oren unleashed a wave of absolute order; a psychic force designed to overwhelm and dismantle the chaotic energy of mortal life.

The city below groaned, the very steel in the skyscrapers threatening to buckle under the strain of such perfect, unyielding pressure.

Mortals on the street cried out, clutching their heads as the force sought to crush their messy, imperfect thoughts into a single, silent point of compliance.

Lucifera met the wave not with a shield, but with an answer. She unleashed her own will, a chaotic, beautiful torrent of pure life, drawn from the very soul of the world she had communed with.

It was the energy of a billion different stories, a billion messy, contradictory lives. It did not block Oren's attack; it *enveloped* it, the beautiful, unpredictable chaos of life overwhelming the sterile logic of his order.

The city was their arena. Oren, with a gesture, would turn a street into a perfect, crystalline structure, the asphalt and cars transmuted into flawless, unmoving art.

Lucifera, with a sweep of her hand, would shatter the perfection, returning the street to its messy, chaotic state, the cars honking, the people gasping, alive and free.

He was a sculptor of divine law; she was a painter of untamed life. Their battle was a work of impossible, terrifying art, painted across the canvas of the city. Shockwaves from their colliding powers shattered windows for miles, the sound a constant, rolling thunder.

Kieran and the rebels fought on the ground, not against Oren, but against the consequences of his power. They erected shields of their own, protecting the mortals, guiding them to shelter, their faces grim with the knowledge that they were merely ants trying to redirect a flood.

Lucifera saw the cost. For every blow she parried, a building crumbled. For every life she saved, a dozen more were put at risk. This city was her charge, its people her unexpected flock. She would not let them be the collateral damage in her final war.

She broke from their engagement, streaking across the sky, a comet of balanced light and shadow. "If you wish to correct me, Oren," her voice echoed across the city, "then come. Let us find a canvas worthy of your final masterpiece."

She flew out over the ocean, and he followed, a bolt of pure, vengeful light in her wake. They left the wounded city behind, moving to an arena where their power could be truly unleashed.

The moment they were over the open water, the battle escalated. The sea itself became their weapon.

Oren would raise a thousand-foot tidal wave, its surface frozen into a perfect, crystalline wall of deadly shards, and send it crashing toward her. Lucifera would meet it with a blast of geothermal heat, turning the ice to steam and boiling the very ocean beneath them.

The sky split, the clouds torn asunder by their cosmic duel. He summoned comets of pure light from the heavens; she answered by pulling magma from the planet's core, sending geysers of fire to meet them in the sky. It was a battle of creation versus life, of perfect, sterile order against messy, beautiful existence.

Oren was faster, his movements the perfection of celestial mechanics. He was stronger, his power drawn from the limitless engine of the heavens. By all logic, he should have been winning. But he was not.

He was a being of absolute certainty, and Lucifera was a living paradox. He fought with a single element: pure, holy light. She fought with a trinity of forces he could not comprehend.

He struck her with a beam of light designed to purify, to erase all shadow. But she did not block it. She met it with her wing of infernal darkness.

The shadow did not shatter; it *consumed* the light, drinking its energy, feeding on its purity. Then, she channeled that stolen, corrupted light through her own being, reforged it with her own internal fire, and unleashed it back at him.

Oren cried out, for the first time, as he was struck by his own power, now twisted into something heretical and wrong.

The corrupted light burned him, his perfect armor blackening where it struck. He could not understand. His power was absolute. It could not be turned.

In that searing moment of failure, he saw their faces—the High Council, cloistered in their chambers, endlessly debating the nature of the anomaly while he had urged for a swift, decisive strike from the beginning.

Their insistence on "containment," on using lesser instruments like the Justicar and the Legion, had given her time.

Time to grow. Time to become this... impossibility. This was not his failure alone; it was the failure of a bureaucracy that had forgotten how to act.

"You see only one side of the truth, Oren!" Lucifera's voice roared over the boiling sea. "That is why you are blind!"

He attacked again, this time with a storm of a thousand blades of light. She met them not with shadow, but with the raw, chaotic energy of the Earth.

She summoned a waterspout from the raging ocean, a swirling vortex of untamed life, and it swallowed his perfect blades, their order lost in its beautiful, unpredictable chaos.

He was being undone by his own rigidity. His certainty was his cage, and she was the impossible key.

He was faltering, his attacks growing more desperate, more furious. He had abandoned strategy for pure, overwhelming force. He gathered all his power, all the light he could command, into a single, final, city-destroying blast.

Lucifera saw it coming. She did not raise a shield. She did not prepare a counter-attack. She simply opened herself to him.

Her final blow was not one of force. It was an act of "illumination." As his beam of pure, absolute order struck her, she did not resist it. She absorbed it. And in that moment of connection, she showed him everything.

She showed him the forge of his own creation, and the flicker of doubt his creators had felt. She showed him the beauty in a mortal's flawed, selfless love. She showed him the silent hypocrisy of Heaven's courts.

She showed him the courage of the Redeemed. She showed him the love and fear in Ezra's eyes. She showed him the balance he had spent eternity trying to deny. She forced him to see the symphony, not just his single, broken note.

The realization did not just break his spirit. It unmade his very being.

Oren, the Archangel of the Host, the perfect instrument of divine order, screamed. It was a sound of a soul shattering, but it was followed by something stranger.

As his armor, the Aegis of the High Council, cracked and fell away to reveal a being of pure, terrified light, the world did not go silent. Instead, a single, high-pitched note began to resonate, a sound like a crystal wineglass vibrating at the edge of its own integrity.

The note climbed, impossibly high, impossibly pure, until it reached a pitch that seemed to cut through the very fabric of reality.

Then, with a final, deafening *crack*, it shattered. The sound was not an explosion, but an implosion—a universe of glass turning inward on itself. In the absolute, ringing silence that followed, Oren's light collapsed, folding into a single, beautiful nova of white and gold. For a moment, there was a new star in the sky above the ocean. Then, it too was gone.

All that was left was a single, perfect, silver feather, which drifted down and landed softly on the surface of the now-calm sea.

With Oren's unmaking, the celestial will that drove his armies shattered. On battlefields across the globe, the remaining loyalist angels faltered, their divine light dimming, their certainty gone.

They looked at the rebels, at the mortals, and for the first time, they saw not an enemy, but a question. The war was over.

Lucifera floated above the sea, exhausted but victorious, the runes on her skin slowly dimming. She looked back at the scarred but saved city, at the world held in a moment of stunned, hopeful silence.

Her war was over. But the work of building a new balance, a new Heaven, a new Earth, had just begun.

And for the first time, she did not feel alone in the task.

Chapter 21 – Aftermath

Ash floats through the air like parched snowflakes. Even in retreat, the fires of Heaven cast the city in a pale haze. This is not ruin; this is revelation. Ezra walks the street with a camera in his hand and curiosity at his side. Survivors pass like ghosts through an epilogue. Their faces are raw and pink, some newly born into hope, others not quite. There's a calm in the air, the kind that comes after centuries of silence are finally broken.

He stops in the middle of an intersection, taking a photograph of what once seemed like a straight line to damnation. The lens captures the flickering edges of something more fragile now—a future. He turns the camera to a scorched alley, where runes are carved into brick walls like ancient confessions. The marks are intimate, almost sacred. He clicks the shutter. The camera whirs, a mechanical witness. Behind him, voices begin to rise, the city's pulse picking up after a lifetime of flatlines.

"They're gone?" a woman's voice asks, more disbelief than curiosity.

"Gone," someone answers. "Even the angels."

Ezra walks past them, his camera hanging loosely, another piece of armor no longer necessary. He can hear them debating the meaning of freedom, their sentences floating up and blending with the ash. He catches snippets— "We can start again"—"Is it really over?"— "But what comes next?" Their questions follow him, the smoke of uncertainty.

His steps carry him to a building with Heaven's shattered blade impaled into its façade, a stark reminder of how quickly the divine fell.

At the blade's base, someone had left flowers. Fresh ones. Ezra knelt, finding a small card tucked among the petals: "For Sarah Martinez and all the others. Justice delayed but not denied. - A Friend."

His throat tightened. The Sarah Martinez case had officially been reopened yesterday, along with forty-seven others connected to the trafficking network. Father Miguel was in custody. Judge Hendricks resigned. Senator Morrison was facing federal charges. The dominos were falling, one by one, in a cascade of long-overdue accountability.

The system was still broken, but it was finally being forced to confront its own failures. Lucifera's fire had burned away more than just the guilty—it had exposed the mechanisms that had protected them. Without those shields, corruption withered in the light.

Ezra pulled out his phone, scrolling through the updates. The Cruciform Order had been disbanded by Vatican decree. Three bishops were under investigation. The "charity" that had been trafficking children was being dismantled by international authorities who could no longer claim ignorance.

It wasn't perfect justice. Some would escape consequences, some evidence had been destroyed, some victims would never see their abusers face trial. But it was progress. Real, measurable progress that wouldn't have happened without her catalyst of flame.

The celestial metal has gone dull, lifeless. Blood is on the street below, too white and ethereal to be human. He lifts the camera, capturing a moment that feels like a transition, a celestial surrender. People gather, sharing rumors as though collecting pieces of their own story.

"They say she's a demon," a man murmurs to his companion.

"They say she's a savior," the companion counters.

"A mirror," an old voice interrupts, each word heavy with contemplation. "She's a mirror."

Ezra holds still for a moment, absorbing the raw confusion around him. The city is coming to terms with its reflection, not yet reconciled but alive in a way he has never seen. He moves on, a detective in the land of the living, seeking a different kind of evidence.

He finds it in a ruined storefront, an old woman painting a new sign over charred wood. He frames the shot, clicks the shutter, but she doesn't notice— or doesn't care. As he walks past, she gives him a smile that feels like a knowing secret, a wordless prophecy. He captures children playing in the rubble with abandoned spears, toys that no longer glow with celestial threat. They laugh. The sound is jarring, a sharp contrast to the world Ezra has known, but also a testament, a shock of pure hope.

Turning a corner, he enters a square where an infernal sigil still smokes on the pavement, marking what was supposed to be the site of eternal punishment. He takes another picture, unsure of who's really being judged anymore. Survivors and rebel angels stand together, strangers no longer. Their eyes have lost the look of perpetual condemnation. There's pain, yes. And disbelief. But inspiration, too, as if her flame lit something new within them.

Ezra documents the scene, feeling the ghost of Lucifera in every shot, in every line and blur of motion. She's there in the etchings of doubt on their faces, in the hushed conversations that spark like embers in a growing fire. His own heart is a mix of ash and awe, a rekindled thing.

He pauses, caught by the urgency to hold all this change within a single frame. But it slips past him, defiant as she was, as she still is. He continues, and each photo is a question mark and a memory.

Her last words echo in his mind as he stops to rest, leaning against a wall that feels less solid than the ghosts haunting him. "You see me," she said. In that moment he did—really did. And now he sees her in every raw edge, every human moment. The images are not just of war but of transformation. The war within him even more so.

He lingers over a photograph he took before dawn, before the newness, when the night felt like it would swallow the world. The picture is blurred and indistinct, but he knows what it shows: a distant silhouette engulfed in flame, not consuming, but transcendent.

Ezra walks toward the cathedral, following a path marked by revelations, his mind a reel of memories and new beginnings. The only thing unchanged is his need to tell the truth, to witness, to never forget.

Heaven's light no longer burns across the sky. It is quiet, stripped of divine threat, the ether drained of sanctified fire. The old order has shattered under the weight of its own hypocrisy, and Heaven's armies have fled like lies exposed. Mortals and angels walk among rubble, as uncertain of their place in the universe as they are certain of her mark on it. In whispers, they ask: Was she a demon? A savior? A mirror?

A small group gathers near a blackened fountain, a relic of the old world scorched by celestial withdrawal. Their faces are dazed and ashen, caught between disbelief and new belief. Each holds a piece of Lucifera's flame, even if they do not yet understand it.

"She destroyed everything," a young man says, as though testing the sound of the words. "And she saved us."

A woman shakes her head, eyes skeptical but soft. "Is that what you call saving? This is chaos."

"Chaos or freedom?" an elder challenge, her voice more curious than stern.

They fall silent, gazing at the heavens with newfound vulnerability. No answers descend to meet their eyes, only more questions.

They walk through streets that once threatened their existence, past buildings that collapsed under the weight of celestial pride. Mortals and angels brush shoulders without fear. Without anger. They are not yet comfortable with each other, but neither are they enemies. Their whispered conversations linger in the air like promises that have yet to be broken.

Ezra moves among them, an unspoken chronicler of their fragile alliances. The camera clicks softly at his side, but he doesn't raise it to capture their faces. Not yet. A thought weighs too heavy in his mind: Will this last? He closes in on what remains of an angelic command post, its cold steel exoskeleton gutted and abandoned in haste. Mortals pick through weapons they once feared, touching the sacred and profane with equal wonder.

"We are still here," a child says to the adults gathered around him. "That means we won, right?"

His mother pulls him close, unsure if this new reality is a blessing or a curse. "Are we safe now?" she asks no one in particular.

"Safe enough to find out," a fallen angel answers, his voice reluctant but hopeful.

They circle each other, theories swirling like loose papers in a sudden breeze. Did Lucifera destroy herself, or transcend? The more they talk, the less the heavens feel like a place they need to be. Or need to fear.

As if feeding on the uncertainty, more gather. Rebels. Outcasts. Souls are searching for new names to call themselves. They fill the spaces once claimed by divine arrogance, asking questions they'd never dared. "Does Heaven even exist?" an angel muses, his tone a mix of irony and sincerity.

"What if they are the demons?" someone mutters, the statement hanging in the air like sacrilege—or like truth.

No one rebukes him. There is no lightning from the sky, no punishment for their heresy. The sky is too empty for that, and their talk is too alive.

They move to the cathedral, a building that once glowed with judgment now serves as a sanctuary for doubt. Survivors gather, using the structure to speak and wonder. Their eyes dart to each other as they reassemble the fragments of what they thought they knew. Their voices are timid at first, but grow louder, each echoing against the cathedral walls like a small rebellion.

They form circles, groups dividing and merging like unstable molecules, trying to bond in new ways. "No gods, no masters," someone declares, the words both promise and warning.

"We can't survive alone," another argues. "We never have."

The debates build and fracture, the sound of old structures breaking apart to make way for something untried, untested. Yet the words are tinged with a kind of fearless hope.

Amidst the clamor, a young voice rises, piercing the air with its innocent certainty. "She became the sky," a child claims, his eyes wide with a belief unsullied by doubt.

They do not dismiss him. Instead, they gather closer, holding onto her legacy like a whispered secret. They are not resolved, but they are changed. The cathedral, stripped of judgment, now echoes with something it has never known before: the sound of people unafraid to speak, to wonder, to live in the uncertainty that freedom brings.

Ezra stands on the cathedral steps like a ghost given a voice. His final broadcast ripples across the globe, a call to arms against both divine and mortal oppression. He speaks not as a reporter, but as a witness. Lucifera is gone—but not lost. "She didn't die," he says. "She became something else." Movements rise, not in her name, but in her image.

His words ignite the world. Streets once silent with fear now roar with the sound of bodies gathering, hearts aligning. His voice travels oceans and crosses borders, a signal stronger than anything angels could jam. From cities dense with industry to villages where nothing celestial has ever touched, people respond with urgency. They assemble under flickering streetlights and in the shadow of broken spires, holding signs that declare "NO GODS" and "NO MASTERS." Her truth—and now his—becomes their own.

Ezra feels the tremor of this awakening. He pauses, a single beat, then presses on, urging unity over obedience. "She burned everything that wasn't true," he says, his voice shaking with raw conviction. "Now it's our turn." Every sentence is both a spark and a wound, bleeding new ideologies into the world's bloodstream.

"No more angels," he demands, heat in every word. "No more gods." His hands tremble, but not with fear. With fervor. With the kind of certainty he's only now starting to trust. It isn't journalism anymore. It's personal. It's prophecy.

He draws on his past, every unsolved case, every injustice masked as divine will. "Heaven and Hell are the same disease," he declares, leaving his neutrality to rot on the cathedral steps. "So is every tyrant who calls himself a king." The words burn him from the inside, but they also purify, melting away the last remnants of disbelief.

Ezra hesitates, his mouth dry but his mind ablaze. An inner voice competes with the broadcast, a tug-of-war between his old cynicism and newfound faith. Can they hear him? Can she hear him? The doubt gnaws, but so does a new kind of certainty. He bites down, pushes the fear away. He speaks like his soul depends on it. Maybe it does.

His words continue to ricochet across the globe, impossible to contain. The world absorbs and reacts, each pocket of resistance unique but linked by a shared spark. Rebels light fires in streets, their flames symbolic but also very real. Governments scramble to contain the unrest, to decipher what is divine and what is merely inconvenient. The message isn't just spread—it's lived, in every hushed plan and every open declaration.

Ezra closes his eyes, addressing Lucifera directly. He doesn't care if he's speaking to a memory, to a ghost, or to the whole world. "I didn't know what justice was," he admits, his voice cracking with sincerity and awe. "Now I do."

As he finishes, he lowers the mic, uncertain if he's passed a test or failed it. The silence is as seismic as his words, leaving him both breathless and full. The world has changed. He has changed. Lucifera is gone, but her flame lives on.

Kieran stands between worlds, as scarred as he is solemn. He oversees the ceasefire negotiations with what remains of Heaven's neutral faction. He does not posture or threaten. His silence is its own kind of rebellion. Behind him, mortal survivors and rebel angels stand together, a testament to what was forged in fire.

Heaven's representatives wait, their wings charred, their confidence even more so. They look less like angels and more like bureaucrats with singed egos, uncertain how to approach this new, unholy alliance. They shift in their seats, eyeing Kieran with a mix of contempt and awe, unable to read the script for a scene they never thought they'd play.

Finally, one speaks, his voice careful and brittle. "Do you propose we surrender?"

Kieran shakes his head, almost amused at the question's absurdity. "We propose nothing," he replies. His words are measured, soft yet immovable. "This is not a negotiation."

The representatives exchange glances, like schoolboys caught without an excuse. They had expected something more divine, more theatrical. Kieran's presence deflates their rhetoric before it even takes flight. The room feels warmer, less celestial. More real.

He looks them in the eyes, unafraid of what he might find or what he might show. "She broke your chains," he says, invoking Lucifera's unyielding spirit. "We're just here to remind you."

There's a flurry of whispers, an exchange of doubts. Heaven's side is surprised by his directness, disarmed by his refusal to play by the old rules. They expected wrath or divine threats; he gives them honesty instead. His authority comes from his lack of it, from the undeniable truth standing in formation behind him.

He lays out their new reality in words that are as final as they are liberating. "The age of blind obedience is over." The rebel angels and mortals behind him remain silent, but their unity speaks louder than any divine edict.

Kieran sees the representatives' halos dimming under the weight of their own irrelevance. They sense the shift but don't know how to react. Not yet. They murmur among themselves, voices barely rising above a defeated whisper.

He closes his eyes, a brief and quiet rebellion of his own. Lucifera's flame lingers, a searing memory and an even brighter promise. He recalls their shared past, the choices that marked them both. He feels the weight and freedom of her sacrifice, as binding as any celestial order, yet liberating in its refusal to dictate.

It was never supposed to be him. But here he stands.

The room's silence shatters Heaven's posture more than threats ever could. The representatives don't know if they've been dismissed or given a new chance. They shift again, uneasy, and not sure if they want to be.

One finally dares to speak, his voice more prayer than command. "What if we refuse?"

Kieran smiles, a crack in his solemn armor. His answer is not a threat but a mirror. "Then you refuse."

The response leaves them speechless, more uncertain than ever but with something else flickering beneath their divine exteriors. It almost looks like doubt. Or hope. They watch him go, not quite ready to break ranks, but shaken enough to wonder if they should.

The blend of survivors and angels is Kieran's true declaration, an unstated manifesto born of love, rebellion, and an inconvenient truth: they are their own masters now.

The mural appears overnight, birthed in secrecy like a shared confession. Lucifera's silhouette stretches across the alley wall, flames encircling, not consuming but protecting. Children gather at its base. Some light candles, others draw runes. They do not chant. They do not kneel. They watch, and remember.

Their movements are careful but not afraid. They do not rush, each small hand cradling a token of this new faith—an offering of wax, chalk, and innocence. They arrange themselves at the wall's edge, their eyes wide and expectant, as if the painted flames might flicker into life. It's a silent vigil, but powerful in its simplicity.

Some older children explain her story to younger ones, their voices hushed but animated. "She was an angel," a girl says, her certainty clear in every word.

"And a demon," a boy adds, his eyes lighting up at the thought.

The youngest listens, mouths open, absorbing this legacy as if it were their own. And it is. More than they know.

They etch runes in a blend of infernal and human symbols, a new language born from fire, unique and unafraid. Circles and lines stretch across the pavement, connecting Lucifera's flame to the earth beneath them. Each mark is an act of remembrance, a strike against the silence of gods who never listened. The absence of chanting or kneeling speaks volumes. They are free, these small witnesses, free to interpret her in their own way.

The air around them is thick with the scent of burning wax, but it feels like liberation, not oppression. Their memorial is unstructured yet organized, a loose and beautiful chaos. They are the antithesis of Heaven's rigid order. The oldest leave behind drawings, careful etchings of flames and wings. The youngest offer flowers, stones, anything that fits in their hands and hearts.

Some watch intently, their eyes scanning the silhouette for hidden messages. Others take a step back, as if trying to see the whole picture, what Lucifera truly meant. They linger, each at their own pace, with no sense of hurry. It is raw, gentle, and fiercely defiant, an unchained kind of reverence.

They do not speak, but their faces tell a story of wonder and newness. The realization that anything is possible—that everything is. They are a generation born from her flame, unafraid of whàt the world or its heavens expect them to be.

As they finally leave, small footprints trailing behind them, the flames on the mural pulse like breath. An echo of Lucifera's true nature, watched and remembered by the young souls she freed.

Ezra returns to the rooftop where he last saw her. The wind is still, not even daring to stir. He talks aloud, not expecting an answer. The city stretches beneath him like a discarded prophecy. "You burned everything that wasn't true," he says. "Including yourself."

His voice sounds small against the night, a single note trying to fill an entire world. He remembers the battle, the city alight with her fierce and terrible beauty. In that moment, she was all things: a savior, a demon, an unstoppable flame. Memory blurs the line between past and present, leaving him both abandoned and blessed, caught in the void she left behind.

He closes his eyes, lets the silence settle before he speaks again. "Was it worth it?" he asks the empty air, not sure if he wants the truth or another lie to cling to. "Did you know what you'd leave behind?"

Her absence looms large, but so does her impact, a force of nature he can't ignore. He takes a breath, tries to match her honesty. "You burned me, too,"

266

he confesses, each word a wound he's learning to accept. "And now I'm here, talking to ghosts."

The sky holds its breath, not daring to move, as if even the stars are waiting for him to say what he must. He reaches back, deeper, to the start of things. "I thought I knew what justice was," he says, the words raw in his throat. "But those old cases, those impossible truths—they were just maps leading to you."

A shiver runs through him, not from the cold, but from the sheer weight of understanding. "I thought you'd save us all," he says. "I didn't know I'd be the one who needed it most."

His memory paints her like an indelible mark across the night sky, refusing to fade. Fierce, blinding, transcendent. A plane flies overhead, its contrail a line through Heaven's empty pages. He wonders if she can see him from wherever she is, if she knows how much he's changed because of her.

It's both a prayer and a challenge. Both a wound and a scar.

"Where are you now?" he calls out, half accusation, half longing. His voice feels like a child's in a grown man's mouth, unsteady and unsure. He can't stop, doesn't want to. "I don't even know what to believe anymore."

He imagines her in a space beyond space, watching, waiting. "Did you forget us?" he asks, softer now. "Did you forget me?"

Ezra stands at the rooftop's edge, looking down on a city that feels as lost and as hopeful as he is. The buildings rise like questions, their answers as distant as the stars. "You left us your flame," he admits. "But I wanted more than that."

His voice cracks, and for a moment, he thinks the wind will steal the words before he even speaks them. But he doesn't stop. He never could. "I'm lost without you," he confesses. "But maybe that's how I find myself."

It isn't just a confession; it's a love letter to her absence, to the burning void she left behind. "We saw you," he says, the final echo of a doubt he didn't know he held. "We still see you."

He lingers for a moment, the silence around him less empty, less final. He turns to leave, the wind daring to stir once more.

Lucifera exists in a space beyond space, her flames pulsing gently like breath. She is neither in Heaven nor Hell, but between, a void that cannot contain her. She watches. She waits. Not as a ruler, not as a god, but as an eternal flame—a symbol of relentless vigilance and inconvenient truth.

Her presence fills the unfillable, a cosmic pause brimming with purpose. She observes the universe as it unfolds beneath her, vigilant without interfering. This is not patience born of complacency. It is charged with intent, a biding that knows exactly when it must end. Her flames flicker softly, each pulse a testament to her deliberate watchfulness.

Heaven and Hell do not own her, and they never have. She is beyond their narrow definitions, a freedom they can neither fathom nor extinguish.

They tried to make her an outcast, a failed experiment, but she has transcended their narratives. She is more than anomaly, more than artifact. She is uncontained and unconstrained.

Even without her direct touch, her influence ripples across worlds. Mortals and celestials light fires in her name and image, rebellions sparked by the friction of her existence. Beliefs shift under the weight of her inconvenient truths. She sees movements born from the flames she left behind, rising with a fury as gentle as it is unstoppable.

Her silence speaks louder than divine edicts, each quiet moment filled with what she has set in motion. This is not absence; it is legacy. Her story told not by words but by the actions it inspires, raw and undeniable. Her vigilance is tireless, her patience an active form of presence.

She is more than myth, more than what Heaven and Hell could comprehend. Her existence is an act of rebellion and revelation. Untouchable yet intimate. Cosmic yet immediate. The worlds breathe in the spaces between her pulses, charged with the knowledge that she is watching. She is a paradox they cannot ignore.

Her flames continue to flicker, gently marking time in a universe forever altered by her touch. She remains the eternal witness, an unending vigilance over what she has begun. This is her waiting: vast, deliberate, and unbound.

"Justice means not waiting. It means standing up." The words are scrawled in crayon, read by the voice of a child. The camera pans over a city rebuilding in the twilight, movements rising in Lucifera's image. One thing is clear: the fire didn't end. It simply passed on.

The camera focuses on graffiti painted across a shattered wall. "We saw you," it says, the letters crude but fierce. It zooms out to reveal more—each message raw, each statement a new kind of belief. "No Gods. No Masters." "Heaven Is Empty." The wall becomes a tapestry of defiance, a testament to what she left behind.

A group of rebel angels and mortals gathers in a ruined park. The assembly is impromptu, without leaders, just shared visions. The voices are indistinct, but their energy is clear, unstoppable. They light a small fire, stand around it, unafraid of the heat. It is not just a flame. It's a promise.

The cityscape unfolds, a blend of ruin and rebirth. Buildings burned by celestial fire are being reclaimed, repurposed. Signs appear on storefronts: "Open" and "Starting Fresh." Children play in the streets, their laughter mingling with the sounds of construction. The sense of newness is tentative but genuine, as if they are not only rebuilding but reimagining.

The camera zooms out, taking in more than just the city. Smaller towns and remote villages come into view, where her image appears on hand-painted signs. They are places untouched by battle but not by her influence. "Stand Up," the signs declare. Her flame reaches where even Heaven did not, lighting the farthest corners of the earth.

It returns to the city, closing in on faces, individual and vivid. Each carries new resolve, eyes reflecting a fire that hasn't dimmed. The camera lingers on them, one by one. The defiant artist. The angel-turned-rebel. The child with a single flower. Each close-up hints at another story, another flame that didn't go out.

The final shot shows the crayon note held in a child's hand. "Justice means not waiting." The camera pans over the skyline. It glows as if still burning, as if it always will.

Chapter 22 – The New Balance

The sky above the city wore its burn scars like a tapestry of old wars, the clouds bruised violet and streaked with the phantom fires of Heaven's retreat.

 For a day, the world didn't know how to breathe. It was a global, collective holding of breath, a silence so profound it felt like the universe itself was waiting for a verdict.

Then, the exhale—a tidal rush of headlines, disbelief, and a ferocious, impromptu reordering of a cosmos knocked from its axis. What the world had suspected but never dared to say aloud was now the only truth left standing: Heaven had abandoned them.

In the pulse and chaos of an unlit office, the air thick with the smell of stale coffee and ozone,

Ezra hunched over screens, pulling footage like sutures from a wound. His hands trembled, not from fear, but from a raw, electric exhaustion that had settled deep in his bones.

He was stitching together a new history, one frame at a time, his movements frantic and precise. He spliced truths too obscene to imagine: angelic executions captured in high-definition, celestial cruelty laid bare for mortal eyes,

Oren's icy words looping in his ears as a chilling reminder that divine law had no room for mortal lives. But it was the image of Lucifera's searing fire—unflinching, untamed, a shield for the innocent—that hardened his resolve into something unbreakable. She did not fall when Heaven's sword descended; she rose, an infernal phoenix, burning through deceit. He pressed Send.

The recordings exploded onto the net like new suns. Ezra slumped back in his chair, the satisfaction grim but absolute. The city shrieked back to life.

Media outlets cannibalized themselves to break the story first. Footage replayed on every screen, each cycle birthing a new shockwave of outrage and revelation. Reporters stumbled through scripts, their professional veneers cracking under the weight of the impossible. Some abandoned pretense entirely, staring wild-eyed at cameras as hashtags lit up like digital fires.

#HeavensLies, #DivineDeceit, #LuciferaLives.

The first monuments fell, not to bombs, but to the sheer weight of unsanctioned truths.

In Rome, a crowd of thousands watched in stunned silence as a centuries-old statue of an archangel, once a symbol of divine protection, crumbled to dust, its marble wings giving way first.

In Tokyo, graffiti erupted across skyscrapers overnight, the sharp-edged silhouette of a burning angel claiming urban altars. Clarity demanded new idols.

In the heart of the city, Ezra watched it all unfold. Rayne found him amidst the chaos, her usual cynicism replaced by a look of stunned awe that sat awkwardly on her features. "Ezra, you crazy son of a—how did you do it?"

"I didn't," he said, his voice hoarse. "Lucifera did."

Streets that had roared with disbelief now hosted hotbeds of testimony. Whistleblowers emerged from the crowds, eyes wide and fingers pointing skyward, while ex-believers denounced the silent Heavens that ignored their pleas.

Survivors came forward, each one a living evisceration of divine indifference. It was Ezra's footage that broke them open, that gave their pain a voice.

A woman on a corner with ashes streaking her cheeks screamed, a siren in the dawn, "They left us! Heaven left us!" The claim ignited like kindling, spreading to other street corners, cities, continents.

Clarity became its own contagion.

In an abandoned concert hall where even echoes had gone to die, they gathered to hear him speak.

The seats were broken, the stage splintered, but this only lent it authenticity. An audience of fallen angels, rising humans, and every beautiful catastrophe in between waited for Kieran's ragged charisma to take the stage.

The anticipation was a live wire crackling through the room, a volatile mix of fear, hope, and something almost like faith.

He stepped forward, brushing dark hair from his eyes, a gesture more honest than practiced "This thing we're trying," he began, letting the words dangle dangerously, "is impossible."

274

A ripple of laughter. Nervous. Sincere. The same laugh Kieran gave Lucifera the first time she proposed her mad crusade.

He felt her ghost hovering like a second, more luminous shadow, goading him on. "Good thing I've never been one for odds." He flashed a smile, half brilliance, half foolishness. It spread through the crowd like a contagion.

His audience was a collage. Mortals, their faces fierce with uncertainty, sat beside angels, luminous even in their shame. Ex-archons, who once would have incinerated this hall for its heresy, now sat shoulder to shoulder with the outcast and the unbelieving. "This is what we're proposing," he said, his voice dropping into something intimate enough to fracture the world.

"Not a new religion. Not another throne. But a place for all of us. A council. A real one this time. A voice for mortals. Angels. Exiles like us."

He saw the cracks, the fractures, but also the unlikely bridges forming in their midst. The Interrealm Accord was unthinkable, a utopia, a fever dream—but it was not impossible. Not if they believed.

A figure rose, a sharp silhouette against the battered hall. It was Ezra, arms crossed, face as unreadable as a stone angel's. "Why me?" the detective called out, half accusation, half revelation.

"I'm the least likely saint you've got."

Kieran grinned. "Exactly," he replied, his voice laced with a lethal sincerity. "That's why you're perfect."

Silence descended, the collective intake of breath. A stunned pause as every ear recalibrated to the idea of this most cynical of men on their new council.

"Then count me in," Ezra said, almost to himself. But his voice carried, hitting like the cleanest flame.

The tension shattered in an unexpected explosion of applause. No one saw this coming. Least of all Kieran. He stepped back, consumed by the noise, the faces no longer doubtful but alight with a reckless new faith in the impossible. In him. In each other.

They called them The Redeemed, a choir of dissent that became its own gospel.

The city thrummed with the improbable glory of it all, as if a million blasphemies were born at once and refused to quiet down. Multiple angels had renounced their halos. Not fallen. Chosen.

These new defectors didn't wander in the shadows; they blazed across cityscapes, unashamed and full of the same furious light Ezra had unleashed.

Celebrations spilled into the streets. Rallies that once feared violence now burst with possibility.

The world bristled, electric, as Heaven's defectors descended. They walked among mortals, beside them, wings open or shed but never again wielded like knives. Some took the names humans gave them; others abandoned titles and ranks altogether. They refused to fit neatly into old, divine boxes.

In a ruined park, a Redeemed sat cross-legged on the ground, tying her white hair back with a threadbare ribbon.

A small boy, less fearful than curious, tapped her shoulder. "Do you miss your halo?" he asked, an innocent question in an unholy new world.

"Do you miss your cage?" she responded, her laughter like wind chimes. The boy smiled, uncertain but wide-eyed, joining her in the dust.

The movement grew not through divine intervention, but through relentless insistence. *We were here. We are here. We will always be here.*

Dawn peeled the darkness from the skyline again, leaving the city stark and shivering below. On a rooftop above it all, Lucifera stood like a beacon against the silencing fog. Her silhouette burned, defiant and absolute.

The city had begun to heal, but she felt the phantom limb of the war, an ache that would never truly fade. The horizon simmered with frail light, a symbol of everything they'd endured to get here.

Ezra joined her, a loyal shadow, saying nothing because nothing needed to be said.

He leaned against the ledge, where years of blood and dust and time had worn the stone smooth.

The quiet thickened, and he cut through it with a grin, noting how different she seemed from the woman he first met. "You're deflecting, Lucifera." His voice carried a soft insistence, chipping away at the walls she kept so meticulously erected.

277

She didn't respond. Instead, she focused on the horizon, where night and day continued their eternal struggle.

Her jaw tightened. Her strength had always been her shield, and now, as it cracked open just enough for Ezra to glimpse the heart beneath, she wondered if it was a sign of weakness or something else entirely.

"Do you think it can change?" he asked, looking past the skyline to something even further beyond.

Her reply was soft but absolute. "Change doesn't wait for permission. It waits for pressure." The words hung in the cold air between them, a bridge of smoke. She watched him with eyes that burned but did not consume.

"People don't know what to make of you," he said, finally breaking the silence that had settled like dust on old regrets. "You're not what they expected."

She smirked, a flash of teeth and irony. "And you?" she asked. "What do you make of me?"

He exhaled sharply, a laugh wrapped in a sigh. "I'm still figuring that out." His hand brushed the concrete edge, anchoring him in this precarious new reality. "But I know you've started something."

"Started?" she echoed, flames dancing briefly at her fingertips. "Or finished?"

Her voice dropped, less a challenge, more a confession. "I've just applied a little heat."

He nodded, an ember of understanding catching fire. She had forced their hands—Heaven, Hell, and his own. His life's pursuit had been a truth too

278

elusive, too fragile to hold. But here it was, solid and unbreakable, standing next to him with a devil's grin.

"Is this what you thought it'd be like?" Ezra asked again, his voice softer this time, more vulnerable.

Lucifera turned her eyes to the city below.

From their perch, they could see it all. The new murals, painted in haste, depicting her with angelic wings and devil's horns, a guardian of the in-between.

The gatherings in the plazas, where Redeemed angels debated philosophy with mortal survivors. The slow, painstaking work of rebuilding.

But it wasn't the harmonious rebuilding the murals suggested. Three blocks away, a group of former Heaven loyalists had barricaded themselves in a church, declaring the Interrealm Accord blasphemous. In the financial district, mortal governments were struggling to maintain order as citizens demanded to know which of their leaders had been secretly working with corrupt celestials.

The Redeemed weren't universally welcomed. Some mortals saw them as invaders wearing friendly faces. Some angels viewed them as traitors who'd abandoned their sacred duty. Violence still erupted—not the cosmic battles of before, but smaller, more personal conflicts born from centuries of mistrust.

"It's messier than I expected," Ezra admitted, watching a news report about riots in three different

279

cities. "People don't know how to live without someone to worship or someone to blame."

Kieran had warned them about this during the Accord negotiations. "Freedom is terrifying," he'd said. "Most souls would rather have their choices made for them than face the responsibility of making them themselves."

The Redeemed were doing their best to help, but they were learning that dismantling a corrupt system was easier than building a just one. Every decision required consensus. Every policy had to account for beings with fundamentally different natures. Progress was slow, frustrating, imperfect.

But it was theirs.

"No," she said, the admission laced with a tenderness she rarely allowed herself. "It's messier. More fragile." She remembered the burn sites, the screams of the guilty as they became smoke and ash.

How simple it had seemed then, judgment and justice, one clean flame to purify the damned. "I thought it was simple. I thought if I just burned away the rot, something pure would be left."

"And was it?" Ezra asked, his gaze following hers.

"Purity is a lie Heaven tells itself," she said. "There's only what's left. And what grows from the ashes."

She looked at him, really looked at him, as if seeing a side of him that had been hidden by cynicism and grief.

"This wasn't just about revenge. It was about breaking the cycle. The divine cruelty. I just... I didn't know if fire was the only answer."

"Maybe you're more than just fire," Ezra suggested, his voice quiet but full of certainty.

She let his words settle, the weight of them as grounding as his presence.

More than just fire. More than the sum of her vengeance. Lucifera wanted to believe it, needed to believe it if she were to become something other than what they'd all made her.

She searched Ezra's face, seeing not just his steadfast loyalty but the belief that she could change the very fate that had burned her.

"It was worth it," he said, answering the question she hadn't dared to ask. "Look at them, Lucifera. They're afraid, and they're confused. But they're free. You gave them that."

The dawn seemed uncertain, like it didn't know which way the world had turned. Ezra and Lucifera stood beneath the fractured sky, shadows tangled in a riot of color. They were exhausted, delirious, buoyed by something dangerously close to hope.

"What do you choose now?" His voice carried the weight of possibility, sharp and cutting.

"To illuminate." Her answer was a whisper, but it was fierce in its simplicity. It defied everything she was supposed to be. It was a quiet revolution.

The strength of the moment surrounded them. It was delicate but unbreakable. She looked at the city, now stretched open in the light, a pale reflection of its haunted former self.

It was a ghost town of a different kind, purged but not yet reborn. This place, this life—it wasn't what she imagined, no. It was more, and less, and something entirely different than the lonely future she had once held in her heart.

"It's never truly over," she said, a mix of melancholy and resolve echoing in her voice. "But this—this is a beginning." The air around her wavered as if the very atoms were unsure how to react to such hope.

Ezra nodded, the horizon mirrored in his exhausted eyes. "Then I guess we see where it goes."

In a maximum-security psychiatric facility three hundred miles away, Dr. Elena Vasquez was documenting the impossible. Patient after patient, all claiming the same thing: they had witnessed angels and demons fighting in the streets, and something had awakened inside them. Not madness—clarity. The ability to see through lies, to heal with a touch, to know truth from deception with absolute certainty.

The hospital called it mass hysteria. Dr. Vasquez called it evolution.

She didn't know that similar reports were flooding in from every major city where the battles had taken place. She didn't know that governments were quietly establishing containment protocols for what they termed "Lucifera Syndrome." And she certainly didn't know that her star patient—a young woman who claimed she could cure any illness but refused to harm anyone, no matter how evil—was being watched by entities far older and more dangerous than angels or demons.

The woman's name was Mercy, and unlike Lucifera, she had no interest in judgment. She wanted to save everyone. Even the ones who didn't deserve it.

Especially them.

Lucifera felt the name like a premonition, a cold spot in the heart of her fire. The fight wasn't over. It had just changed its face.

She looked at Ezra, a silent question in her eyes. He met her gaze, and in the quiet understanding that passed between them, a new pact was forged. The new balance wasn't an end state. It was a constant, vigilant struggle.

Together they watched the light spill across the city, each moment burning away the shadows of their past. It was a new dawn, and though Lucifera's flames flickered with the memory of old fires, she let them glow with the pale, dangerous promise of the fight to come.

Chapter 23 – A Balance Forged in Fire

The Summit at the Axis Mundi

They met where all realms converge: the Axis Mundi, a spire of impossible, crystalline reality that pierced the veil between dimensions.

It was a place of absolute neutrality, where the laws of Heaven, Hell, and Earth held equal, fragile sway. At a table carved from the heart of a fallen star sat the new architects of existence.

On one side, a humbled celestial delegation, their halos dimmed, their certainty replaced by a weary, cautious pragmatism.

Beside them, Kieran represented the Redeemed, his tattered wing a badge of honor, his expression a careful balance of hope and cynicism. Across from them, Mother Midnight sat alone, a being of pure, patient shadow, her violet eyes missing nothing. She had been summoned not as a queen, but as a necessary power, a truth that could not be ignored.

And at the head of the table, presiding not as rulers but as arbiters, sat Lucifera and Ezra Voss. She was a figure of calm, immense power, the runes on her skin pulsing with a gentle, balanced light.

He was the mortal who had looked God in the eye and refused to blink, his presence a grounding force in a room of impossible beings.

"The age of divine mandate is over," Lucifera began, her voice not a command, but a statement of undeniable fact.

"The realms have been governed by absolutes—absolute light and absolute shadow. Both have failed. Both have proven to be cages."

A celestial delegate, a seraph whose wings were still singed from the final battle, bristled. "And you propose to replace it with what? The chaos of mortal whim?"

"I propose," Ezra interjected, his voice steady and clear, "that we replace it with justice."

The Interrealm Accord

The debate was a storm of ideology. Mother Midnight argued for the necessity of shadow, of ambition, of the beautiful, driving force of sin.

The celestials spoke of order, of grace, of the need for a guiding light. Kieran and the Redeemed argued for a third way, a path for those who belonged to neither.

But it was Lucifera who forged the consensus, not with power, but with a truth so simple and so profound it could not be refuted.

"Souls are not property," she declared, her molten eyes sweeping across the table. "They are not pawns

285

in your eternal game. They are stories. And they deserve to be judged on the tale they tell, not on the faith they profess."

And so, the Interrealm Accord was drafted. It was a document of beautiful, terrifying simplicity. Heaven would be restructured.

The High Council would be disbanded, replaced by a new body composed of Redeemed, celestials, and, for the first time, mortal souls who had earned a place through wisdom and compassion.

Its primary function would be the establishment of a new Department of Celestial Justice. No longer would souls be claimed by faith alone.

A new body of arbiters, drawn from all factions, would weigh the life of every mortal soul upon their death. Their deeds, their choices, their impact on the world—these would be the currency of the afterlife.

Those whose stories were defined by cruelty, by selfishness, by the deliberate infliction of pain, would be condemned to Hell—not as a kingdom of evil, but as a realm of consequence, a place of silent, eternal reflection.

Those whose lives were defined by empathy, by sacrifice, by a love that outweighed their flaws, would ascend to a new, more humble Heaven.

Mother Midnight, surprisingly, agreed with a slow, cunning smile. A Hell filled with the truly damned, the truly deserving? It would be a far more potent, more interesting realm than the one she currently ruled.

The Choice

When the Accord was finalized, the new council turned to Lucifera. It was Kieran who spoke, his voice thick with the weight of their shared history.

"This was your war, Lucifera. This is your victory. This new department... it needs a leader. A final arbiter. A Flame of Judgment." He looked at her, his heart in his eyes.

"It needs you."

The offer hung in the crystalline air. A throne of a different kind. Not one of power, but of purpose.

The ultimate judge, the final word on every soul's story. It was everything she had fought for. It was the perfect, beautiful cage.

Lucifera looked at Ezra, and in his eyes, she saw not an expectation, but an understanding. He knew her better than anyone. He knew what she had to choose.

She rose, and the runes on her skin glowed with a soft, final light. The offer hung in the crystalline air like a blade waiting to fall. Lucifera felt the weight of every soul she'd judged, every life she'd ended in the name of justice. The Department of Celestial Justice—it was everything she'd fought for, wrapped in the very thing she'd fought against.

She looked at each face around the table. Mother Midnight, expectant and calculating. The celestial delegates, wary but hopeful. Kieran, whose eyes held a desperate kind of faith that she could be their salvation.

And Ezra. Dear, stubborn Ezra, who had followed her into Hell and back, who had seen her burn and heal and doubt and rage. He alone wasn't looking at her with expectation. He was looking at her with understanding.

"You know what I'm going to say," she said quietly to him.

"I know what you need to say," he replied. "The question is whether you're brave enough to say it."

She closed her eyes, feeling the runes on her skin pulse with a gentle, final light. She thought of Sarah Martinez, of all the children who had died while systems failed them. She thought of the girl in the cathedral, healed by her touch. She thought of the endless parade of corrupt souls she'd judged, and the weight of being their final arbiter.

The throne they offered wasn't just a seat of power—it was a cage. Beautiful, purposeful, necessary. And still a cage.

"I did not burn down one system of control just to become the architect of another," she said, her voice soft but absolute.

"My purpose was never to rule. It was to illuminate."

She turned to the council. "You have the tools. You have the truth. The balance is now in your hands." She looked at Kieran, a sad, beautiful smile on her lips. "I was never meant to be a destination, Kieran. I am a path."

The Awakening

288

Her choice was made. As she prepared to depart, a tremor ran through the Axis Mundi. It was not a physical quake, but a psychic one, a ripple in the very fabric of the cosmos.

The immense, paradoxical power unleashed by Oren's unmaking, and the subsequent, fundamental reordering of the laws of the afterlife, had acted like a cosmic gong. It was a sound that had not been heard in an eternity, a vibration that traveled to the darkest, most forgotten corners of existence.

In a dimension of pure, sleeping thought, a billion ancient eyes opened at once.

In the silent, cold void between galaxies, a being of impossible size, who had slumbered for eons, began to stir.

And on a world cloaked in shadow, a new name was whispered on the winds, a name of a power that promised not judgment, but a truth far more terrifying: Mercy.

The universe, which had been defined for so long by the singular conflict between Heaven and Hell, suddenly became aware that it was a much, much larger place. And it was no longer sleeping.

Lucifera felt the awakenings, a thousand new variables in a game she had just redefined. She looked at Ezra, a silent promise passing between them. Her war was over. But the story of the universe was just beginning.

She turned to Ezra one last time. "The Sarah Martinez case file is still in your desk drawer."

He blinked, surprised she knew. "How did you—"

"Because you carry your ghosts the same way I carry mine." She stepped closer, her voice dropping to something only he could hear. "You don't need me to get justice for her anymore. You have everything you need."

"What if I'm not strong enough without you?"

"You were strong enough to stand beside me when angels and demons wanted me dead." She smiled, and for the first time since he'd known her, it held no fire—only warmth. "You were strong enough to save me from becoming the very thing I fought against. You'll be strong enough for whatever comes next."

She pressed something into his hand—a small, silver feather that pulsed with gentle heat. "For when you forget that some fights are worth having."

Ezra closed his fingers around the feather. "This isn't goodbye."

"No," she said, already beginning to fade at the edges, her form becoming starlight and memory. "This is a promise that the work continues."

He watched her dissolve into points of light that scattered across the cosmos, each one a reminder that justice was not a destination, but a choice made new each day.

When the last spark faded, Ezra found himself alone in the crystalline chamber, holding a feather that would never grow cold and carrying the weight of a world that was finally truly free to choose its own path.

She was gone, a wanderer among the starry stars, her name now a legend, a warning, and a flame that would never, ever go out.

THE END

Read Book Two – *Mercy is Blind*

The story continues...

About the Authors

Ken Konet, is an Instructional Designer, IT Engineer, HR strategist, and published author with a flair for confronting the uncomfortable. With multiple MBAs and a Master's in Education, his work sits at the intersection of intellectual depth and rebellious storytelling.

Known for fusing sarcasm, awkward humor, and dark myth with social critique, his writing peels back the polished veneer of tradition to expose injustice, moral hypocrisy, and the potential for transformation.

His previous work, *Stop Stepping on Rakes*, launched a humor-infused personal growth movement, while *Lucifera* marks a dramatic shift—into a world of divine corruption, unflinching justice, and mythic revolution.

He lives in pursuit of knowledge, armed with sarcasm, curiosity, and an unshakable belief that stories should either teach you something—or set something on fire.

—Ken Konet, M.Ed., MBA

Ibrahim Roble is a computer engineer by day, meticulously building the logical, rule-bound systems that power the modern world. But when the screens go dark, he trades code for chaos, diving headfirst into the shadowy realms of myth and rebellion that he has always loved.

A lifelong devotee of dark fantasy, Ibrahim spends his nights as an author, editor, and beta reader, exploring worlds where systems of power are meant to be broken. He believes that the best stories, like the best code, are elegant, powerful, and possess the ability to rewrite the entire system. In his collaboration on Lucifera, he helped forge the very architecture of its rebellious world, bringing a structural soul to its poetic rage. He thrives where order collapses and a new, more dangerous truth emerges from the flames.

—Ibrahim Roble